"Grandpa won't take me away if he thinks I have a sheriff for a dad."

Beth pulled her son close and over his head met Sheriff Ethan Drum's eyes. She understood the man's appeal for her son, because at the moment she'd like nothing better than to run into his arms and let him deal with her in-laws, and all her other troubles, too.

Then she sighed and held Jason at arm's length. "Jase, your grandparents are just making threats. But we can't involve the sheriff in a lie to make those threats go away."

Jason shrugged. "Why can't we just make believe he's gonna be my dad until Grandma and Grandpa go home?"

"Because of what you told Grandma and Grandpa, they're not going home until *after* the wedding." Beth shook her head. "But there's not going to be a wedding. So they'll know you lied, and then they'll *really* think I'm a terrible mother."

"Then let's have a wedding." Jason turned to the sheriff.

Beth turned to him, too, hoping against hope that he would have a solution.

Sheriff Ethan Drum smiled. "I guess we have a wedding."

ABOUT THE AUTHOR

Muriel Jensen, the award-winning author of almost thirty-five novels, began writing romance fiction in the ninth grade. She realized she'd found her niche in life when her classmates started gathering around her desk every morning for the latest installment.

Muriel, who is the mother of three adult children, lives in Oregon with her husband.

Books by Muriel Jensen

HARLEQUIN SUPERROMANCE

422—TRUST A HERO
468—BRIDGE TO YESTERDAY
512—IN GOOD TIME
589—CANDY KISSES
683—HUSBAND IN A HURRY
751—THE FRAUDULENT FIANCÉE

Don't miss any of our special offers. Write to us at the following address for information on our newest releases.

Harlequin Reader Service
U.S.: 3010 Walden Ave., P.O. Box 1325, Buffalo, NY 14269
Canadian: P.O. Box 609, Fort Erie, Ont. L2A 5X3

THE LITTLE MATCHMAKER
Muriel Jensen

Harlequin Books

TORONTO • NEW YORK • LONDON
AMSTERDAM • PARIS • SYDNEY • HAMBURG
STOCKHOLM • ATHENS • TOKYO • MILAN
MADRID • WARSAW • BUDAPEST • AUCKLAND

ISBN 0-373-70764-9

THE LITTLE MATCHMAKER

Copyright © 1997 by Muriel Jensen.

This edition published by arrangement with Harlequin Books S.A.

® and TM are trademarks of the publisher. Trademarks indicated with
® are registered in the United States Patent and Trademark Office, the
Canadian Trade Marks Office and in other countries.

Printed in U.S.A.

THE LITTLE MATCHMAKER

CHAPTER ONE

SHERIFF ETHAN DRUM swept his flashlight in a wide arc in front of him, willing the missing little boy to appear out of the rainy darkness. The three-hour search had become desperate and very personal. As a parent himself, he didn't have to guess at the anguish of the mother who waited at home; he knew it all too well.

His daughter had once disappeared at a family picnic, and he could still remember how the unthinkable possibilities had driven him and Diana to the brink of madness. Then a Search and Rescue volunteer had walked out of the woods with her, and Ethan's heart had almost stalled with relief.

He wanted to bring that same relief to this boy's mother. It wasn't that he wanted to be a hero. He'd been the sheriff of Butler County long enough to know that the job wasn't about heroics, but about maintaining peace and order in a little corner of Oregon, where the Columbia River met the ocean.

Generally people weren't the problem here; nature was. The pine, fir and cedar woods that ran along the beach could hide a boy in their dense undergrowth so that a man could walk right by him in daylight and not see him.

Tonight there was no moonlight, and a steady soaking rain served to blot out any remaining visibility.

At least the temperature was on his side—a reasonably moderate midforties rather than the just-above-freezing levels usual for early February.

And nothing was impossible. Ethan's ancestry was Portuguese, French-Canadian and, somewhere way back, Mohawk, which was as hardheaded an ethnicity as could be created in any gene pool. It meant he liked to have his way and was willing to go to any lengths to see that he did. He was damned if he was going to be deprived of delivering this boy alive and well, home to his mother.

He flipped the switch on the shoulder mike connected to the radio at his belt and called the office. "500," he said, indicating his call number.

"500," a woman's voice answered. "Go ahead."

"Ebbie, it's Ethan."

"You found him?" she asked hopefully.

"No," he replied. "I was just checking to see if he'd turned up at home."

Evelyn Browning, secretary and reliable source of gossip both in and out of the office, sighed audibly. "No. His mother left a friend waiting at home and came into the office. She, ah…she'd like to borrow a car."

Ebbie's tone suggested that the mother was standing within earshot. He frowned at the darkness as rain dripped off the brim of his hat and into his jacket. "What?" he asked.

"Well…you know…she wants to help. But she doesn't have a car."

Ethan could imagine Ebbie smiling reassuringly at the woman as she spoke to him.

"She was thinking," Ebbie went on, "that she could go up the dump road while you're—"

"No."

"She says she's an excellent driver."

"No! I don't care if she's Michael Andretti. Do *not* give her a car. I know she's upset, but it's an abso—"

"Sheriff Drum." This was a different voice—younger, deeper. "This is Bethany Richards. I know the idea might sound foolish to you, but your assistant here tells me that Search and Rescue is all tied up looking for a group of missing campers and you're searching for Jason alone. We could cover twice as much ground if I was searching, too. And please don't tell me the county's insurance wouldn't cover me. I don't care. I'll sign a waiver."

He'd been about to bring up the safety rules governing county vehicles until he'd heard the fear and the end-of-her-rope torment in her voice. To mention such practical matters in the face of that seemed insulting.

"Mrs. Richards," he said patiently, "I'm going to find your son. You've got to have faith."

"I've *got* faith!" she said, her voice rising as she lost the calm with which she'd come on the line. "What I want are wheels!"

"You don't need wheels, Mrs. Richards," he said firmly. "You need to stay right where you are so that when I bring Jason back, I can put him right into your arms. I don't want to have to tell him when he's cold and scared that you're driving around somewhere and we don't know where *you* are."

He heard an inrush of air—a swallowed sob, he guessed. "But you *aren't* finding him, Sheriff," she disputed hoarsely. "And he's only seven—he'll be eight tomorrow—"

"But I *will* find him," he insisted. "You told us

that Forest Beach is one of his favorite places. I've walked the beach and checked the woods. He must be on the hill." The road at the top of the gradual thickly wooded slope behind the woods was a favorite parking spot of teenagers because of the seclusion it provided. He prayed that was where Jason Richards had gone to hide.

There was a moment of silence. "What if he isn't?" she asked finally. The question had an edge of despair. The mile of darkness and woods that separated him from the voice on the radio disappeared, and Ethan knew exactly what she was feeling.

"I thought you had faith," he chided gently, rubbing the chest of his bulky jacket with a gloved hand. Inside him, frustration was burning a hole.

He heard that sound again, the little inrush of air.

"What time is it?" he asked her.

She hesitated. He imagined her looking up at the ancient round clock on the wall over Ebbie's desk. "Ah...five minutes after ten."

"All right," he said, knowing this was risky but unable to stop himself. "You watch that clock, and by five minutes after eleven, I'll have Jason back to you."

He heard her sigh of acceptance. He knew it didn't mean she believed him; it just meant she'd give him the hour because she had nothing *else* to believe in.

He switched off the radio and headed for the hill, sweeping the beam of his flashlight methodically from side to side.

"YOU JUST SIT right there." The plump middle-aged woman in the beige-and-brown county uniform, whose gold badge was inscribed with "E. Browning," pointed Beth to a chair. Beth had avoided it since she'd walked into the office an hour earlier, because she'd been afraid that if she sat down it would be an indication she was prepared to wait—and she wasn't. She wanted Jason back now!

The woman pressed a steaming mug of coffee into her hands. "Drink this and watch that clock just like Ethan told you. If he said he'd be back with your boy in an hour, he will be. Ethan Drum is a man of his word."

Beth wanted to believe that, but it was a night out of a horror movie. Jason, just a day short of turning eight, had been frightened and angry when he'd left; if he wasn't already unconscious from hypothermia, he might hide from the sheriff rather than be brought back home to face the risk of being taken away by his grandparents.

Beth took a long sip of the coffee. Her eyes widened when the generous dose of brandy in it hit her tastebuds.

The sheriff's staff assistant had gone back to her desk and now turned to wink at her. "Nothing like a good medicinal cup of coffee."

Medicinal, indeed. There was enough alcohol in the cup to pickle her for posterity! Still, the warmth of the brandy brought a measure of relaxation to muscles that had been clenched in terror ever since darkness had fallen. Ever since she'd realized that Jason had followed through on his threat to run away.

Beth had explained to him over and over that her mother-in-law's threats to take her to court for custody of Jason were a bluff, and that nothing and no one would ever separate them.

She and Jason had moved here to Cobbler's

Crossing three months ago. Some bully at the school, who'd overheard Jason expressing his fears to a friend, had been teasing and tormenting him. And all her assurances that his grandparents had no legal cause to take him from her hadn't comforted him. She imagined that when a boy's father died, his sense of security died, also, leaving him to feel that everything else he held dear could be taken, too.

Beth looked at the clock. Ten-fifteen. She took another sip of the coffee-cum-brandy, or rather, the brandy-cum-coffee, leaned her head back against the wall and closed her eyes, remembering the man she'd been married to for thirteen years.

They'd met in high school. Steve Richards had been of average height, with a handsome face and muscular build. She'd admired his drive to achieve and accomplish, especially when other boys seemed to spend much of their time avoiding homework and skipping classes. It was in wood shop that they'd become fast friends; they were the class misfits—she, because she was the only girl, and he, because he had no skill for carpentry.

Her parents had died in an automobile accident when she was six, and she was raised in a Seattle suburb by a grandmother who was loving and supportive, but possessed slender financial means. Steve's parents were indulgent but overbearing, and he'd been anxious to strike out on his own.

And so Steve and Bethany had married right out of high school. He'd gone to work at a furniture store, part of a retail chain, while she'd worked in the office at the community college—which enabled her to take art classes without charge.

For two years they were very happy. She'd produced painted wooden art and worked every craft show in the area, and he'd worked long hours at the store, eager to get ahead.

Beth became pregnant with Jason at the same time Steve was put in charge of the chain's newest and largest store, in downtown Seattle. And then everything changed.

By working night and day, catering to all his customers' needs and demands, and keeping costs down by serving as both clerk and manager, Steve put the store in the black the first year.

Over the next two years he made enough in bonuses and stock options to strike out on his own. Though Beth knew he loved her and Jason, she also accepted that he put them second to his career. What had once seemed such an admirable trait had become, in her eyes, an insatiable and obsessive drive to succeed at any cost.

In search of some adult contact, she'd joined a co-op of artists that required each member tend the small neighborhood shop several mornings or afternoons every week. But many of Steve's contacts called him at home, and he resented their having to deal with an answering machine rather than a person. He wanted Beth there.

"Steve, the co-op is important to me," she'd tried to explain.

He'd made a sweeping gesture with one hand that encompassed the vaulted ceiling and floor-to-ceiling windows of their new house on Puget Sound and said, "The store means this house and the way we live. If I land the deal to furnish the redecorating of the convalescent home on Markham Road, it's going to mean two weeks in the Caymans for us."

She'd sighed, tired of the argument. "If you don't slow down, Steve," she'd warned, "you're going to land *in* the convalescent home on Markham Road."

"That's what it takes to build a business, Beth," he'd said. "You have to work at it all the time."

It had been on the tip of her tongue to tell him that what built a business could also destroy a marriage, but Jason adored his father and she'd made a vow. She'd looked around—at the oversize sofa with its distressed-velvet slipcovers, the Scandinavian pine dining table under the iron rope chandelier—and decided that she was caught in a very elegant trap.

So she'd left the co-op and worked on her art at home, unwilling to discard the time and emotion she'd invested in her marriage or to dismiss the love Jason felt for his father.

Then one day a little more than a year ago she'd received a telephone call from a client with whom Steve had a lunch meeting. He told her Steve had collapsed as they were leaving the restaurant and had been taken by ambulance to the hospital.

She'd left Jason with a neighbor, and by the time she'd arrived at the emergency room, her thirty-two-year-old husband was dead of a heart attack.

She'd grieved for months over the loss of the man that driving ambition had robbed of his potential as a husband and father. The bank holding Steve's loans took everything, including most of the money Beth made by selling the house, which, thank God, had been paid off by mortgage insurance.

When she'd signed the check over to the bank and was given only a small fraction of it back, she'd stood on the sidewalk in front of the bank with Jason beside her. A curiously quiet happiness stole over her.

She was free.

For the first time in years she was free of Steve's crippling need to do more, to have more. Free of the terrifying debt that resulted. Free of all the pressures that suppressed who she really was and who she really wanted to be.

She'd called Kelly Braxton, one of her co-op friends who'd moved to the Oregon coast and with whom she'd kept in contact. Kelly had sent her the newspaper from Cobbler's Crossing, population two thousand, and Beth had seen the picture of the old cannery that was for sale at the end of a pier on the waterfront.

Kelly had checked it out with the Realtor for Beth. She reported that a previous owner had tried to put shops into the old building, and that some of the interior had been painted; plumbing and wiring had been installed, along with a furnace. Then the small-town entrepreneur had run out of money.

"But the rest of it's pretty primitive," Kelly had warned over the phone. "The walls to break it into shops are up, but they're not painted. There's flooring, but the roof leaks on the river side. The dock would probably also have to be checked for safety before you could allow any commercial traffic."

Beth had looked at the photo of the cannery and seen everything she'd always wanted—space for a studio combined with living space so that she had only one set of expenses. And if she was willing to work hard, the place had income potential as a location for rental studios. Artists were always looking for big inexpensive spaces.

She put a down payment on it sight unseen and moved with Jason to Oregon, sure it would be a fresh start for both of them. But Steve's parents, who adored their grandson but only tolerated Beth, had come to visit two weeks after she and Jason moved into the cannery. They'd been appalled by the general condition of the building, by its location at the end of a pier and by the tiny living area, which was the size of a very small apartment.

Beth took them through the rest of the building in an attempt to show them its possibilities. But all they'd seen were the ceiling and walls stained with water from the leaky roof, and the stark bareness of the building, not the happy little art community she envisioned.

Joanne, her imposing, haughty mother-in-law, had met Beth's eyes and said ominously, "We can't let Jason live like this. Steven would be appalled. We'll see you again when we've looked into our options."

Beth had swung her gaze from Joanne to Zachary, her father-in-law. "You have no options, Jo," she said. "Steve let you intrude on our lives, but I won't. I want Jason to be able to see you, but don't think for one moment I will let you take him from me. Jason is *my* son, and he's not going to replace Steve in your lives."

Her in-laws had left in a huff, Zachary making threats of suing her for custody.

Beth hadn't know Jason had been listening until they'd slammed the door behind them and she'd turned to find him in the doorway to his tiny bedroom, his eyes wide with fear.

She'd done her best to reassure him, but he'd been convinced that, since his grandfather was a judge, he'd be able to carry out his threat. When Zachary had called yesterday to tell Beth that he and Joanne were coming to Cobbler's Crossing for Jason's birthday tomorrow, Jason had been sure they were coming to take him away.

Now Beth was wondering if indulging her dream had been selfish and irresponsible. It was one thing for an adult to leave family and friends and flirt with poverty to fulfill an ambition, but had it been right to uproot her son? At this moment she wasn't sure. She'd gladly go back to life in Seattle if it meant the sheriff would walk through the office door right now with Jason by the hand.

THE GRASSY HILL was slick with rain and difficult to negotiate, but the muddy trail was worse. So Ethan tacked across the face of the hill, swinging his light in wide arcs, careful not to miss anything.

"Jason!" he shouted. "Jason, are you here?"

For the first time in hours of searching, he thought he heard a faint response. His heart lurched and he swung the beam of his flashlight up the hill in the direction of the sound.

But the wind was howling and the rain was noisy; he couldn't be absolutely sure. The light revealed nothing.

He waited for a lull in the wind, then shouted again. "Jason! Where are you?"

So weak he wondered if he'd imagined it came, "Over here!"

"Where?"

The answer was a little louder. "In the tree at the top of the hill!"

Relief surged through Ethan as he pressed on up the slope. He knew precisely what tree Jason meant.

The lone mangled fir that leaned east from a lifetime of being buffeted by the wind.

He stopped under the tree and shone his flashlight beam upward. About fifteen feet above his head he saw a small sturdy figure in jeans and a red waterproof parka. The boy was straddling a branch and holding on to the trunk with both hands. He was crying.

"Hi," Ethan said, propping the flashlight in the fork of a branch so that its beam remained on the boy. "I'm Sheriff Drum."

"Yeah," the boy replied, his voice shaking. "I know."

Ethan reached for a branch above the one in which he'd propped the light. He pulled himself up, then bracing himself against the trunk with his feet, reached for the next branch.

"You mean we've met," Ethan said when he was only a few feet below the boy, "and you'd make me come out on a night like this to find you?"

"You...you came to school to talk to us," Jason said haltingly. "And the other kids told me all about you...."

"Ah." Ethan's head was now level with Jason's feet. He could see that the tree had kept the boy reasonably dry. "Okay, just hold the branch above your head and swing your leg over the branch you're sitting on."

Instructing the boy step by step, cautioning him to always keep a hold on the branch above, Ethan soon had him down to his level and clinging to his neck.

"Well done," Ethan said, pleased. "You okay?"

Jason, teeth chattering, wailed, "I want my mom."

"Right. I know." Ethan was afraid to risk freeing

a hand to comfort him, so he had to use his voice, instead. He spoke quietly and with confidence. "She's waiting for you in my office. All we have to do is get down this tree."

"I'm okay," Jason said after a moment, tightening his grip on Ethan's neck and wrapping his legs around his waist. "I'm ready."

Ethan smiled into the darkness. At fourteen his daughter was fiercely independent and resisted all his efforts to help or counsel her. And though she never said so directly, he suspected she considered him generally useless and unable to function competently in her world. So having a child willingly depend upon him was a treat he hadn't experienced for a while.

"Here we go. Hold on tight." Ethan moved slowly, the boy's sixty or so pounds a challenge to his balance. Still, he reached the bottom branches without incident.

"Okay," he said into Jason's ear. The boy's cheek was pressed so tightly against his that conversation was easy. "Now I need you to let go of me and hold on to this branch so I can jump down and catch you."

"No," the boy said adamantly, fearfully.

"Jason," Ethan explained, "if I jump holding on to you, we'll get hurt."

"I don't want to let go!"

"It'll only be for a minute. If I bring you back to your mom with a broken bone, she'll be really mad at me."

The boy apparently considered that something to think about. "She's gonna be really mad at *me*."

"I talked to her on the radio," Ethan said. "She sounded much more worried than angry."

"Yeah, but after she doesn't have to be worried anymore, she'll be mad."

Probably true, Ethan thought. "Well, running away isn't the best way to handle whatever the problem is."

"But *he's* coming for me."

"Who's 'he'?"

"Grandpa Richards. And Grandma. He's a judge and he's gonna take me away." Jason began to cry again.

Ethan decided it was time to be firm. "Look. I want to hear about this, but you're going to tell me about it in the car after we get out of this tree and down the hill. So listen to me."

Jason sniffed. "Okay."

"Take your right arm from around my neck and hold the branch that's over our heads."

"I don't want to!"

"I know, but you have to. Just do as I say, and this'll be over in a minute."

Still whimpering, Jason freed one hand, reached up and grasped the branch just above his head. The pudgy face now visible in the light from below was pinched and pale, and the blue eyes were wide with fear.

"Good," Ethan said. "Now reach up with the other hand and catch the other branch." Jason complied.

Ethan's neck was free, but the sturdy legs around his waist felt riveted to him. "Great." Ethan uncoiled one of Jason's legs and placed that foot on a branch.

"Feel that?" he said.

"Yeah," Jason replied thinly. "It's wobbly."

"It only has to hold you for a minute."

He did the same with the other leg, and before the

boy could realize what he was doing and complain about it, he jumped backward to the ground.

"Hey!" Jason shouted.

Ethan clapped his hands and reached up for him, bracing himself to take his weight. "Come on. Just—" Before he could complete the command, the boy fell into his arms. Ethan, his hat dislodged and rolling away, landed on his back on the wet grass with the boy on top of him.

"We did it!" Jason said exultantly, sitting up on Ethan's stomach. "And I didn't even get a broken bone! Did you?"

"No," Ethan replied with a half laugh. "I'm squished. You want to get off me so we can radio your mom that you're all right?"

"Oh. Yeah." Jason scrambled to his feet, found Ethan's hat in the process and handed it to him.

Ethan drew the boy back under the shelter of the tree and called Ebbie.

"You found him?" she demanded.

It gave Ethan great pleasure to be able to say yes. "Put Mrs. Richards on," he said. "Here's Jason."

Ethan disconnected the mike from his shoulder and held it to the boy's mouth. "Mom?" Jason said, then he whispered to Ethan, "Am I s'posed to say, 'Over'?"

Ethan bit back a grin. "No. Just talk."

"Mom? Hi. It's me."

Ethan heard the voice he'd spoken to half an hour ago laughing and crying at the same time. "Jase, are you okay? Where are you?"

"I was in a tree, Mom, only I couldn't get down 'cause it was too slippy, but Sheriff Drum came up and got me. He jumped down at the bottom and then he caught me. It was really cool!''

Cool, Ethan considered, shaking his head. That's not what *he'd* have called it.

Jason's voice lowered and he asked gravely, ''Mom, are you mad?''

''Jase, right now I'm just happy and grateful you're alive and all right,'' she answered. ''But by tomorrow I'm going to be mad. It doesn't mean I don't love you, it just means...'' There was a sigh. ''But we won't talk about that until tomorrow.''

''Tell her we'll be there in twenty minutes,'' Ethan prompted.

Jason repeated the information.

''I'm waiting for you, sweetie. I love you.'' Her voice was a comforting sound in the roaring blackness. Then she added softly, ''Tell Sheriff Drum that I love him, too.''

Jason handed the mike back to Ethan. ''She said—''

''Yeah.'' Ethan had to cope with a weird sensation in the pit of his stomach. ''I heard her.''

It had been five long years since a woman had said those words to him—his wife, Diana, only days before she'd died of ovarian cancer. And this time, of course, the words were simply an exaggerated expression of gratitude. All the same he found them touching.

CHAPTER TWO

ETHAN LED THE WAY down the muddy trail, one hand holding Jason's, the other holding the flashlight. They slipped and slid and finally arrived at the small parking lot, which was empty except for the brown-and-white patrol car.

Ethan put Jason in the front seat, retrieved blankets from the trunk, then took the boy's jacket off and wrapped him in one of the blankets. He pulled the seat belt over him, then covered him with another blanket, unmindful of the mud that caked him from foot to thigh. At last he climbed in behind the wheel, cranked up the heat and turned the car toward the road.

The wipers beat hard against the rain sheeting the windshield.

"Warm enough?" Ethan asked. When Jason didn't answer, Ethan glanced over to find the boy staring at him.

"Yeah," Jason said finally. Then he fell quiet, but continued to stare at him.

"How'd you get this far from home?" Ethan asked.

"On my bike," Jason answered. "But I crashed on the trail when it started to rain and bent my front wheel. Then my bike fell down the hill."

Ethan turned his full attention back to the road.

They were approaching a long series of hairpin turns that led to the state highway. Ethan could still feel the boy's eyes on him.

"What?" he asked. "You worried about your mom coming down on you when you get home?"

Jason sighed. "No. Well, yeah, but that's not what I'm thinking about."

"What are you thinking about?"

"I was thinking," Jason said hopefully, "that you could maybe...arrest me."

Ethan glanced at him again. The blue eyes looked serious. "If it was up to me," he replied, "I *would* put you in jail for scaring your mom like that. Unfortunately the law doesn't consider running away criminal."

"But you're the sheriff." The boy shifted in his seat, turning toward him, his voice going to a higher pitch as he warmed to the idea. "You can do whatever you want."

"No, I can't," Ethan corrected. "I can only do what the law tells me."

"Well...you could say I resisted arrest. I'd tell everybody that I really did."

"But you're not *under* arrest. You haven't committed a crime."

"You could say I stole something."

Ethan shook his head. "Now, how do you think your mom would feel if I told her that?"

"She'll feel worse if Grandma and Grandpa take me away! And if I'm in jail, they can't get me, right?"

Ethan heard the very real anguish in the boy's voice. "What makes you think your grandparents want to take you away?" he asked.

"They told Mom it's 'cause of the cannery."

"What cannery?"

"Mom's an artist," Jason said, wiping rain off his cheek with an edge of the blanket. "We bought the old cannery out on the pier."

Ethan nodded, remembering his brother mentioning that some gullible out-of-towner had bought the old Baldwin Cannery building.

"We're gonna make an art mall out of it," Jason went on excitedly. "And when it's all rented, we'll make enough money to send me to college. But right now it looks pretty awful. And just one little part of the building's fixed up, and that's where we'll live till Mom gets the rest of it done. Grandma said my dad would be *appalled.*" He gave the word dramatic emphasis.

"Pretty strong word."

"Yeah, well. Grandma doesn't like a lot of stuff. She doesn't like artists, so she doesn't like Mom."

"Your mom and dad are divorced?"

"No. My dad had a heart attack and died." Jason's voice became very faint.

Ethan turned to the boy and was encouraged to see that he looked sad but not destroyed. He reached over to pat his knee. "I'm sorry. It's hard to lose a dad."

"He wasn't home that much, but when he was, I really liked him. My mom says he loved me a lot."

"That's a good memory to have."

"Yeah."

Ethan heard the lack of conviction in Jason's reply and realized that a memory, especially to a little boy, was a poor substitute for the real thing.

"I bet you miss him a lot."

"Yeah." Jason heaved a sigh. "I used to miss him

a lot *before* he died, too." He shifted in his seat, then asked, "Where do *you* live?"

"In a big old house in town. In fact, you can see it from the cannery. It's gray with green shutters."

"That one?" Jason's voice was reverent. "Wow! It has that tower thing?"

"That's the one."

Jason sighed again. "I wish I lived there."

"Oh, I don't think your grandmother would like it any more than she likes the cannery. It's not very fancy, just comfortable." Jason grinned at the boy. "You warm enough?"

Jason nodded, then sat straighter. "Hey. Maybe you could arrest my *grandpa!*"

The boy definitely had a future in law enforcement, Ethan thought. He was determined to have someone arrested—anyone. "But he hasn't done anything against the law."

"If he tries to take me, wouldn't that be stealing?"

"Ah...that would be kidnapping," Ethan said. "And if your grandfather's a judge, I'm sure he wouldn't try to take you away without first getting a judgment from the court. And to do that, he'd have to prove that your mother wasn't doing a good job of being your mother."

"She does a great job," Jason said staunchly.

Ethan could believe it. From the way she'd sounded on the radio, it was clear she was very caring.

"Then you probably don't have as big a problem as you think you have."

"Yeah, I do." Jason's voice was anxious again. "Taylor Bridges's dad is a lawyer, and he says my house is awful enough to prove my mom's a bad mother.''

"Taylor said, or his father said?"

"Well, Taylor."

Ethan sighed as he turned off the highway and down the road into Cobbler's Crossing. "Think about it, Jason. What does an eight-year-old kid know about it, even if his father *is* a lawyer?"

"Taylor's nine." Jason seemed to think that was significant. "He's in the fourth grade."

"Well, I don't think you learn much about the law in the fourth grade. He probably just likes to rattle you."

Jason looked at him in surprise. "That's what Mom says. How did *you* know that?"

"Evreybody's got somebody like that in his life. You just have to let them talk, but you can ignore it and hold to what you know to be true." Ethan turned into the parking lot of the small complex that held the sheriff's office and the jail. "If your mom's a good mom, you don't have to worry about what Taylor Bridges says."

"I wish Grandma and Grandpa weren't coming for my birthday," Jason said plaintively. "Then I could have a pizza party like the other kids have. With balloons and video games."

Ethan brought the car to a stop directly in front of the office's back door. "I'm sure your grandparents love you a lot and just want to help you celebrate."

"Uh-oh," Jason said. His voice had a despairing note.

Ethan turned off the engine and unbuckled his seat belt. "What?"

Jason pointed to the white Cadillac two spaces over. "That's Grandma and Grandpa's car."

Ethan removed the blanket he'd put over the boy and unfastened his seat belt; Jason was wrapped too tightly in the other blanket to do it himself. "When your mom came to the office tonight, she left a friend at your house in case you came home. Your grandparents probably got there, heard you'd run away and came down to the office because they were worried about you."

Jason shook his head adamantly. "But don't you see? Now they're really gonna think Mom's bad!"

"We'll explain everything," Ethan promised. He reached for his door handle and found his neck caught in Jason's death grip.

"Let me stay with you," the boy pleaded. "Just till Grandma and Grandpa are gone. You can tell them you had to arrest me, even though it isn't true. And I'll wash your car and sweep out the jail. I can paint, too. I helped my mom paint the bathroom. Please?"

Ethan held the boy close and let him absorb the comfort he seemed to need so desperately. But he had to be honest. "Jase, if I had a way to help you, I would. But your mom's been worried to death about you, and we can't keep you away from her any longer. Now let's go in there and explain what happened."

Jason groaned and clung to his neck.

Ethan backed out of the car, holding the boy to him, and ran the few short steps to the door. Once inside the vestibule, he grinned at the still-clinging Jason and said, "You can stand now." But the boy only wrapped his arms and legs around him even more tightly.

Loud voices from the office filtered back to them.

"Yes. Well." The two simple words were spoken perfunctorily and in a high disdainful voice. "You can make all the claims to good motherhood you want, but the fact remains your eight-year-old son has been missing for hours in a raging storm and the police had to be called out to find him."

"That's Grandma," Jason whispered.

"We're the sheriff's office, ma'am," Ebbie said in the no-nonsense tone she used on drunks and attorneys, "not the police. Search and Rescue is a county function. Though we do have a very small police force and we often back them up."

"Moving here was irresponsible, Bethany," a man's pompous voice accused. "You should never have taken Jason from Seattle."

"Grandpa," Jason whispered to Ethan.

"Steve always said you had no sense of what's important in life," the man went on. "You snatch a child away from all that's familiar less than a year after his father's death and drag him to this godforsaken place. You make him live in a hovel where he can't even play outside for fear of falling in the river!"

"The sheriff found Jason," Ethan heard the beleaguered Bethany reply mildly. "I'm sure it was frightening for you to arrive to such confusion, but he let me talk to Jason and he sounded fine. They'll be back anytime now."

Ethan waited for her to tell them that they were the reason Jason had run away. But she didn't.

He felt a sense of outrage he couldn't have explained, except that in the dark stormy night he'd made a connection with that voice on his radio and knew with a certainty born of long experience that she hadn't been careless about the boy he now held in his arms.

And he felt guilty about trying to minimize the boy's fears about his grandparents. They did indeed sound like people to be feared.

Jason clung to his neck. "Can't you tell them you lost me again?"

Ethan smiled grimly, then settled Jason on his hip and pushed his way through the door into the office.

A young woman ran at him instantly, a blur of red coat and dark hair pulled back in a disheveled ponytail. For a moment, he had a second pair of arms around him, crying and clinging.

"Jason! Oh, Jase." The woman buried her face in the boy's hair, then looked up at Ethan, her head just topping his shoulder. Her eyes were enormous in a face that was pale with worry. "Is he okay? Is he hurt?"

"Just a little scared," Ethan replied, having to think about words with those blue eyes so like her son's, on him. "He had a warm coat and the good sense to take shelter in a tree."

Jason looped an arm around her, but his other arm remained securely fastened to Ethan's neck. "Yeah, Mom," he said, "I'm okay."

"Sheriff, thank you!" A portly balding man in glasses and a raincoat came forward to clap Ethan on the shoulder. "I can't tell you how grateful we are. Jason. Come see your gramps."

The man tried to pull Jason out of Ethan's arms, but the boy held on to Ethan with one arm while retaining his hold on his mother with the other. "Hi, Grandpa," he said.

Jason turned his gaze to Ethan and looked him in the eye. Ethan recognized it as a man-to-man communication. He and the boy had shared a lot tonight, and something in Jason's eyes told him he was going to test their developing friendship.

A tall full-figured woman in a silky lavender raincoat came near, her features hard—until she put a hand on the boy's back. Then the contours of her face softened.

"Jason," she said in a gentle, yet wheedling tone, "why did you run away? You can tell Grandma. Are you tired of living in that awful cannery place?"

Jason stiffened. "No. I ran away because I thought you and Grandpa were gonna try to take me away from Mom, but Ethan says you can't."

The older woman looked momentarily horrified. Then the horror dissolved into confusion followed immediately by suspicion. "Oh, really?" she asked. "And who is Ethan?"

Jason pointed in the vicinity of Ethan's nose. "This is Ethan. The sheriff."

The woman assessed Ethan haughtily. "I have rights as a grandmother," she said, then redirected her gaze to Jason. "And it's not that I want to take you away. It's that I want to make sure you're well taken care of."

"I am," Jason insisted. He looked at Ethan, and Ethan couldn't fail to notice the strange plea in his eyes. Then the boy said, "And now that Ethan and Mom are getting married, I'll have a dad to take care of me, too. So now there's no problem, right?"

For the tick of ten seconds there was absolute silence. Through his own shock, Ethan felt the woman in his arm clutch at the back of his jacket.

So that's what Jason's man-to-man look had meant—*Watch it, buddy. I'm about to shaft you.*

"He has a neat house on the hill where you can see the cannery," Jason went on, undeterred. "We live there now."

While Ethan tried to decide how best to cope with the situation without denying Jason's claim and humiliating him in front of his pompous grandparents, Bethany Richards looked up at him, her eyes stunned.

The press of bodies around Jason had forced her right into Ethan's arms. Jason's grandfather took a step back and looked at them in shock. The grandmother made a strangled sound.

"So you don't have to worry anymore," Jason said, adding to his little fiction. "We have a dad now and a great house."

Jason's mother looked from man to boy, and Ethan saw understanding dawn in her eyes. She knew what her son was doing. The eyes she fixed on Ethan were suddenly sad and apologetic.

At last she turned to her in-laws, apparently prepared to refute Jason's claim, but Ethan interrupted her to introduce himself.

"Ethan Drum," he said, offering his hand to the older man. "How are you, Mr. Richards? I'm sorry it's been such a harrowing night for you."

He had no idea what in the hell he was doing. He was an agent of the law, for God's sake! He couldn't make up stories to deceive people. But he also couldn't shatter Jason's story or let this woman admit to her bullying in-laws that her son had lied.

Jason's mother was staring at him. He evaded her by tipping the brim of his hat at the grandmother.

"Mrs. Richards. Did my assistant, Ebbie, give you some coffee?"

"I don't believe it!" the woman said, drawing herself up like some kind of dangerous blowfish. "I don't believe it for a minute!" She turned accusing eyes on her daughter-in-law. "You never said a thing about seeing anyone. You never even *hinted* you were getting married. This is just a trick to try to stop us from getting custody of Jason."

Before Bethany Richards could speak, Ebbie got to her feet from the other side of the counter. "Oh, it's true, Mrs. Richards," she said with a smiling glance at Ethan and Beth. "In fact, the wedding's taking place at my house."

Joanne Richards's expression tightened.

"Next Saturday," Ebbie added.

"I don't believe it," the woman repeated.

Beth Richards stared at Ebbie as though she'd lost her mind. Then she turned to her mother-in-law. "Jo—" she began.

"Guess you'll have to come and see for yourself, won't you?" Ebbie interrupted.

Ethan hadn't a clue what his staff assistant was doing, either. He only knew she was everyone's self-appointed mother, and she must have taken a real liking to Bethany Richards.

Jason's grandmother turned to her husband, who shrugged helplessly. Then she spun toward Ethan, who still had Jason on his hip and Bethany in his arm, and said adamantly, "No. You're all lying. And just to prove it, Zachary and I will stay and attend...the wedding." She spoke the last two words with scornful disbelief.

"Great." Ethan decided, now that he'd been drawn

into Jason's scheme, the only way to play it out was with all sincerity in the hope that the Richardses finally believed them and—God willing—remembered some previous appointment that conflicted with the wedding day. "Meanwhile," he said, "you'll want to come to Jason's birthday party tomorrow. We're having it at Dinosaur Pizza."

Jason's eyes ignited with pleasure and he tightened his grip on Ethan. "All the kids have their parties there!" he said.

Bethany Richards frowned at her son. But before she could speak, Jason grinned convincingly. "At three-thirty," he said. "Right after school."

Bethany gasped.

Ebbie smiled at the grandparents. "I'll add two more to the reservations."

Joanne Richards studied the staff assistant closely, obviously suspecting collusion. But Ebbie met her eyes with that same friendly smile. The other woman finally turned away.

"We'll be there," she said. Then she turned her attention to her grandson. "Jason, are you sure you're all right? Where are your shoes?"

"They were muddy and wet and Ethan pulled 'em off me." He strangled Ethan with a hug. "'Cause he's gonna be my dad."

Ethan was treated to that disbelieving stare again, then the woman began to button her coat. "Dads don't usually lose track of their children."

"I sneaked away," Jason said quickly. "It wasn't his fault. He's prob'ly gonna spank me. Aren't ya?"

Ethan tried to back him up. "No. I don't spank. But I do yell and take away privileges."

Jason looked pleased and relieved. "That's what

Mom does. Only she doesn't yell. She talks like a queen.''

Ethan couldn't quite interpret that. "Like a queen?"

Jason lifted his chin and assumed an expression of royal displeasure. "'Jason Peter Richards,'" he said in a deeper adult tone, "'I've warned you about that before. This time I have to take action.'" He relaxed and assumed his own voice again. "And then I can't watch TV or go out and play."

Joanne Richards put her purse over her arm and pulled up the collar of her coat. "I'm happy you've agreed on parenting techniques," she said with a disdainful lift of an eyebrow, "but I think they'll have to improve considerably before we're convinced they're good enough for our grandson. We'll see you at your party, Jason."

"We're gonna have a cake from the bakery!" Jason called after them, thespian skills at full throttle.

Ebbie exchanged a grinning glance with Ethan.

At the door Zachary turned to add, "We're staying at the Coast Motel if you need us, Jason." Then he slammed the door behind him.

Beth took her first full breath in hours. She extracted Jason from the sheriff's arms and let him slide through her hands to his feet. The blanket puddled on the floor.

She pulled it up over the boy again and gave him a little shake. "Jason Richards, what do you think you're doing?" she demanded. "You've been lying like Pinocchio since you came through that door!"

The anguish of this interminable night was still very clear in her mind, and added to this incredible little drama her son had just performed—with the help of the sheriff and Ebbie—she felt as though she'd lost complete control of her life.

"Grandpa won't take me away," Jason replied simply, somewhat subdued in the face of her displeasure, "if he thinks I have the sheriff for a dad."

She pulled her son close for a moment, in sympathy with his fears of being taken away. Over his head, she met the eyes of the wet and muddy sheriff, who was the lead in Jason's drama. He seemed to be studying her.

He was a big man, with a good solid look about him. And he'd rescued Jason—possibly even saved his life. She understood his appeal for her son, because at the moment she'd like nothing better than to run into a pair of arms like his and let him deal with her in-laws and all her other troubles, too. But unlike her son, she was a grown-up and understood that real life had to be dealt with in a real way.

She held Jason at arm's length and looked into his eyes. "Jase, I understand why you ran away, because I would rather die than be separated from you." She swallowed hard, as emotion and the strain she'd been under threatened her composure. "But I promise you that isn't going to happen. Your grandparents are just making threats. But we can't involve the sheriff in a lie to make those threats go away."

Jason shrugged. The blanket slipped and he caught it and pulled it tightly around himself again. "Why can't we just make believe he's gonna be my dad until Grandma and Grandpa go home?" He turned to look up at the sheriff. "Why can't we?"

Beth caught the boy's chin in her hand and turned him back to face her. "Jason, because of what you told Grandma and Grandpa, they're not going home until *after* the wedding." She shook her head. "But there's not going to be a wedding. So they'll know you lied and then they'll really think I'm a terrible mother."

Jason smiled cautiously. "Then let's have a wedding."

"My house is too small," Ebbie said, "but my garden is available."

Ethan frowned at her. "It's February."

"So I'll borrow the Ladies of Law Enforcement's tent. We use it at the Winter Festival and everyone stays dry."

Beth turned condemning eyes on the sheriff's staff assistant. "And you, Ebbie, *what* were you thinking?"

The woman smiled, obviously unaware she'd probably just blown a hole right in the middle of Beth's life. "That you needed a little help against a pair of bullies, however well-meaning they are."

"But you told them I was getting married." Beth was trying to sound reasonable. Difficult when you were on the verge of panic. "What do you think they'll do when I *don't* get married? They'll tell one of Zachary's judge friends that I'm delusional and a liar, and they'll get custody of my son!"

Ebbie folded her arms, looking concerned at last. She unfolded them, frowned at the sheriff and sighed penitently at Beth. "I'm afraid I didn't think that far ahead. In the time I've spent with you, I got to sympathize with you and wanted to help."

Beth reminded herself that this woman had come back into the office after a full day's work to man the radio and keep in touch with the sheriff while he searched for her son. Anger seemed out of place.

She moved to the counter and put a hand on Ebbie's. "Thank you. I know you meant to help."

Ebbie placed her other hand atop Beth's and patted it. "Don't worry. The sheriff's always got a solution. When the county cut our budget, he found a way to keep me on. When the van died and we didn't have money to replace it, he bought one at an auction and got his brother to overhaul it. He shut down the drug house near the middle school when the police department claimed they didn't have enough manpower to do it. We only had four people in the department at the time."

Those accomplishments enumerated, she looked up at the sheriff expectantly. "So, how about it, boss? How do we get Beth and Jason out of this mess?"

Beth turned to him, too, hoping against hope that Ebbie was right and he would have a solution. He looked capable of it. He pulled off his muddy jacket to reveal a muscular chest and broad shoulders. But in his dark eyes and the thoughtful lines of his mouth were a wit and intelligence that said he wasn't just another set of pretty pecs.

He tossed the jacket at a chair, removed his hat and flung it atop the jacket. His dark hair was a little too long and curled just above his ears and at his neck. It was still wet from his hours outdoors.

Beth watched him run a hand through it and was surprised to find herself wondering if it was as coarse and thick to the touch as it looked.

She pushed the thought away, equilibrium held on to by a thread. She focused her attention on the sheriff's face as he smiled. Thank God! He had a solution.

"I guess," he said, "we have a wedding."

CHAPTER THREE

JASON THRUST a fist in the air. *"Yes!"*

Beth's heart began to thump wildly, not with joy and excitement, but thanks to a surge of adrenaline brought on by her body's "fight or flight" reaction.

An index finger raised in protest, she began, "Ah—"

"You come with me." The sheriff caught Jason by one arm, then pushed open the gate in the counter with the toe of his boot and urged him through. "You, too," he said to Beth. "We have to get this guy into some dry clothes and then we have to talk." He glanced at Ebbie. "You can go home, Eb," he said firmly.

"But I want to know what's happening," she said, then added righteously, "After all, I'm hosting the wedding."

When his response was a darkening of his expression, she reached for her purse. "Fine. I'm out of here. But don't worry about the cake for the party tomorrow. I'll pick it up."

The sheriff's inner office was a small beige room furnished with a plain oak desk littered with paperwork, four gray metal file drawers and two old ladderback chairs. A venetian blind covered the room's only window, and there were certificates, maps and a wildlife calendar on the wall.

The sheriff pointed Beth and Jason to the chairs and opened one of two doors. A small closet was revealed.

Beth sat, but Jason stayed glued to the man's side and peered into the closet with him. She watched the sheriff pull a brown sweatshirt off a shelf and turn, prepared to walk toward the chairs with it, only to find himself nearly tripping over the boy.

With a look of amused exasperation, he pushed the blanket off Jason's shoulders and dropped to one knee to pull the sweatshirt on him. Its hem fell almost to the boy's knees. Then he cuffed the sleeves back until they were inches thick around her son's small wrists.

She felt an almost physical pain at the sight of them together. Jason glowing with the attention and a full-blown case of hero worship, and the sheriff a seemingly perfect male specimen who obviously related to children, this one particularly.

The sheriff rose to his feet, reached into the closet again, snatched another pile of fleece and turned, only to find once again the boy standing squarely in front of him.

"You know, you're like a wart on my knee," he said to Jason with a grin, handing him what turned out to be a pair of sweatpants. He pointed to the door beside the closet. "Bathroom. Put those on, tie them as tight as you can around your waist—see the string?—and roll up the cuffs."

"Cool," Jason said. "These yours?"

"Yes. I get muddy a lot in the line of duty. I usually have a change of clothes here."

Jason walked into the bathroom, carrying the brown sweatpants as if they were royal robes.

The minute the door closed behind her son, Beth

got to her feet and confronted the sheriff. "I appreciate your willingness to help me and Jason," she said to his back as he reached into the closet for another sweatshirt. "But there's no way out of this mess." She moved a little closer, afraid he hadn't heard her. "The only thing I can do at this point is explain to my in-laws why Jason told such a tale and pray they'll understand."

He turned suddenly in the doorway of the closet and had to catch himself from tripping over her, just as he'd done with Jason. For one protracted moment her nose was a fraction of an inch from his second shirt button.

She could smell the outdoors on him, the rain in his hair. She could feel the warmth emanating from his big body.

She took two quick steps back and said flatly, succinctly, "It'll never work, so thank you for all you've done, but I'll just take Jason home and get on wi—"

"How?" he asked. He walked past her, the sweatshirt thrown over his shoulder as he unbuttoned his flannel shirt.

"How what?" she asked, a little impatient with him because this evening had been all too frightening and then weird, and he didn't seem to notice.

"How will you take Jason home?" The shirt unbuttoned, he pulled it off, revealing a rock-hard torso tightly clothed in simple white cotton.

Beth saw the jut of his chest and the concavity of his stomach, which disappeared under his belt. "My friend...at the cannery. She'll come and get us."

He pulled the sweatshirt over his head and yanked it into place. "You go home to the cannery," he warned, "and you'll make a liar out of Jason in front of his grandparents."

"Well, he *did* lie." She walked around the office, arms folded. "That's the problem here. And anyway, they've gone back to the motel. In the morning I'll—"

"No, they haven't," he said. He threw the flannel shirt at the bottom of the closet. "I just saw the white Caddy turn into the trees across the road. They've doused the headlights."

Beth frowned. "What do you mean?"

He caught her wrist as she started toward the window. "I saw the car through the blinds when we walked in here. I imagine they decided that a little simple spying might tell them something and get specific evidence on you, so they thought they'd hang around and watch us leave. *Don't* turn around. Relax."

It was just a touch, a hand on her wrist, but it claimed control of the situation.

It wasn't that she wanted to give over control of her life for any length of time, but it would be delicious to let someone else be in charge for a little while. After an absolutely hideous year, she'd been trying against overwhelming odds to rebuild her life in a simpler, cleaner pattern. Then her in-laws had intruded, casting a pall over her newfound happiness and, worse, stealing Jason's comfort in his new surroundings.

Now there seemed to be more wrong with her life than she could ever fix.

"If you can see them," she said, the emotional knot inside her tightening, "they can see us."

He drew her toward his desk and sat on a corner

of it, retaining his grip on her wrist. "That's my point. Your taking comfort in the arms of a loving fiancé will only lend believability to Jason's story. And you look as though you're going to dissolve into a puddle any minute."

"I don't need comfort," she denied as he drew her closer. Everything in her was trembling now.

"What *do* you need?" he asked quietly. He was watching her with gentle dark eyes that moved over her face feature by feature. There was no judgment in them, no demand, no criticism. It seemed forever since she'd looked into a man's eyes and found simple interest there.

Her composure unraveled. She had no idea why this man should even ask the question, much less care about the answer. "Why does it matter to you?" she asked. Instinct told her to pull away from him, the warm serenity he represented had never been her destiny. All her life she'd moved from one demanding, unsatisfying situation to another. A tempting taste of comfort and security would only remind her of what life *could* be like, but wasn't.

As though sensing her need to pull away, he put his free hand to the middle of her back and used it to draw her between his knees. "This is my county," he replied. "Everyone in it matters. You can cry if you want to. I think that's what you need."

She sniffed resolutely. "Thank you, but I'm fine. Maybe you could just...walk over and close the blinds."

He ignored her suggestion. "My daughter was lost once for a couple of hours," he said, rubbing gently between her shoulder blades. "When she was finally found and my wife and I took her home and put her to bed, we cried for hours. The fear of what could have been just sits in your gut if you don't.''

Yes, Beth thought. She could feel it there, hot and heavy, with barbed edges that continued to hurt even though the danger was over.

Ethan had never seen a woman—or a man, for that matter—under such tight control yet with an urgent need for release in her eyes. And he guessed it had to do with more than just this night.

The rigidity in her back had to be tension of very long standing. His father had been gone a lot, Jason had told him, and then he'd died.

Had she gotten what she needed from her husband? he wondered. If she had, he knew from personal experience that the death of a spouse was like a fresh wound every day for years.

If she hadn't, that was a different kind of tragedy. Either way, he couldn't imagine having to cope with grief and then having to deal with the threat of someone trying to take your child away.

"Jason's safe now," he said. Her fists were clenched between her breasts and she'd closed her eyes. There was a frown line between her eyebrows that seemed to deepen as he rubbed gently up and down her spine. "And we can deal with the issue of his grandparents."

"How?" she whispered.

"I don't know. We can talk that over, explore the options. But if you're going to stand up to it, you have to do two things."

"What?"

"You have to let this tension go and let yourself be human." She opened her eyes to look at him, the anguish there so great he swore he could see sparks.

"And you have to trust someone to help you. It looks like I'm it."

He felt something snap in her. She lifted a hand to cover her eyes, and below it her mouth contorted on a sob. "All I want," she said in a high desperate voice, "is to be left alone to make a life with Jason. That's all! Is that so much to ask? Is it?"

He knew he didn't have to answer. He simply pulled her the rest of the way into his arms. She wrapped hers around his neck with a strength that might have surprised him if he hadn't seen the intensity in her eyes close up.

She clung to him and sobbed and he held on, sure the Richardses were watching. The way they operated, he'd probably be brought up on charges of sexual harassment if they weren't convinced that he and this woman had a relationship.

He couldn't believe the bizarre turn the missing-child call had taken tonight. He'd been able to relate to Jason and hadn't wanted to make a liar of him when he'd made those outrageous claims in front of his grandparents. And then he'd looked into Beth Richards's blue eyes and known he had to help. He wasn't sure why, except that he cared about everyone in his jurisdiction, and she'd touched the same chord in him Jason had. What could he say? He was the paternal type. That was what had led him to law enforcement in the first place. It hadn't been the excitement of high-speed chases or pistol-drawn stand-offs. It had been the simple desire to keep safe the people and the place where he'd grown up.

But when Beth Richards drew back from his shoulder and shifted her weight, her hip brushing the inside of his thigh, he experienced a reaction that was decidedly not paternal.

He absorbed the startling impact of it for an instant, then cleared his expression when she sniffed and looked into his eyes. Her own were like a turbulent sea, her eyelashes wet and spiky against her pale skin.

"Are they still there?" she asked.

"Who?"

She frowned at him. "My in-laws. Are they still watching?"

He pulled himself together. "Ah…yeah, I think so. The car hasn't moved."

"So what do we do now?"

"I guess," Ethan answered, thinking it was going to be interesting explaining this to Nikkie, "we go home."

The bathroom door burst open and Jason came out, his muddy jeans over his arm and more of the sweat-pant legs rolled up than not. In spite of his ordeal, he looked pink-cheeked and clear-eyed.

Until he noticed that his mother had been crying. He crossed to her. "What's the matter, Mom?"

She took him in her arms and held him, resting her cheek on top of his still-damp curly hair. "Nothing," she replied, putting her concerns aside to reassure him. "I'm just very glad you're all right."

"I'm sorry I scared you." He gripped her tightly around the waist. "I was just gonna hide out till Grandma and Grandpa were gone, but then it got raining so hard." He leaned away from her to smile at Ethan. "I was really glad when you came to find me. Are you gonna take us home with you?"

Ethan suspected the little devil's penitence stretched only so far. Jason was getting what he wanted, at least temporarily, and he was unashamedly pleased about that. Well, hell. What lonely little kid didn't deserve to pretend he had a father who cared about him?

And what lonely frightened woman didn't deserve a buffer between herself and the bullies in her world?

"Yes, I am," Ethan said, getting to his feet. "Then tomorrow, while you're in school, your mom and I are going to decide what to do about all the fibs you've told." Ethan gave him back the blanket he'd been wrapped in earlier. "Put that around you. We'll get your jacket washed tomorrow."

Jason did as he was told, then said, "Ebbie fibbed, too."

Ethan took a clean jacket out of his closet for himself. "I know. And I didn't bother to correct either one of you. I'm not saying it's all your fault. I'm just saying it's going to take some doing to straighten it out."

"Why do we have to?" Jason asked, watching Ethan as he put on his hat.

"Because they're lies, Jason," Beth said.

"But the sheriff doesn't have a wife," the boy said reasonably. "And you don't have a husband. Why don't we just have a wedding? He's got that house on the hill with the cup thing. Grandma would like that."

Beth looked at Ethan in surprise. "The cupola? That's your house?"

She smiled. He'd seen enormous relief and gratitude on her face when he'd walked into the office with Jason. But he hadn't seen pleasure there before. "That's a wonderful house," she said. "Jason and I used to imagine who lived there. We thought maybe the mayor.''

"Nope.'' Ethan caught her arm and drew her with him to the front office. Jason followed. "Just the sheriff. You want to call your friend and tell her where you'll be? You might want to invite her to Jason's birthday party so we can get some bodies in the pizza place to make our story look good.''

She made a wry face but finally seemed resigned to going home with him. "This is all so unreal,'' she said, dialing the number while Ethan put a clean pair of big tube socks on Jason's feet.

Her friend Kelly did not understand the simple explanation Beth gave.

"What do you mean, you're going home with the sheriff?'' she asked. "You mean he's...holding you or something? Your in-laws have filed charges?''

"No,'' Beth said. "Jason sort of told them that...that we're...''

"Yeah?''

"Getting married,'' she said in a rush, watching the sheriff cuff the long socks on her son's ankles.

"Who?'' Kelly demanded.

Beth turned away and lowered her voice. "Me,'' she replied, "and the sheriff. Jase told my in-laws we were getting married, and they didn't believe him. They think he did it just to make them leave me alone—which he did—so they're hanging around outside waiting for me to go home.''

There was silence on the other end of the line. "So you're really going home...with the sheriff?''

"Yes.''

"I see.'' There was a note of interested speculation in Kelly's voice.

"No, you don't," Beth said. "It's just a stopgap measure until we can talk it over and figure out what to do."

Kelly cleared her throat. "It's odd that telling the truth hasn't occurred to anybody."

That was true. And it was something Beth didn't care to give much thought to because, in retrospect, she realized she should have firmly denied her son's claims at the time.

But Jason had seemed so thrilled with his solution to the problem of his grandparents, and frankly, she'd rather enjoyed their shocked surprise. Throughout her married life they'd cajoled and coerced Steve into doing what they wanted rather than what *she* wanted, and since she'd moved here they'd bedeviled her with their threats of taking Jason away.

It had been thrilling to see them outsmarted, if only for the moment.

She sighed. "I'm sure it'll have to come to that, probably tomorrow at Jason's birthday party. Oh. You have to come. Okay? Dinosaur Pizza at three-thirty."

"Ah...sure. But I didn't know you were planning a party."

"I wasn't. It was all rather impromptu. Kelly, listen." Beth wished she had her friend in front of her to give her a hug. In the blackness of her despair when she'd realized Jason was gone, she'd had no one to turn to but Kelly, who'd hurried to help. "Thank you so much for coming over and for staying so late. I owe you big. Go into the gallery on your way out and take that welcome sign you've been admiring."

"No, I—"

"Kelly, please. Take it." Beth glanced over her

shoulder and saw the sheriff sitting in a chair by the back-vestibule door, her son in his lap. "I've got to go. See you tomorrow for pizza?"

"I'll be there. Beth?"

"Yeah?"

"You know...be careful. The sheriff's a hunk and all, but this is all kind of...sticky."

"I know. Don't worry."

The ride to the sheriff's house took less than ten minutes. Ethan checked the rearview mirror and grinned without looking away from the road. "Guess what?"

Beth played the game. "We're being followed by a white Cadillac?"

"Yep. And they're coming with us up the hill."

The neighborhood was old and comprised of beautiful turn-of-the-century homes. The old sidewalks were broken by the roots of oaks and cedar trees that had probably been there when the town was settled 150 years before.

It was now almost midnight, most porch lights were off, and only the occasional light glowed in an upstairs window. Ethan's house was dark as he pulled up in front of it. He checked the rearview mirror again.

"Are they still with us?" Beth asked.

"They're maybe two hundred feet back. Just turned off their lights."

Beth held the car door open while Ethan pulled Jason out of the vehicle and into his arms. "I hope we don't wake your daughter," she said. "You must worry about her when you have to leave her alone at night."

When he looked surprised that she knew about his

daughter and that the girl was alone, she explained. "Ebbie told me that your wife died and you live alone with your fourteen-year-old daughter."

He shook his head. "It's a good thing Ebbie works for me and not the CIA," he said. "National security would be a thing of the past."

"It was a long wait," she said in Ebbie's defense. "We exchanged confidences."

"To her that's like oxygen. No wonder she offered her garden for our wedding. Follow me."

Beth trailed Ethan up the porch steps and waited while he held Jason with one arm and fitted his key in the lock with his free hand. "My brother lives next door," he said, indicating a large Craftsman-style house on the neighboring lot. "He watches out for her."

The door open, Ethan set the boy on his feet just inside and flipped on a light.

Beth saw a short-haired calico cat race down the stairway to the right, then stop abruptly at the sight of strangers, big green eyes peering at them through the balusters.

Ethan went to the stairway and reached a long arm up to scratch the cat between the ears. "This is Cindy Crawford," he said with a light laugh.

Beth noticed the small black spot above the cat's mouth. It did indeed look like a glamorous mole.

Jason went forward to get acquainted, but Cindy meowed once and darted upstairs.

"My daughter's a cat lover." Ethan led the way up and beckoned them to follow. "She also has a big gray Persian named Simba, but he's usually too lazy to investigate visitors after he's gone to bed. Cindy, on the other hand, has to know everything."

Beth noticed the subtle green-and-yellow-flowered wallpaper and dark woodwork as she and Jason followed Ethan. They proceeded down a corridor softly lit by a night-light in a bathroom, and Ethan paused to look behind a partially open door. His daughter's room, Beth guessed.

Apparently satisfied that all was well, he continued to the end of the hallway where he pushed open a door and reached inside to flip on a light. He ushered Beth and Jason inside.

The room was fairly large, despite a sloping wall under the eaves. The walls were white, the curtains blue-and-white gingham, and a pair of maple bunk beds had red-white-and-blue bandana-print coverlets.

Jason launched himself gleefully at the ladder. "I get the top one!" he declared.

Beth shushed him, aware of the sleeping girl down the hall and the major inconvenience their presence in the house had to be to the sheriff.

"It's not ideal," Ethan said, indicating the bunks, "but it should do for tonight. I'll get you some pajamas. You saw the bathroom?"

"Yes, thanks."

Ethan disappeared and Beth looked around, experiencing a strange sense of distance from the situation. She felt as though she was watching her son move around on a stage as he shed his blanket and crawled, still wearing the oversize brown sweats, under the blankets of the top bunk.

"Isn't this cool?" he demanded in an exaggerated whisper. "Bunk beds!"

Beth looked at the narrow bottom bunk and decided that even a king-size water bed could not have been more inviting at the moment. She was exhausted.

"Every woman's dream," she said, pulling off her jacket. She opened a door under the eave and found a garment rod, several empty hangers dangling from it. She hung up her jacket, feeling as though she was establishing at least a modicum of order to the chaotic jumble her life had become.

She picked up the blanket Jason had draped over the ladder and folded it at the foot of the top bunk. She turned to find Ethan standing behind her, a pair of gray pajamas in his hand.

"Nikkie could probably lend you something more suitable," he said, "but I hate to wake her."

"Of course." Beth took them from him. "These'll be fine."

"There's a fourth bedroom, but at the moment there's no bedding in it and not much furniture."

"The bunk will be fine. Thank you, Sheriff. I—"

"If you call me Sheriff in front of your in-laws," he interrupted, "it's not going to help sell our story."

"Right." She held the pajamas to her, feeling suddenly as though she needed a shield. Ethan looked comfortable and relaxed in his home environment, and she felt as though she'd landed on an alien planet. Not an unfriendly one certainly, but far removed from where she'd thought she'd be spending the night when she'd awakened that morning.

She felt compelled to chatter. "Of course. Ethan, thank you for spending hours in the cold and rain looking for Jason. And thank you for trying to help him with his grandparents. I know you've put yourself out on a limb and probably turned your household upside down. I'm very sorry we got you into all this."

"I'm not," Jason said, chin resting on his folded arms on his pillow. "This is gonna be fun!"

Beth turned to her son in complete exasperation. "Jason—"

Ethan chuckled. "He's not going to see it your way, so don't even try. Just sleep well and we'll sort it all out in the morning."

She couldn't imagine how they could sort it all out without either admitting the truth to Zachary and Joanne or staging a wedding. But she was too tired to think about that now.

"All right. In the morning."

Ethan turned to Jason. "You have everything you need?"

"Yeah." Jason reached out and caught Ethan around the neck. "Thanks. Are Grandma and Grandpa still watching from outside?"

Ethan shook his head. "I checked out my bedroom window when I got the pajamas. They're gone."

Jason freed Ethan and grinned broadly. "So they're probably thinkin' right now that everything's going to be okay with Mom and me."

Ethan imagined they were thinking they were going to hang around and see how this all played out on the supposed wedding day. But Beth didn't look as though she could deal with that right now, so he said nothing.

"Do you think I could have Buzz Lightyear on my birthday cake?" Jason asked. He fell back against his pillow. Ethan stepped forward to pull up his blankets and tuck him in.

"Sure. Who's he?"

"A space hero in *Toy Story*," Beth explained.

When Ethan still looked puzzled, she added, "The Disney movie."

Ethan nodded. "We'll see what we can do. I'll call Ebbie in the morning."

Jason kicked his feet under the covers as though his delight with the prospect of his birthday party couldn't be contained. "Thanks. This is gonna be so cool!"

Ethan turned away from the bunk to find Beth standing behind him, the pajamas still clutched to her chest. She looked uncomfortable.

"I'll pay for the party," she said.

He took her by the arm and pulled her with him to the doorway. "Good night, Jase," he called, flipping off the light.

"Night, Ethan," Jason called back.

Ethan drew Beth into the hallway and said quietly, "We'll work that all out later, all right? Why don't you just change into the pajamas and try to get some sleep."

"But I don't want you to—"

"I do pretty much as I please," he said mildly, pointing to the bathroom. "You're welcome to shower if you want to, take a bath, whatever. Just try to relax and don't sweat the details."

"Life, Ethan," she said, a little prudishly, he thought, "is all about details."

He folded his arms and shook his head. "No, I don't buy that. Life is about the big picture and not getting all hung up on the details. And right now the big picture is seeing that Jason has a great birthday."

She folded her arms, too, over the pajamas. "I agree, but I just want to make it clear that I'm the only family Jason has. Therefore I will pay for the party.''

''I'm afraid I don't buy that, either.'' He watched her sigh and firm her jaw, as though intending to resist whatever he was about to say. He found something challenging, even stimulating, about that. ''Jason and I developed a friendship tonight. I know from what he told me about you that you've done your best this past year to be everything to him. But he's coming to a point in his life where he needs more than you can give him. Maybe you're going to have to share him a little. So let's not worry about who pays for the party.''

Her eyes widened in the shadowy hallway. ''Did he say he's unhappy? I mean, besides the worry about his grandfather?''

''No,'' Ethan assured her quickly. ''He seems to understand and accept his situation. And he was proud to tell me about the cannery and all you intend to do with it. But he said he missed his father. In fact, he said he used to miss him even *before* he died.''

Beth heard those words and felt the impact of them right in the middle of her chest. So much of her grief over Steve's death was because they'd had so little of him the last few years he was alive.

''His father loved Jason very much,'' Beth said gravely. ''But he failed him.''

Ethan spread both hands in an expansive gesture. ''So let's indulge the kid a little. Let him have his fantasy for a while. We'll do his party up big and between us, try to convince the grandparents we're making a cozy home for him.''

''That sounds reasonable,'' she said on a sigh, ''but if you carry that plan to the conclusion my in-laws will demand, you may very well find yourself married to me.''

He leaned a shoulder against the wall and grinned. ''Are you suggesting I might find that unpleasant?''

Beth did her level best to quell the spark of excitement those words generated in her. For the last five or six years of her marriage, she'd wondered what it would be like to live intimately with someone who was aware she was there.

And she had the feeling the sheriff was always sharply conscious of who was around him and what went on.

''I'm an artist,'' she said, thinking she could erase that grin from his face, ''and not very domestic. I'm a marginal cook and I often forget things like laundry and shopping.'' She let her eyes run lazily over the attractive length of his body. ''I imagine a man like you pictures the perfect wife as a cross between Martha Stewart and a Playboy bunny.''

He laughed softly. ''I had a perfect wife,'' he said, ''and she was nothing like that. She often forgot to do laundry, too, though she was a lawyer and not an artist. She was loving and funny and forgiving.'' He sighed, his voice taking on a moody quality. ''And I had her for only twelve years—she died five years ago. I miss her often, but it's never her domestic skills I think of, only the warmth and laughter she brought to my life.''

Beth felt small for having tried to force him to a distance by suggesting he was in any way typical.

''I'm sorry,'' she said. ''I guess it's because I haven't been appreciated as anything but a business prop for a very long time. It sounds as though you had a wonderful marriage.''

"I did. I'm sorry you didn't."

She shrugged, having long ago accepted that domestic bliss would never be hers. "It was good in the beginning, I learned to live with what it became, and now it's over. Art and marriage aren't compatible, anyway."

Now he shrugged. "A lot of people think law enforcement and marriage are incompatible because the job comes first." He grinned again. "So that makes cops and artists compatible, doesn't it?"

She blinked. "I believe that's a flawed equation," she said. "I think it means neither of us should get into a relationship. Anyway—" she squared her shoulders and cleared her throat "—thank you again for finding my son. And for being his friend. I...I do appreciate your concern for him. I just don't think it has to extend to me and my problems with my in-laws." She smiled at him hesitantly. "So, good night. We'll organize the party and the...the problem in the morning. Okay?"

It was a moment before he nodded. She got the distinct impression he was simply humoring her. "Okay," he said. "Sleep well."

"Thank you. You, too."

She stepped into the bathroom. She'd change into the pajamas and shower in the morning. As she closed the door and stood in the dark, her heartbeat skipped erratically. She attempted to analyze her feelings and finally concluded that they didn't appear to be caused by worry or fear.

Her racing pulse was caused by excitement. She groaned, knowing that suggested big trouble.

CHAPTER FOUR

BETH TURNED OFF the shower and stood for a moment in the warm steamy space, pulling her arguments together. After a good night's sleep and in the sunny sanity-restoring light of day, she felt in control again.

Her in-laws were forceful and demanding and single-minded, but she was sure she could make them see reason if she was calm and logical. That was certainly a more acceptable solution to her problems than marrying the sheriff.

She reached beyond the shower curtain surrounding the old tub, caught a towel off the rack and wrapped it around herself, wondering what had happened to her that she'd even considered such an outrageous scheme.

Actually the answer was simple. Her son had been missing for hours in rain-filled darkness, and when he'd finally been restored to her, she'd have done anything to ensure she'd never be parted from him again.

But such dramatics weren't necessary. Last night the storm had heightened the dangers of her situation. But this morning she was thinking more clearly. She would thank the sheriff for his help and be on her way.

Wrapped in a fluffy green towel, she pushed the shower curtain aside—and found herself face-to-face with a girl in a red chenille bathrobe with tabby-cat faces embroidered on its big patch pockets.

The girl was probably as tall as she was. Her long curly mass of dark hair was disheveled, and the expression in her dark eyes as she stared at Beth was one of complete disbelief.

Beth stared back, searching her mind for some brief and reasonable explanation to give the girl for her presence there.

The girl smiled suddenly. "Hi," she said in a voice still groggy with sleep. "I'm Tanika. But nobody calls me that. It's Nikkie." She laughed a little nervously, then indicated Beth's towel. "So. You stayed the night?"

"Ah...yes," Beth replied. Then realizing what the girl was suggesting, corrected her quickly. "Oh. No, no. Not like that. I mean...my son was missing and your father searched for him for hours. Then...well, he brought us home because—"

"Hi!" Jason burst into the little room, still wearing the brown sweats. His thick dark hair stood up in spikes, and his blue eyes were as filled with excitement as they'd been the night before when he'd discovered the bunk beds.

Nikkie's friendly smile turned to confusion.

"Nikkie," Beth said, stepping out of the tub, "this is my son, Jason. Jase, this is Ethan's daughter, Tanika."

Jason looked at her as though assessing her worthiness to associate with his hero. "Weird name," he said.

"It's American Indian," the girl replied somewhat stiffly. "My mother liked it." She looked from Jason to Beth and asked, "What are you doing here?"

Beth opened her mouth to explain, but before she could form the words, Jason said with considerable pride, "The sheriff's going to be my dad!"

Nikkie stared at him for a full ten seconds, then demanded in an over-my-dead-body tone of voice, "What? *What?*"

"Hey." A quiet male voice spoke from the doorway of the crowded little room. "I see you've all met. Who needs a family room when you've got a bathroom? Good morning, Nik."

He was already showered, Beth noticed, and dressed in a beige shirt with all the brass buttons and pins of his office, a brown tie and brown slacks.

"Daddy." Nikkie turned to her father, a formidable picture of indignation not at all diminished by the kitty faces on her bathrobe. "I want to know what's going on. *Now.*"

Beth clutched the towel closely, feeling her cheeks redden as Ethan's eyes ran over her. "Good morning," he said, his attention diverted from his daughter. "Sleep well?"

"Yes, thank you," Beth replied awkwardly, feeling apologetic that his daughter was upset, wishing desperately that she was anywhere but this tiny packed room. "I, ah, was hoping to be out before Nikkie got up, but—"

"The kid says you're going to be his father!" Nikkie indicated Jason with a disparaging wave of her hand. "Is he delusional or was I left out of the loop on something important?"

Jason threw his arms possessively around Ethan's waist. "Tell her," he said, wrinkling his nose at Nikkie. "Tell her about you and Mom getting married."

"What?" Nikkie shrieked.

"We are *not* getting married!" Beth told Nikkie, hoping to defuse what was rapidly becoming a little war. The source of the dispute, she accepted wryly, was the sheriff. Nikkie felt he belonged to her, and while she might have been willing to share him with a woman who'd spent the night in his bed, that generosity didn't extend to another child.

And Jason, who didn't want anyone or anything to endanger the flimsy hold he had on security, was also staking his claim on Ethan.

Beth couldn't help but feel left out. She was the only one in the room with no claim on the sheriff, and her own son didn't even seem to notice her presence in his determination to make sure that Ethan noticed *him*.

Ethan put a hand to Jason's back, then extended his free arm to Nikkie. "Jason, why don't you get ready for school while I catch Nikkie up on what's going on," he said. "Beth?"

"Yes?" She looked up, a little surprised to be noticed after all, even if it wasn't by her son.

"Brodie'll make you breakfast."

"Brodie?"

"My brother comes over every morning to eat. Don't let him scare you. He's all talk."

And with that he patted Jason's shoulder and left the room with Nikkie.

Jason stared after them longingly. "You don't think he'll change his mind, do you?" he asked, his voice small and pitiful.

Beth, her early-morning confidence shaken by the volatile confrontation, found that she could neither reassure him that Ethan wouldn't change his mind, nor explain to him that it would probably be better all around if he did. At the moment she wasn't sure of anything.

And there'd been something friendly, even... needy, in Nikkie's eyes when she'd introduced herself to Beth. As though a woman in her life might be welcome.

But that tentative extension of friendship had been shattered when she'd thought Beth—and particularly Jason—might be intruding on her life with her father.

Beth closed her eyes for a moment, wondering how things could possibly get more complicated. She quickly dismissed the thought, afraid maybe they would.

"Take your shower," she said briskly to Jason, "and remember, when you're a guest in someone's home, it isn't polite to tell them you think their name is weird."

Jason sank onto the closed lid of the toilet. "She doesn't like me. Do you think Ethan'll change his mind because she doesn't like me?"

"I don't know what will happen, Jase," she said frankly. "Take your shower and get ready for school, and I'll try to figure everything out today."

He looked at her doubtfully. "You'll tell Grandma and Grandpa the truth because you won't want to lie. Then...then it'll all be over."

She took his face in her hands and leaned over to kiss the tip of his nose. "Sweetie, it never began. The sheriff is *not* your father, even though you'd like that very much. And you can't make it happen, just because you want it. He belongs to Nikkie, not to us."

Jason's eyes brimmed with tears. "Well...how come we don't get a dad?"

"We had one," she reminded gently. "Remember?"

A tear spilled over onto Jason's cheek. "Not very much. Mostly it's just been you and me. I love you and all, Mom. But he's...he's got muscles."

Beth wrapped her arms around her son and hugged him. "The heart's a muscle, too, Jason. And mine works just for you."

He returned her hug and giggled. "It's funny to think of a heart being bulgy."

Now she laughed, relieved to hear the humor in his voice. "At my age, Jason, everything gets bulgy, only not in a good way. Now hurry up and get showered and dressed so you can have breakfast before you go."

"Okay." Momentarily distracted from his problems, Jason pulled off the brown sweatshirt as Beth hurried to the bedroom to put on the undies, old jeans and sweater she'd been wearing last night before this whole drama had begun.

ETHAN SAT on the blue-and-yellow coverlet on the edge of his daughter's bed and watched her pace in front of him, much as he'd seen her mother do during opening or closing arguments in court. He felt a bittersweet pang in his chest.

"I thought we were in this together," she said with an air of injured pride as she marched past him. Her cats watched her movements with interest, one on each of her two pillows. "That's what you're always saying when you want to learn something from me. 'Nikkie,'" she quoted him, "'we're in this together. There isn't anything you can't tell me or ask me.'" She gave him an angry glance as she went past him again, headed in the other direction. "I thought that applied to you, too."

He caught her arm and pulled her down beside him onto the bed. "It does apply to me, too." He put an arm around her shoulders. "But I just explained what happened. Jase was a little kid in trouble, and Beth looked like she was at the end of her rope last night. And while I imagine the grandparents have the boy's best interests at heart, they were terrifying. I had to do something."

"So you brought them home." Nikkie sighed with exaggerated patience. "Fine. But what's this stuff about you becoming the little twerp's father? You're not going to do that, are you? Marry her just so the grandparents won't go to court to get the kid?"

Ethan rubbed his forehead. He hated starting the day with a headache. "I don't know what I'm going to do. I thought I'd wait till the birthday party this afternoon and see how the grandparents react."

Nikkie played with the belt of her robe, knotting and unknotting the ends. "You always wanted to have a boy, didn't you?" she asked moodily. "Only, Mom died before you could do it."

"No," he replied honestly, pulling her closer. "We never talked about having another baby. You were great and your mom had a busy career. You were enough for us."

"But you always took me fishing with you and out to cut wood and to football games at the park."

"I thought you liked coming with me."

"I did. I do. But it'd be more fun for you with a son. All your friends bring their boys and you just have me."

He wasn't sure where this was coming from and

he tried to tread carefully. "You're a good sport. They all like you. It's never been a problem, has it?"

"No," she replied with a certain lack of conviction. "But I'm getting older now. Worms are losing their thrill for me, and I hate having to go to the bathroom in the woods."

He laughed. "Your mom did, too. But the point is, you never gripe and that makes you one of the guys."

She leaned into him and put her arms around him. He knew he had her sympathy if not her understanding. "I think it'd be a little scary around here if you got married—even if it wasn't for real. I mean, they'd have to *live* here, right?"

"Beth and I are going to talk about that later." He squeezed her to him and kissed the top of her head. "But you must know you're the most important person in my life and I'd never do anything to hurt you."

"I know. But you have to fall in love again *some*time. I mean, you're still a young man." She said the words seriously and with some surprise.

He bit back a laugh. "Thank you."

"But it'll be hard for me to share you. What if she doesn't want to go to Bailey's for breakfast on Sunday mornings and read the paper while we eat? What if she doesn't like 'NYPD Blue' and wants to rent some mushy movie?" She sat up, her eyes wide and horror-filled. "What if she doesn't like cats?"

"Then," he said with a theatrical sigh, "I guess you'll have to make pancakes on Sunday mornings, sit through *Love Story* on Tuesday nights and...I don't know, give the cats to some lab-animal bounty hunter who—"

That earned him a doubled fist to the chest and an indignant "Da-ad!"

He laughed and dodged a second punch, catching her wrist. "Come on. You know I'd never let anyone deprive you of your cats. And the rest of the stuff is something all families have to deal with. Sometimes you give up something to get something else. It's life."

"I like *this* life," she said petulantly.

"I know." He grew serious. "I do, too. And I promise not to do anything that'll change it too radically. Trust me, okay?"

She appeared to consider that. "I always trust you. But I never got up to take a shower and found a woman wrapped in a towel in the bathroom before."

Yes, he thought with a slight quickening of his pulse. That had been quite a sight. Soft breasts pressed under the enveloping edge of the towel and two long shapely legs visible below. He'd had to force himself to focus on Nikkie and Jason.

"Right. But everything happened too suddenly last night, and too late for me to explain it to you. I thought I might get to you before you got up this morning, but apparently Beth's an early riser."

"So." Nikkie went to a dresser drawer and pulled out a pink sweater. "Her name's Elizabeth."

"No." He stood. "Bethany. Bethany Richards. She's an artist. She bought that old cannery on the waterfront."

Nikkie pulled a pair of jeans out of the closet and turned to frown at him. "An artist? You mean, paintings and stuff?"

"Yeah, I guess. I'm not sure." He went toward the door, then turned as he opened it and asked, "What are you doing after school?"

"The drama club's meeting to decide what play to

do for the Winter Festival weekend.'' She retrieved a pair of fat-heeled boots from the bottom of her closet. They were the ugliest things he'd ever seen, and he remembered paying a fortune for them. ''Why?''

''We're having a birthday party for Jason at three-thirty at Dinosaur Pizza. If you have time to come, it'd help his story in front of his grandparents.''

She rolled her eyes. ''You want me to come to an eight-year-old's birthday party?'' Then she huffed impatiently. ''And how come *you're* giving him a party? You just met him last night.''

Ethan nodded. His daughter definitely had some of her mother's gift for argument. ''He happened to mention when I was returning him to his mother that he wished he could have a birthday party like all the other kids have, rather than one where his grandparents come to bully his mother. So when he started telling his story about me becoming his father, I backed him up by inviting them to the party—which hadn't really been planned but which Ebbie's supposed to put together this morning.''

Nikkie tossed her boots at the bed, then yanked open a drawer and pulled out a pair of thick flowered socks. ''And it'd help your story if I show up and act like a big sister.''

''You don't have to act like anything. But it'd be great if you could come. And pizza will likely be dinner tonight.''

She tossed the socks after the boots and moved toward him. ''The meeting'll probably break up too late for me to make the party,'' she said with little visible sign of regret. ''But maybe you could bring me home a couple of pieces of pizza. Sausage, pepperoni and onion—no olives.''

"Right." He leaned down to kiss her cheek. "Have a good day."

She hugged him briefly. "You, too. And, Daddy?"

He stopped in the hallway and leaned back into the room. "Yeah?"

She hesitated, as though considering what she was about to say, then blurted, "Did you and...Beth have sex last night?"

It always startled him when his daughter brought up the subject of sex. He understood that she was no longer his *little* girl and that it was far healthier for her to bring him her questions than talk about them to someone else, but the subject was so important it unnerved him.

He was always tempted to tell her horror stories about how sex at too young an age ruined lives and futures, but that wasn't smart. He didn't want to frighten her into never discussing sex with him again. Still she was pretty and shapely already, and he knew that several of her classmates were experimenting. The prospect that she might terrified him.

"I prefer the term 'making love,'" he said, trying not to betray his fears. "But no, we didn't."

"You'd only known her a few hours." Nikkie studied him gravely. "You couldn't possibly have learned to love her in that amount of time. So you couldn't have made love to her. But you could have had sex. People have recreational sex all the time."

Dear God! He leaned a shoulder against the wall as much for support as to appear casual. "*I* don't. Sex is for love...and for communication and procreation, but not recreation."

"She's very pretty," Nikkie persisted. "And you've been celibate a long time."

He closed his eyes briefly. He certainly could never be considered guilty of having stifled his child's curiosity. "Like I said, love's important. I had it with your mom, and that's made it impossible for me to ever use sex just for fun. Though it certainly can be."

She sighed, apparently satisfied. "I sure would like to know what it's all about," she admitted wistfully.

He found relief in her admission that she didn't know. "It's all about things that are just too big to deal with at fourteen," he said, leaning down to kiss her again. "Even for a fourteen-year-old as smart as you are."

She gave him a rueful and knowing look. "But someday I'll be ready. Right now, though, there's enough going on in my life."

"Amen to that," he said. "See you tonight."

He went into his room to retrieve his utility belt and jacket, praying he would be much older and wiser by the time she *was* ready.

BREAKFAST BRODIE-STYLE was bacon, eggs and hash browns with onions and garlic. Beth considered herself lucky that she had a preference for onions and garlic, because Ethan's brother had been generous with them. She poured coffee while he brought their plates to the table.

Brodie Drum was a little taller and leaner than his brother, but had the same rich dark hair and eyes. He wore a blue-and-white-striped shirt with a large sewn-on patch on the back embroidered with "Drum's Garage." His name was on the front pocket.

He exuded energy and a confident sexuality that Beth concluded was the reason for Ethan's warning, but he was friendly and welcoming. She guessed he was four or five years younger than Ethan.

They sat across from each other at the small table in the middle of the sunny yellow kitchen. Ethan had explained her presence to his brother earlier, and Brodie had commiserated with her while he cooked.

"So what we have to do now," he said, sounding eager, "is convince your in-laws you're marrying into a solid loving family. I'll come to the birthday party."

"Thank you," she said, shaking salt and pepper on her egg and potatoes. "I'd like that, but we're not sure what we're going to do about the...the wedding thing."

Brodie seemed surprised. "But what other solution is there? And you can't do better than Ethan, even if it's just a temporary thing. He's a solid citizen, good provider, and he knows all that—" he waved his fork over his plate "—all that sensitive stuff. He shouts only when he's exhausted every other option, and he's willing to lend a hand to people everybody else has given up on."

Brodie's eyes softened. "His wife, Diana, I know, was very happy with him. And he's great with Nikkie. She's a good kid and he's raised her by himself the last five years."

"Hi!" Jason burst into the kitchen, jacket held by its collar and dragging on the floor. Someone had laundered it already. It was easy to guess who.

He came to Beth's side and smiled at Ethan's brother.

Brodie pushed his chair back and reached across the table to shake Jason's hand. "Hi, Jase," he said, pulling a chair out for him. "I'm going to be your uncle. Sit down. I'll get your breakfast."

Beth opened her mouth, prepared to remind him that the wedding issue was undecided. But Jason followed him to the stove and said excitedly, "Wow! I never had an uncle before."

"Well, you're going to like it," Brodie replied, carrying the warm plate to the table with a hot pad. Then he went to the refrigerator and poured a glass of milk. "Uncles spoil you. They let you do things your father won't. Want some chocolate in that milk?"

"Yeah!"

Jason sat in the chair at a right angle to Beth and dug into his breakfast while Brodie poured a generous amount of syrup into a dessert spoon, then stirred it into the milk.

"I'm coming to your party this afternoon." Brodie resumed his chair. "What'll I bring?"

"What do you mean?"

"For a present."

"Oh! You know those *Toy Story*..." Jason began a complicated description of the movie's action figures, then caught Beth's reprimanding eye and stopped. "You don't have to bring me anything." The denial was offered with a smile but lacked conviction. "I'd just like you to come so I can introduce you to Grandma and Grandpa."

"I'll be there," Brodie promised.

Beth had difficulty taking issue with her son's ear-to-ear grin of delight. Brodie was as comfortable to be with as Ethan was and just as indulgent with Jason. But he also seemed as bent as his brother on believing that marriage to Ethan was the solution to her in-law problems. She'd tried to stop him from letting Jason think that was going to happen, but he hadn't seemed to notice her protests.

"Hi!" Jason said when Ethan entered the room.

The concern that Ethan would no longer like him because Nikkie didn't showed clearly in his expression. But Ethan touched Jason's shoulder as he passed him, and the expression evaporated.

Ethan went to a far corner of the kitchen where a large bag of cat food was tucked away. He lifted it easily and shook food into two bowls.

Cindy and a gray ball of fur Beth presumed to be Simba ran into the room and began to eat. Ethan stroked each down-bent head, then crossed to the oven to retrieve his plate.

He poured a cup of coffee and brought it and his plate to the table. He grinned at Jason as he sat opposite him. "Mm," he said. "Smell those onions and garlic."

He picked up his cup without using the handle and took a sip, smiling at Beth over the rim. "Did Brodie ask you to run away with him to the Seychelles yet?"

"I was saving that for after she gets to know me." Brodie winked at Beth. "Think you could take to island living?"

"Easily," she replied. "I like the thought of warm beaches and blue water."

"But Gauguin already did the island thing in his paintings," Ethan said. "Don't you want to do something else?"

Beth laughed. "I wouldn't complain about where I was if I had the time to paint." She chewed and swallowed a bit of crisp bacon. "But I don't, at least not right now. All my dreams of being a real artist—you know, doing oils on canvas—have to take second place to paying the rent, so to speak. I make signs, plaques, decorative boxes, children's chairs, stuff like that."

"In the Seychelles, you could make those little figures you see made out of shells in tourist shops." Brodie drew a picture in the air with his fork.

Beth made a face. "I don't think so. But we could make our living pearl-diving or something. Maybe you could open a garage there."

Now Brodie made a face. "No. When I make it to the Seychelles, the only thing I'm doing is beachcombing. No more squeaks you can't find, brakes that don't act up when I'm test-driving them, no customers unwilling to pay for the time it takes to repair a transmission…"

"You mean you'd be expecting monthly checks from me," Ethan said, clarifying his brother's daydreams. "Or Beth would have to support you."

Brodie chewed thoughtfully on a mouthful of potatoes, then shook his head. "No, I don't want Beth to have to lift a finger. And you owe me for all the times you beat me up when we were kids."

Ethan made a scornful sound. "You deserved it. You were such a whiner, always running to Mom over every little thing. Like the time I gave you a little tap on the nose in the grocery store."

Brodie sat up indignantly. "That wasn't a tap. It was a punch! My nose was bleeding all over the candy aisle!"

"You tried to steal a package of bubble gum."

"It might have had a trading card in it that would have made me a rich man today!"

Ethan shook his head at Beth. "I wouldn't go anywhere with him if I were you. No matter how inviting he makes island living sound."

"Me, either." Jason grinned from brother to brother, happy to be part of their banter. Then he said staunchly to Ethan, "I'm staying with you."

"Well," Brodie said, pretending to be affronted, "Forget getting any *Toy Story* character for your birthday."

The three of them laughed and Beth forced a smile, but she felt a mild resentment over how quickly her son's allegiance was switching from her to Ethan.

Nikkie flew through the kitchen calling goodbye to her father and her uncle as she reached into a cupboard, snatched a granola bar and headed for the door. To Beth and Jason she threw a polite smile and a casual "See ya."

The door closed behind her just as a school bus pulled up in front of the house.

Brodie pushed his empty plate away and made a conciliatory face at Jason as the boy downed his last swallow of milk. "My shop's a couple of blocks from your school. Do you want to come with me or do you want to wait for Ethan to drive you?" He turned to Beth. "Is it all right?"

"Of course." She smiled gratefully. "I'd appreciate that."

"Good." Brodie stood and carried his plate to the counter. "Then I'll pick him up after school and bring him to the party."

Jason followed his example with his own plate. "Even though I won't go to the seashells with you?"

"The *Sey*chelles," Brodie corrected. "And I'm sure you'll eventually come to your senses. I'm a much nicer guy than Ethan."

Jason cast an adoring look at Ethan. "Nobody's nicer than Ethan."

Ethan gave him a thumbs-up. "You're okay, Jase," he said.

CHAPTER FIVE

"YOU LOOK RESTED," Ethan said as he got up to get the coffeepot off the warmer and bring it to the table. His gaze skimmed Beth's face and lingered on her hair before he topped up her coffee mug and then his own. "If you can sleep in a bottom bunk with a squirmy kid over your head, you can sleep anywhere."

She added cream to her coffee, then pushed the small jug toward him, resisting the impulse to touch her hair. She'd combed it and left it swinging free this morning because she had no idea what happened to the pins and fastener she'd had in it the day before. "You've had the experience?"

"Brodie and I had bunks," he said over his shoulder as he returned the coffeepot to the counter. "He sleeps with the same energy he displays when he's awake. And he makes great hash browns."

"That he does." She kept her eyes on her plate, wondering how best to explain to Ethan what was on her mind.

"So, do you want to talk about the birthday party and the problem with your in-laws?" he asked between forkfuls of food.

She put her own fork down and squared her shoulders, his direct question reminding her that the only

way to deal with this man was with the same direct-
ness.

"Yes," she said, "but *I'm* going to talk and you're
going to listen." She waited for him to object. When
he didn't, she was surprised into silence for another
moment.

He pretended to cock his ear. "I don't hear anything."

"I expected an argument," she admitted.

He raised an eyebrow. "Arguments are generally
two-sided. 'I'm going to talk and you're going to listen' doesn't really encourage that."

She felt her shoulders sag a little. "True. But you
saved my son's life and I'm a guest in your home and
at your table. I...I guess I'm having second thoughts
about the way I phrased that."

He grinned at her. "I'm not that delicate, Beth. If
I want to argue, I'll argue, whether or not you try to
stop me. Speak. I'm listening."

She collected her thoughts, the corner of her mind
not occupied with her son and his grandparents thinking that this man would be interesting company if her
circumstances were different. And if she didn't mind
always being in a dither. But they weren't. And she
did.

"All right." She pushed her plate away and leaned
toward him on folded arms. "I could never repay you
for all you've done. I can't tell you what my son
means to me, but I don't suppose I have to because
I can see how much you and Nikkie care for each
other." She smiled, despite her determination to make
her point. "She's lovely, by the way. Before Jason
managed to annoy her, she was very warm and polite
to me."

He smiled, too, the gesture filled with pride and amusement. "Thank you. That was because she thought you'd spent the night." He gave the phrase significant emphasis.

Her smile widened. "I know. And then Jason flew into your arms and she became Warrior Woman, protecting her home."

"I'm sorry."

"Don't apologize. It's a quality that admits her to our sisterhood—even at fourteen." Beth's expression sobered. "But that's not what I wanted to talk about."

"I'm still listening," he said, then took another sip of coffee and leaned back in his chair.

"I wish it was possible for me to let Jason go on thinking he can have you for a father," she said quickly before she could lose track of her arguments. Ethan's quiet dark eyes were focused on her, and she found their intensity unsettling. "But let's face it. Getting married to keep my in-laws out of my hair would be ridiculous."

"Why?" he asked. "Or is it my turn to talk yet?"

She sputtered, wondering how he could possibly ask such a question. "What do you mean, why? Because you don't love me and I don't love you. We don't even know each other. And even if we did it just to appease them for now, Joanne and Zachary will be a threat to me until Jason's an adult. You'd have to be married to me for at least ten years!"

Ethan watched the fire in her eyes, saw the color tinge her creamy cheeks, saw her eyebrows disappear under rich brown bangs as she strained to make him understand her position. He remembered how her voice had sounded over the radio when her son was lost and she wanted to take one of the county's cars and go look for him herself.

He was beginning to think she was wrong in believing he didn't love her.

Well, maybe *love* was too strong a word. Maybe it wasn't love at all. But he had feelings for her. A very powerful...*like*. And that seemed a pretty good basis for a relationship.

"Fifty percent of the marriages supposedly based on love," he said calmly, "end in divorce. And many of the couples who stay married do so out of laziness. Even *you* said you'd simply gotten used to what yours had become."

"That's right!" she said fervently. "And that's precisely why I've sworn I'll never get married again."

"Maybe something more reliable than love should be the reason for marriage. Like a mutual need."

"I'm thirty-two years old, I'm finally free to do what I want to do with my life, and I'm determined that no one is going to get in the way of that."

"What makes you think I would?"

She looked heavenward in supplication. "You would. I'm sure it would upset you if I didn't cook and forgot to do laundry and stayed up all night finishing a project for a craft show."

"I can cook," he replied reasonably. "Nikkie does our laundry, my uniforms go to the cleaners, and I wouldn't care how late you stayed up if you finally came home to me."

She stared at him in disbelief, opening and then closing her mouth several times as she apparently considered, then discarded one argument after another.

"Are you forgetting the kids?" she asked finally, her voice high and a little desperate. "Do you think it'd be good for them to know we married to perpetrate a hoax?"

"I think," he said, "that Jason really likes the idea of having me for a father."

"But Nikkie," she argued, "*doesn't* like the idea of sharing you, which is perfectly understandable. And I seriously doubt it would be good for a fourteen-year-old girl to have her life upended like that."

"Nikkie's been without a mother for five years." He leaned his elbows on the table, cupped one hand over the other and looked at her, his eyes reflecting that he, too, had been without someone he loved. "That was an important time for her. I did my best to be there for her and I think we've held our own, but I know she's lost out on some things because I can't be what Diana could have been to her. And now I'm looking at an even more critical time in her life. A time when she should have a woman to turn to."

Beth felt her arguments growing fuzzy in the face of his emotional honesty, but she struggled to clear them. "Ethan, I can't be what Diana could have been to her, either. I'm me, and unfortunately I'm not at all a typical mother. And, anyway, if you married me, I think she'd see me as a threat, rather than someone to turn to and confide in."

"Maybe in the beginning," he agreed, "but she's a smart kid. She'd see how much you have to give to our lives."

Beth shook her head in disbelief. "Why do you *say* that? I just told you—"

"I know. You don't cook, you forget to do laundry, and you hang out in your studio all night." He sighed, lowered his arms and leaned toward her. "I guess because your husband resented the artist in you, you have trouble understanding that when a man really loves a woman, he wants her to be who she really is. Whatever inconvenience that brings him is tolerable—particularly if she loves him back."

"But you don't *love* me!" she said emphatically, slapping both hands on the table so hard the crockery shook.

He didn't even blink. He smiled, instead, and that completely unsettled her. "I like you a hell of a lot, though. And you like me."

She closed her eyes and put a hand over them. "What I really like," she said with quiet exasperation, "is a man who listens to me when I'm talking."

He laughed softly. "I've heard every word. I think what you mean is that you like a man who listens, then does what you want him to do. Which seems to be in direct contrast to how *you'd* like to be treated by *him*."

Beth dropped both hands to her lap, fell against the back of her chair and eyed him with weary frustration. "If we were married," she said, "I'd probably kill you the first time we had a fight."

He grinned wickedly. "I don't think so. I'm BPST-trained."

"Who trained?"

"Board of Police Standards and Training. But I might let you wrestle me down just to see what happens."

"You're impossible."

"You're not the first to tell me that."

"I can't marry you."

"Okay."

For all his wily arguments, he made that concession easily and with seemingly little regret. Beth felt a strange pinch of disappointment in the suddenly quiet aftermath of their head-to-head confrontation.

"No hard feelings?" she asked.

"Of course not." He pushed away from the table and picked up his plate and mug. "Come on. I'll give you a ride to the cannery."

She followed him with her dishes. "And I'm paying for the party," she insisted, hoping to take advantage of his amenable mood.

He nodded, putting his things in the sink. "Whatever you want."

"Why?" She put her dishes in after his, then turned to face him suspiciously.

He appeared confused. "Why what?"

She put a hand on her hip. "Why are you suddenly saying yes to everything? To show me what an easygoing husband you'd be?"

"No," he replied, reaching up to button the collar he'd left undone under the loose knot of his tie. "To show you how dull and unfulfilling it would be to have such a husband."

So, he was using reverse psychology on her. She felt warmed and amused. "Ah." She smiled. "The toothless-tiger theory."

"Pardon me?"

"Challenge. Where's the glory in taming a toothless tiger? Is that what you're trying to tell me?"

He considered that a moment, then shook his head. "I don't think so. Generally men don't like to hear the word 'tamed' used in a sentence about them. Some of us can be domesticated but never *tamed*."

"Then what was your point?"

"That you'd be bored in a week by a man who did exactly what you wanted him to do."

She laughed. "That's a myth put forth by men who want everything their *own* way."

"Really?" He shifted his weight and she had the skin-prickling awareness of being hunted. "Do you want me to kiss you?"

She parted her lips to answer, but couldn't decide on yes or no. In her current state of confusion, either answer seemed a lie.

Then with a swiftness that validated her notion of being hunted, his hand went under her hair and caught her nape, gently but firmly. He tilted her head slightly as his came down to block out the sun streaming in through the kitchen window.

And he kissed her. He wasn't forceful, but he wasn't tentative. His lips had the same gentle but confident strength as the hand at her neck, as well as an artful mobility that made her put both hands on his waist to steady herself.

She felt the tip of his tongue against her lips and opened to admit it. But all he did was explore the rim of the inside of her lips. Then he withdrew, ending the kiss with the lightest nip of her bottom lip, effectively erasing any comparison of him to a toothless tiger.

When he raised his head, she felt as though someone had worked her over with a foam bat.

He frowned down at her, looking a little unsettled himself. "I expected you to say no." His voice was quiet, thoughtful. "And because I was sure kissing you would be wonderful, I was going to make the point afterward that you'd have missed the pleasure if I'd done as you asked." His frown deepened. "But you *didn't* say no."

Still shaken, she pulled his hand from her neck. "I didn't say yes, either." Then because she knew he'd won that one, she admitted with a thin smile, "But your point was made, anyway."

He cleared his throat. "Good. Get your jacket. I'm leaving in five minutes."

ETHAN FOUND a sales receipt on his desk for a sheet cake. There was a note scrawled on it that said, "Pick up at three." Beside it was a bag that contained paper plates and napkins with *Toy Story* figures on them, as well as a giant package of colorful balloons.

"Your share is seventeen dollars," Ebbie called from the outer office, her telephone receiver cradled on her shoulder. "I'm holding for Chuck. He's rousting a pair of homeless men out of that empty house down the street from your place. I wish that somebody would buy it and restore it, or that the city would condemn it. Between the drifters who break in for a refuge from the rain and the kids who dare each other to go in, the damn thing's on the log every other day. Yeah, Chuck?" She responded to a question on the other end of the line, logged the call on the computer, then called the shelter to tell them Chuck was bringing them a couple of clients.

At last she hung up the phone and grinned at Ethan, who stood in his doorway. "I bought Jason a basketball. You think he'll like that?"

"Sure." He pulled the right number of bills out of his wallet and put them on Ebbie's desk. "You made the reservations at Dinosaur?"

"Yes. But I couldn't tell them how many. I guessed twenty, with kids from school. What do you think?"

"Sounds good to me." He patted her graying curls. "Thanks. Even if his grandparents foul up his life, he'll have a party to remember."

Ebbie looked concerned. "I thought you and the mother were getting along when I left. The wedding's off?"

He shrugged, trying to ignore the feeling of something important missed, of two lives destined to entwine, yet somehow evading each other and moving in opposite directions.

But that was ridiculous. This time yesterday he hadn't even known Beth or Jason Richards existed. He'd known Diana a lifetime. He and she had planned on Nikkie for years.

Last night had just been a strangely emotional accident. Jason's fantasies about a father couldn't be safely indulged without completely upsetting four lives.

The hell it couldn't.

"Her last marriage wasn't great," he told Ebbie, then went into his office and stood beside his desk, pretending to study the calendar. "She's determined not to do it again. It was an outrageous idea, anyway."

Ebbie got up from her desk and crossed to his doorway. "Well, *un*determine her. She's afraid of you, that's all."

Ethan looked up from his calendar, eyes narrowed. "What?"

"Afraid of you," she repeated, folding her arms over her matronly bosom. "Because you...light her fire, so to speak. I don't understand it, but I suppose a competent in-charge sort of man could appeal to a woman who was ignored by her first husband.''

He shook his head over her homegrown psychology. "Apparently not. She was very emphatic about it. No wedding.''

Ebbie studied him for a moment, then asked, "Disappointed?''

He turned a few pages on his calendar. "No. Nikkie doesn't like Jason and was annoyed that he and Beth spent the night. It was just that..." Ethan abandoned the calendar and sat down in his chair, trying to look busy. "The notion put a little excitement in my life for a few hours, that's all. When you've lived in the same place for thirty-seven years and have nothing in your life but work and a daughter who's trying hard to keep you out of *her* life, there's a certain seduction in a change of pace. Now beat it, all right? I'm busy.''

"No, you're not," she said. "I keep your calendar, remember? What does she intend to do about her in-laws?''

He pulled a file toward him. "I'm not sure. I think she intends to tell them the truth at the party this afternoon.''

Ebbie looked horrified. "You saw them. You know what they'll do with that bit of information.''

Ethan shuffled papers. "It's her decision, Eb. Our job was to find her missing child and we did. The rest of her life is up to her.''

"Your job's not over yet," she said.

He looked up at her with strained patience. "Why not?''

She angled her chin with that superior maternal air

she assumed when she thought he was being dense. "Because now *she's* the one who's lost."

Her telephone rang and Ethan shooed her away. "And close the door!" he called.

She did.

Ethan forced his mind from thoughts of Bethany Richards, from the woman who looked at him with eyes that seemed to devour him, then told him she'd vowed never to marry again and was sure they'd only make each other miserable.

He'd see what the musts were on today's schedule, give serious thought to Jason's birthday present— Then it hit him like a bolt out of the blue. A bike! Jason had said he'd bent the wheel on his bike and that it had fallen down the hill. He could use a new one, Ethan was sure.

The bike would need a light, a bell, a water bottle. Jason would need a helmet. He resolved to check out Bike-King on his lunch break.

KELLY SAT on a stool beside Beth and hung over her as she painted a whimsical angel with patchwork wings on a yellow-painted pine board. It was for the door of a little girl's room.

She watched as Beth rimmed the patches with a fine black line and added broken lines to look like stitches.

"You are so clever," Kelly said, propping her elbow on Beth's worktable and resting her cheek in the palm of her hand. "I should order a couple of those for my nieces. The name goes there, right?" She pointed at the expanse of bright empty yellow to the right of the angel.

"Yes. Julia Marie. But I won't let you order any

more stuff from me.'' Beth dropped the brush in the water, then selected a wider one for the lettering. "You do it just to make work for me so you can pay me. I appreciate it, but *you're* an artist. You can make signs for your nieces yourself.''

"I'm a potter.'' Kelly delved a hand into a bag of microwave popcorn at her elbow. "And don't tell me what I can and can't buy. I hate painting. It's so tedious.''

"Then I'll paint you a couple gratis.'' Beth dipped an inch-wide brush into bright pink acrylic paint.

Kelly groaned in disgust. "You know, that's what's wrong with you,'' she said, continuing on a theme she'd begun earlier, before she'd paused to admire the angel. "You're too generous. You're also too honest.''

Beth concentrated on forming a simple block-letter capital *J.* "And that's a bad thing?'' she said absently.

"It is when you turn down business, refuse to let a friend rent space in your art mall and decide to come clean about the sheriff to your in-laws when you know they'll probably end up taking you to court over it! That's...*stupid* honesty.''

Beth made a face at her as she dipped the brush in paint again, a perfect *J* executed. "There's no such thing as stupid honesty. Honesty is always smart.''

"Then why,'' Kelly asked smugly, "when I asked you if these narrow-legged jeans made my backside look fat, did you say no?''

Beth bit back a smile and concentrated on the lower-case *u.* "Because they don't.''

"Liar.''

"Diplomat,'' Beth corrected with a grin as she

dipped for more paint. "And anyway, they don't make you look fat. They make you look...lush."

Kelly waited while Beth formed the *l*, *i* and *a*, then expelled a breath. "Well, I'm not being diplomatic with you. You're insane."

"You don't need to rent space in my mall," Beth said, dipping the brush again. "You have that enormous garage, which you don't have to share with anyone."

"It doesn't have north light."

"You don't need it. You're a potter."

"I want to have a studio in your building!"

"You're just trying to give me money."

"You *need* money."

"Not yours."

Kelly groaned and watched her dot the *i* in Marie with a tiny heart with a patch on it.

"You know," she said, pointing to the heart, "that's your problem right there."

Beth leaned back to get a better perspective. It looked fine to her. "What's wrong with it?"

"Not that one—*your* heart. I swear to God, Beth, sometimes you're such a blonde! Your heart has a patch on it—that's why you won't let me help you and why you've decided against marrying the sheriff."

Beth dropped her brush in a jar of water and snatched the bag of popcorn from Kelly. "My heart does not have a patch on it. I'm heart-whole, and you've helped me too much already. You have to support yourself and your house and studio. My cannery is *my* responsibility. And I'm not marrying the sheriff because..."

Because for a few hours it had been a delicious

notion to share her problems with someone else, to see Jason blossom under the man's attention and to speculate what it would be like to be noticed. Not loved necessarily, just noticed. But thinking she could have that under these circumstances was absurd.

"Because it was a dumb idea. In fact, if you recall, last night when I phoned you to tell you Jason and I were going home with him, *you* told me to be careful. That he was a hunk and all, but the situation was sticky."

Kelly looked her in the eye. "I think you know you need a man, and you're afraid of that."

Beth slid off her stool and reached into the bag of popcorn. "No, I don't. I can live without it."

"It?" Kelly looked smug again. "I wasn't talking about sex. I was talking about the need for companionship, emotional support."

"I have you for that," Beth said with a smile as she crossed to the small refrigerator against the wall. She opened it and took out two bottles of juice.

"Yeah, well, I'm about to withdraw my companionship and emotional support if you don't wise up," Kelly threatened. "Come on. Don't tell your in-laws anything, team up with the sheriff and see what happens. I've asked around. Everyone has nothing but the highest praise for him. Maybe you shouldn't be careful at all. Maybe you should go for it."

"We're talking *marriage,* Kelly. That's a little different from a simple 'teaming up.' And what happens to my son and his daughter when it doesn't work out?"

"Maybe it would."

Beth handed Kelly a bottle of juice and hitched herself back up on the stool. "Yeah, right. You're an artist and you know what happened with *your* marriage. Your husband left you because he was sure you were having an affair with some guy named Art. He couldn't believe you could find a clay pot more interesting than he was.''

"That was my mistake," Kelly said after a moment's moody reflection. "If I'd truly loved him, I *would* have found him more fun than a clay pot. I'd have done my pottery, but I'd have wanted to go home to him.''

Beth shrugged and took a long swig of her cranberry-apple juice. "Look, the way things are for us now, neither of us is forced to make the choice. That's the safest thing.''

"Is life supposed to be about being safe?''

Beth put her juice down and picked up another brush. "It's about being able to do what you want to do. And we are.''

"But we're doing it alone.''

"I'm happy about that," Beth said, touching up a patch on the angel's wing. "But if you insist on complicating your life, I've got just the man for you. He's going to be at Jason's party.''

Kelly put her juice down. "Really? Who?''

"Ethan's brother, Brodie. He owns a garage and he's a great cook. Seems very nice, too.''

"Well." Kelly looked interested, then cast a disparaging eye at her jeans. "Well, you can just bet I'm not wearing these. Lush and fat *are* the same thing.'' She was silent a moment, then said, "You know, if you married the sheriff, we could double-date.''

Beth pushed the plaque out of her way and put her head in a hand stained with pink acrylic. "Kelly,'' she pleaded, "if I let you rent a studio, will you leave me alone about the sheriff?"

Kelly's cell phone rang before she could reply. She dug in her big suede backpack for it, pulled up the antenna and pressed the talk button.

Beth glowered at her friend as she addressed her caller. "Gone to Pot. This is Kelly."

Beth left the plaque to dry, then pulled another similarly designed board toward her, the angel already painted, the empty expanse for the name in blue. She dipped a brush in white paint while forming the name Jessica by eye. Now she was preparing stock for the Winter Festival Art Fair.

"Ah...yes," Kelly said hesitantly.

Beth looked up at the odd note in her friend's voice. Kelly pointed to her phone and made a face. Beth raised an eyebrow in question.

"Yes," Kelly said. "Yes, I knew her in Seattle. Why?" She listened, then blinked and shook her head at Beth. "Yes, I know you're asking the questions, but if you expect me to answer them, you'd damn well better tell me what this is about."

Beth dropped the brush back into the water and felt her shoulder muscles tense. Someone was talking to Kelly about *her.*

"Yes. She bought an old cannery to turn it into an art mall." Kelly's voice grew increasingly antagonistic. "Yes, that's a formidable venture, but the woman is very smart, hardworking and a fine artist herself." She paused to listen. "Yes. He's healthy and bright and a real credit to his mother."

Now they were discussing Jason. A little frisson of fear inched up Beth's spine. "Who is it?" she mouthed.

But Kelly was concentrating on another question from whomever was on the other end of the line.

"Rush Weston!" she said in surprise, her eyes widening at Beth. "Yes, I imagine she knows him. He teaches at the college and we've both taken classes there. I believe he'll be renting studio space in her mall when it's ready. No! No, there is nothing romantic between them."

Kelly's mouth worked uncertainly, her eyes rested on Beth in grave concern, then she swallowed and said with singular firmness in her voice and apology to Beth in her eyes. "I don't care who told you that, it isn't true. She's about to be married to Ethan Drum, our sheriff."

Oh, God. Beth put both hands to her face. "And if you want to know any more about them," Kelly continued, "I suggest you call *him* and see how he reacts to your snooping!"

Beth guessed by the sudden silence that the conversation had been terminated. She lowered her hands and asked with a sense of dread, "Who was it?"

"He said he was a reporter for an art magazine, but I'm sure the name he gave me was phony. I subscribe to everything, and I've never heard of it. And why wouldn't he have called you? My guess is he's a private detective hired by Joanne." Kelly looked reluctant to impart that information and she put an arm around Beth's shoulders as they slumped.

"I'm sorry about telling him you were getting married," Kelly continued, "but he seemed to be trying to make something out of your relationship with Rush Weston."

Beth spread her hands helplessly. "But I don't have a relationship with Rush, except as a fellow artist and possibly as his landlord when the building's ready.''

"I know that, but you know what a flamboyant gasbag Rush is. This guy had already spoken to him because he knew about his participation in the art fair. Apparently Rush was indulging his fantasies again and told him that he'd be renting space from you and the two of you would be sharing more than that very soon.''

"Oh, God, oh, *God!*" Beth paced across her studio, a knot of panic forming in her stomach.

As though reading Beth's mind and her fears, Kelly said, "Imagine what Joanne could do with that. Jason tells her you're marrying Ethan, Rush tells her detective you're marrying him. She could use you for a hockey puck in court with that!''

Beth put a hand to her chest where terror was building up a full head of steam.

"Do you hate me?" Kelly asked warily.

They'd done it, Beth thought. They'd actually put a private detective on her with the intention of discrediting her. Or they'd hired an attorney and he'd hired the detective. Either way, the result would be the same.

She couldn't believe it. She'd worried about her in-laws' interference, but she'd never thought they'd go this far.

She was confident they'd find nothing on her that would prove her an unfit mother, but if she fought them, she was looking at probably months of litigation, months that would be even harder on Jason than on her and her efforts to get her art mall going. And that would incur more expense than she could possibly pay for even if she sold the cannery.

"You *do* hate me," Kelly said, her miserable expression reflecting what Beth felt.

Beth went to her friend and put her arms around her. "Of course I don't. You were trying to help."

Kelly hugged her tightly. "You've got to do something about this, Beth."

"Yes," Beth said, dread and fear like a lead ball in her stomach. "I intend to."

CHAPTER SIX

ETHAN PULLED the red-and-silver Blazer into the parking lot of Dinosaur Pizza and drove around the back. He parked beside Ebbie, who was lifting a wide pink bakery box out of the trunk of her old Toyota.

She came around to greet him as he climbed out, then lifted the lid of the box to show him the contents. Buzz Lightyear had been formed in the middle of a cake with green-and-white icing, his features perfectly drawn with piping gel and a little dome of plastic serving as his helmet.

Jason's name was written on the cake with Buzz's highly quoted "To infinity and beyond!" under it.

"Think he'll like it?" she asked.

Ethan nodded. "If he doesn't, it's mine. Good work, Eb. Thanks for doing all the running around this morning and for making the arrangements."

"No problem," she said. "My grandkids are so far away I don't get to do this stuff. See you inside. I've already brought the cups and plates in, and we're going to need your help with the balloons."

He grinned. "I'm ahead of you. I borrowed the helium tank the Red Cross used for the blood drive."

"Clever devil." Ebbie backed away toward the restaurant's rear entrance. "See you inside."

"Right." Ethan opened the Blazer's tailgate and pulled out a blue bike with all the pertinent accessories and a giant silver bow attached to the handlebars. The bike shop had put the helmet in a box, wrapped it in colorful paper and attached another silver bow. With the box on the flat of one hand, Ethan lifted the bike by its frame with the other and was halfway toward the restaurant with it when a little yellow MG convertible came whipping around the corner at a speed that suggested the driver hadn't slowed for the turn. It screeched to a halt inches from him.

He was about to threaten the pretty redhead behind the wheel with arrest for reckless driving when her passenger leaped out of the car and ran into his arms.

Well, not precisely into his arms; both were occupied with Jason's gifts. But Beth caught the front of his tweed jacket in both fists, her blue eyes wide and troubled. He was about to tell her to give him a minute to put the bike down when she said anxiously, "Ethan, I *have* to talk to you."

He sighed. "Is this one of those all-I-get-to-do-is-listen things?"

She didn't seem to mind his sarcasm. "No. Actually your input will be very important. Please. Can we talk before we go in? Brodie just pulled up in front with Jason."

"Want me to take that?" The pretty redhead had backed up and pulled into a parking spot with the same speed and screech of brakes and now stood beside Beth.

She smiled and offered her hand. "Hi. I'm Kelly Braxton, a friend of Beth's. I'm invited to the party. Want me to walk the bike in so you can talk?" Then realizing he didn't have a free hand to shake hers, she said, "Oh, sorry," and took the wrapped box from him.

Ethan shook her hand. "Hi. Ethan Drum."

Her smile was wry. "Yes, I know. Center of the vortex." She handed him back the box.

"Vortex?"

"Beth will explain." She took the bike from him with both hands and set it on the pavement. Then she grasped the handlebars and pushed it toward the restaurant's rear entrance.

Ethan stood face-to-face with Beth, her hands still clutching the lapels of his jacket. She looked a little like she had the night before when Jason told his grandparents she was getting married.

"You want to sit in the Blazer?" he asked, gesturing toward it with the gift-wrapped helmet.

"No," she said. "I need fresh air. Can we just walk up the block?"

"Sure. Let me get rid of this." He sat the gift on the back of his vehicle and closed the tailgate. When he turned to her, she slipped her arm into the crook of his and led him out of the parking lot and up the street. Lined with a print shop, a dog groomer's, a furniture store and a supermarket on one side, and an old brick turn-of-the-century post office on the other, it was surrounded by ancient maple trees, their bare branches like lace against the blue sky.

She leaned into him slightly, her tone quiet but urgent. "I don't have time for small talk, all right?"

He put both hands in the pockets of his gray cords, her arm still looped in his left. Things were looking as though she might have changed her mind about marrying him, after all, but he'd been a cop long enough to guard against too optimistic a view.

He kept walking at a leisurely pace, careful to keep

what he thought to himself. "As I seem to say often when I'm around you—I'm listening."

She sighed. The wind blowing from the direction of the river had a sharp bite. She didn't seem to notice. "While Kelly was visiting my studio today," she said, her breath puffing out ahead of her, "she got a call on her cell phone. Someone was full of questions about me."

"Who?"

She shook her head, her hair moving in loose waves with a gloss and grace that caught his eye. He looked his fill for a moment while she stared ahead, a pleat between her eyebrows, then concentrated on her eyes when she looked up at him. They were filled with fear.

"He said he was an art-magazine reporter, but she thinks he was a private detective. He knew that Kelly and I had known each other in Seattle, and that Jason had run away." She shook her head and added with a mocking twist of her lips, "And he tried to make something out of my relationship with Rush Weston."

He felt instant and profound annoyance, but he kept that, too, to himself. He'd picked up Rush Weston while breaking up a brawl in a waterfront tavern on a Friday night a couple of weeks ago. The man had behaved with scornful superiority, and Ethan had enjoyed pinning him to the bar and cuffing him when he'd resisted arrest.

"What about Rush Weston?" he asked calmly.

"Nothing. Well, you could say we're friends. He's an artist, too, a sculptor, and when he's not being obnoxious, he can be very nice. He's renting a spot in my art mall when I open."

Although Ethan knew his attitude was unwarranted, he resented that she even knew Weston. "That doesn't sound like anything a detective could use against you," he said, sounding mature and magnanimous. What he really wanted to do was warn her to stay away from the guy, but he could imagine how that would go over. And anyway, depending on the point she intended to make with this conversation, he might have very little to do with her life from now on.

They stopped at the corner where the pedestrian light read Don't Walk, and she took the moment to lean her forehead against his upper arm. The wind stirred her hair and strands of it drifted across his chin and throat. He felt a stalling of his brain function. When she lifted her head again, her cheeks were pale and pinched with the cold.

Without giving thought to the action, he reached down to pull the zipper of her red jacket up from between her breasts to her chin.

The light changed. They crossed the street and started back in the direction of Dinosaur Pizza. "You might have guessed by the fact that I'm walking you around like some fraternal organization sergeant-at-arms that there *is* something the detective can use against me."

"And what's that?"

Her grip on his arm tightened. "When the detective spoke to Rush, he implied that there was something between us. He said we'd be sharing studio space and that soon we'd be sharing...more."

That fanned Ethan's annoyance. "How did Rush get that impression?"

Beth stopped walking and looked into his face. She

dropped her arm from his and jammed her hands in the pockets of her jacket. Her eyes were speculative, surprised. She'd detected his irritation and it seemed to have sparked her own.

"I don't know," she said finally, her tone a bit stiff. "He did ask me out a couple of times and I refused. Some men have difficulty taking no for an answer. Certainly a man like you who generally does as he pleases can understand that?"

He narrowed his eyes at her for using his words against him. She looked at him in all innocence.

"I'm acquainted with Rush Weston," he said, then added with relish, "professionally."

Her look of innocence vanished. "What do you mean?"

"It made the paper."

"I don't subscribe," she said impatiently. "It's a way to pinch pennies. I count on gossip. How do you know him professionally?"

"I picked him up in a brawl at a tavern on the waterfront." He provided that information with satisfaction. "If you're trying to present a squeaky-clean image to your in-laws, Weston is not the way to go."

"He and I are not..." she began angrily, a little loudly, then remembering where they were, lowered her voice. "I said he's a fellow artist, that's all. His suggestion that there's something more between us is just a lot of bull. Everybody who knows him understands his tendency to fantasize."

"Your in-laws," he reminded her quietly, "don't know him."

Her lips firmed and she shifted her weight. "You're absolutely right," she said. "That's why I need you to marry me."

Beth spoke the words quickly before she could lose courage, then resisted the impulse to cover her eyes and watch for his reaction between her fingers. Instead, she squared her shoulders, held his seemingly unsurprised gaze and waited for his reaction.

If she'd expected something dramatic, she was disappointed. He simply started walking slowly back toward the restaurant. She had no choice but to follow.

"What exactly did you have in mind?" he asked when she caught up with him.

"I'm desperate," she admitted candidly. "So, I guess, pretty much whatever you want. If you really hate the idea, if you'd just do it for me for now to get us through this week, we can annul it the moment they leave town and I'll find a way to disappear with Jason. Or...something." That wasn't fair to anyone, she knew, but right now her need for a solution was too immediate to allow contemplation of future consequences.

"Or," she continued, trying hard to sell him on the idea, "if you want someone to cook for you and keep house, I'll do it for as long as you want me to. And I'll do my best to help with Nikkie, if she'll let me, provided you do the same for Jason."

He stopped to look down at her with open skepticism. "What about all your denials of domestic competence?"

She nodded, willing to grant him the right to wonder. "I have no domestic competence, but I can do anything I set my mind to. And I'm a damned good mother. I'll do my best for Nikkie."

He moved on again. She kept pace with him.

"Well, so far," he said, "we've talked about your

abilities as a housekeeper and a mother, but not as a wife.''

''In my experience,'' she said, doing her best to keep up with his long strides, ''that's all a wife is. Maybe an answering service, too.''

They'd reached the corner opposite the restaurant and another Don't Walk light. He frowned down at her. ''What kind of a marriage did you have, anyway?''

She'd been trying to avoid thinking about those days. Cobbler's Crossing was supposed to be a fresh start for her and Jason. But now that opportunity sat squarely in the hands of Ethan Drum. So she answered his question with one of her own—the only one that mattered now.

''What kind of a marriage do you want?''

His dark eyes told her in detail. To her horror she blushed. He noted that and groaned.

The light changed. He caught her arm and pulled her with him across the street and toward the Blazer. They could hear the excited sounds of children's voices and the lower notes of adult laughter coming from the restaurant.

Ethan stood her squarely in front of him against the back of the Blazer, then put a hand to the roof on either side of her. Her heartbeat accelerated and all the air seemed to leave her lungs.

''What I *don't* want in a wife,'' he said quietly, ''is a woman who blushes at the mention of sex.''

She tried to fold her arms to put some distance between them, but he was too close. She dropped both arms and flattened her hands against the cold metal of the car behind her. That was steadying somehow.

"You *didn't* mention it," she said, "but I saw it in your eyes. That made it more intimate. I'm sorry."

He seemed annoyed with her apology. "So you hadn't considered intimacy as part of our marriage?"

It was hard, she decided, to allow a fear to surface that she'd suppressed for years. Particularly since it was a fear she'd never shared with anyone except Kelly. She'd borne it for a long time, then when Steve made it clear there was little need to deal with it, she'd simply put it away. And her choice never to marry again allowed her to let it remain hidden.

But her present situation changed all that.

"Frankly..." Her voice came out thin and reedy, and she cleared her throat. "Frankly, I hadn't thought that far. When Kelly repeated what that caller said about Rush Weston, I knew there was only one way out of this, so I came to you. But—" she cleared her throat again, blushed again and closed her eyes when he watched her in obvious confusion "—there's something you should know."

She was hyperventilating and she felt as though she was about to faint. She opened her eyes and found that he still appeared confused, but not angry. He simply waited.

"Do I have to tell you again that I'm listening?" he asked quietly.

He didn't. But a man who listened to her was something new; she suspected that that was why it unsettled her so much. That, and the nature of what he was waiting for her to explain.

"I'm not very good sexually," she said at last.

There was a long moment of silence in the parking lot. Children laughed and shrieked in the restaurant, cars drove by on the street, a siren whined somewhere in the distance. But Beth felt as though she'd been covered with a glass dome, as though she could see out but was isolated.

Ethan studied her for an endless moment, as though that remark might make sense to him if he stared long enough at the woman who'd made it. At last he stepped back, folded his arms and asked, "What do you mean?"

That was the very question she dreaded. She looked at him imploringly. "I mean," she said, her blush draining, pallor replacing it. "I'm not...very skilled at...making love." Her lips twisted in self-deprecation. "I think I'm even worse sexually than I am domestically."

Now that he'd moved away, she could fold her arms, too, but it didn't seem to work as a defense mechanism. She still felt exposed. She dropped her arms and put her hands in her pockets. "It doesn't mean I won't do it," she said, her eyes miserable with humiliation. "It's just a warning that you shouldn't expect...great things."

He studied her another moment, then turned and leaned against the Blazer, too. "What makes you say that?" he asked, his voice filled with disbelief.

When she tipped her head back and looked up at the sky, agonized by the thought of going into detail, he said gently, "I'm sorry. I can see that this is difficult for you, but I want to understand. So tell me. When did you arrive at this conclusion?"

She was asking this man to let her into his life for her own purposes, she reminded herself. She had an obligation to let him into hers. Even into the places she didn't like to go.

"About five years ago," she said, staring at the

toes of her shoes. "I...never found it wonderful, although it was all right the first couple of years of my marriage. But then Steve became very busy and, when he did think about me, sex was always after he'd made some lucrative deal—and then it was sort of quick and triumphant. I sort of...lost interest."

"And it never occurred to you that it was his fault and not yours?"

"I'm not sure it was entirely," she said, remembering the humiliation she'd felt at the time. "I...I'd suggested we try something new. He was disgusted by it and I was embarrassed. Then I realized somewhere along the way I'd lost all appeal for him." She sighed. "And then, I guess, I gave up."

Ethan turned to face her, but she couldn't meet his eyes. "He was disgusted?" he asked incredulously.

She shook her head. "Please don't ask me to tell you what it was."

"I won't." He reached up to catch her chin with his index finger and turn her face toward him. She found his expression gentle and surprisingly easy to look into. "But I want you to know that if you ever want to tell me, I like to consider myself... adventurous."

He pushed away from the Blazer, drew her a short distance from it, then opened the tailgate again. Handing her the gift-wrapped bicycle helmet, he closed and locked the door, put an arm around her shoulders and led her toward the restaurant.

"We'll get married on Saturday," he said. "You can do your art, not worry about the housekeeping, we'll do our best with the kids, and we'll let sex take care of itself."

She stopped him a few feet from the door, her expression serious. "Ethan, I appreciate how well you're taking my news, but...I can't let you get into this if you don't understand that there's a real problem here."

He shook his head, apparently failing to grasp the severity of her warning. He tapped her temple with his index finger. "I think the problem's here, not anywhere else."

She blinked at him, torn between exasperation and admiration. "How could you possibly know that?"

"Because I kissed you this morning," he replied with a grin, "and you kissed me back. The interest is there. Maybe you just need more inspiration than you've had in the past." He pulled the door open. "But some things are better done than analyzed. Come on. Jason's waiting for us."

CHAPTER SEVEN

BETH WATCHED her son surrounded by school friends cheering him on as he maneuvered around monsters in a video game. She guessed there was not a happier child anywhere that sunny afternoon.

A couple of teenage boys in white aprons with triceratops printed on them cleared two long tables of the debris generated by eight large pizzas and four pitchers of soft drinks.

In one corner of the room was a veritable treasure trove of presents. Because of the party's short notice, Jason's friends had not had a chance to buy gifts, but Brodie had arrived with the entire set of *Toy Story* figures down to the barrel of monkeys and the green rubber soldiers. Ebbie had bought a basketball, and Kelly had wrapped several videos in a backpack. Several sheriff's deputies in uniform, whom Ebbie or Ethan had probably commandeered to fill out the party for the sake of the grandparents, appeared with a fleet of toy trucks and a set of Goosebumps books.

The deputies had left early, explaining that they were on a dinner break, and Beth and Ethan had walked with them out to the parking lot.

"Thank you for coming," Beth said sincerely, shaking their hands. "I know you were bullied into this. You really shouldn't have brought gifts."

The taller of the two, whose badge read "Curtis"

shrugged off her thanks. "What's a birthday party without presents?"

The other deputy, shorter, stockier and a few years older, was Billings. "And when Ethan speaks, we obey," he said in a heroic tone. "Right, Chief?"

"Yeah, right." Ethan's tone suggested that wasn't true at all. "Has it been a quiet afternoon?"

Billings nodded. "Yeah. We feel neglected, but we'll adjust."

Ethan put a hand on each man's shoulder. "That's the spirit of the department, gentlemen. Now get out there and make me proud."

"But, Chief," Curtis said gravely, "pride's been your problem all along."

Ethan gave him a shove toward their county car. "Goodbye, Curtis."

As they moved off, Curtis could be heard asking loudly, "Did that shove qualify as boss brutality?"

"No," Billings replied as they separated to walk around opposite sides of the car. "But I'm getting out of here before he does something that does."

Ethan and Beth went back into the restaurant. "Incidentally," Beth said quietly as the boys continued to carry on loudly at the video game, "why did you buy Jason a bike? An expensive bike, at that."

There was scolding in her tone, and he turned just before they reached the tables to fix her with a silencing frown. "His was totaled," he said, "and I wanted to buy him a bike. All right?"

She glanced in the direction of the table and saw that Zachary and Joanne were watching them. Kelly and Brodie seemed completely absorbed in each other, and Ebbie was busy slicing and packaging left-over cake.

"I just don't want you spending a lot of money," she said.

"What *is* it with you and money?" Ethan demanded, keeping his voice low. "Were you frightened by a savings-and-loan bailout or something?"

She gave him a speaking look. "My in-laws are watching," she warned, "and don't get smart with me. I used to have a lot of money and nothing else. Now I have only a little and...and many concerns. But Jason and I do not require much, so there's no point in your indulging every extravagance he—"

She stopped because he'd run a hand over his face as though he'd had about all of her he could take.

"If you play your cards right," he said, smiling—which she was sure he did for Joanne and Zachary's benefit, "you can have everything I have. It's not a lot of money, but usually enough. And you can have everything else—all that was missing in your life before. But not if you keep ragging on me."

"I wasn't ragging, I was—"

"You were ragging."

A glance toward the table told her that her in-laws were still watching. "Now you've probably made them think we're not getting along," she accused him.

"Then maybe," he suggested under his voice, "you should do something to make them think otherwise."

She studied him with suspicion. "Like what?"

"Your call," he said mercilessly. "What comes to mind?"

In view of what she'd explained to him just before they joined the party, her mind was blank. Then she realized that all her in-laws needed to see was a loving touch.

She drew a breath and looped her arms around his neck. His came to her waist. She felt the press of his leg between her thighs, the hardness of his chest against the softness of hers, the hair at the back of his neck against the inside of her wrist.

She smiled in the interest of her performance and asked sotto voce, "How's that?"

Apparently also performing, he returned her smile. "A little lukewarm."

"We're in a pizza parlor."

"I don't think passion has a sense of place. It's as combustible in a downpour on a street corner as it is in the bedroom."

And with that he pulled her against him. She was sure her body's instant clamoring response was only one of surprise.

Then he nuzzled under her hair and kissed the side of her neck, and she knew she was wrong. Her heart jolted and sent what felt like a little stream of lava right down the middle of her being. The pulse of excitement she felt had nothing to do with surprise.

But before she could analyze it further, Ethan said in amused warning, "Uh-oh. Incoming."

She began to step back out of his arms, but Jason collided with them, wrapping an arm around each of them. His face was almost too bright to look at.

He took a fistful of the sleeve of Beth's sweater and pulled her down to his level. "Is Ethan gonna be my dad?" he whispered. "Be real quiet, Mom. Grandma and Grandpa are looking this way, and I think they're trying to listen."

She kissed his cheek. His happiness was infectious,

and it would be easy for the sake of today's performance for her in-laws, to let herself believe as her son did—that her marriage to Ethan was the best thing that could possibly happen.

"Yes," she said, smiling into his hopeful expression. And with that admission, she let go of all the potentially grievous problems the situation presented. If she was going to do this, she would have to do it with certitude and enthusiasm, to be both convincing to her in-laws and fair to the man who was giving her this chance to avoid messy and expensive litigation. "Yes," she said again, "he is."

With a whoop of delight, Jason leaped at Ethan, who bent slightly and caught him in one arm. The boy reached up and gave him a strangling hug.

"I'm gonna really like being your kid," he said in a loud whisper. "And thanks for the bike and the helmet! And the cool party! I've never had so much fun. Never, never, never!"

"Well, good." Ethan straightened and exchanged a wry glance with Beth. "'Cause I think the fun's just starting."

Half a dozen of Jason's friends who were crowded around the video game shouted that it was his turn. Jason raced back to join them.

Ethan wrapped an arm around Beth's shoulders and led her to the table where Brodie, Kelly and the Richardses sat. Ebbie stood at the end of the table, still wrapping up leftovers.

Brodie and Zachary were enthusiastically discussing basketball scores. Ethan joined the men on one side of the table, and Beth sat between Kelly and Joanne on the other.

A young man in a Dinosaur Pizza apron arrived with a tray filled with cups and a pot of coffee.

"We're soft drinked out," Kelly explained, helping the boy distribute cups. "But it doesn't look as though the kids are ready to go yet." She pointed to the knot of little boys cheering excitedly in the corner as Jason turned a wheel with one hand and operated a joystick with the other. His laughter was loud and gleeful.

Kelly laughed just watching them. "Have you ever seen such unbridled delight? Ah, to be eight again!"

"When I was eight," Brodie said, holding his cup out as the waiter poured, "Ethan made me slide down the banister into the basement of our parents' house."

Ethan passed him the cream, his expression unrepentant. "You could have refused."

"You had my Tonka dumptruck and wouldn't give it back."

"Because you had a fear of the basement stairs and wouldn't go down. I was trying to help you deal with your problem. Get past it."

"Sure."

"It worked, didn't it? You no longer have a fear of basements."

"That's true. Now I have a fear of sliding down a banister, falling off and losing my front tooth."

"Lighten up. The implant looks great. Women love your smile." Ethan turned to Kelly. "Don't they?"

"Ah...um..." Kelly stammered. Beth watched with interest as her usually quick-witted friend seemed to lose the power of speech. Beth looked at Brodie, who was giving Kelly the reputed smile, then at Ethan, who also appeared to be studying the action with interest. "Yes," Kelly said, finally pulling herself together. "It's a charming smile."

"See?" Ethan said to Brodie. "Quit whining." Then he turned to Zachary and asked politely, "Did I overhear you say you're having trouble with your car?"

Zachary stirred sugar into his coffee and eagerly launched into a detailed explanation of the Cadillac's behavior.

"When did you meet Ethan?" Joanne asked, her arms folded on the table.

"It's a small town," Beth replied carefully, certain the question was a trap, "everyone gets to know newcomers pretty fast, and Ethan's job requires him to be very involved in the community."

Joanne nodded, her smile suggesting acquiescence, but her eyes suggesting suspicion. "But when exactly? How?"

Aware that a lie of any kind could mean trouble, Beth took a sip of coffee to give herself a moment to think. Had Joanne already asked Ebbie how they'd met? Or Jason? Or Kelly? Was she just waiting for Beth to contradict that information?

Beth suddenly remembered something Jason had told her and decided that a grain of truth in her reply was better than none at all.

"Ethan went to Jason's school to talk to the kids about the sheriff's office. I volunteer there a few hours a week."

She hadn't been there the day Ethan visited the school, but that wasn't what she'd claimed, anyway. She'd simply stated two separate truths.

Joanne glanced across the table at Ethan, who was deep in conversation with Brodie and her husband, then turned back to Beth. "You've only been here three months. That isn't very long to know someone."

"Well," Beth said, thinking fast, "when it's right, it's right."

That, too, was true. Saving herself from litigation over her son was very right.

Joanne's dark eyes focused on her with disapproval. "Can it *be* right when you've just lost Steve?"

"That was a year ago, Jo," Beth replied, thinking that she'd really lost him years before his death. But his mother didn't know that.

"One can't help but wonder," Joanne said, raising her coffee cup, "how deeply you felt about him if you can get over him in a year."

Mercifully Beth was saved from having to respond by Ebbie, who leaned between them and placed a foil-wrapped package in front of Joanne. "There you go," she said. "A little cake to enjoy tonight in your motel room."

Ebbie offered another foil package to Brodie.

He accepted it with a smile, then pursed his lips in imitation of a kiss. "When are you moving in with me, Eb?"

"When Mel gets tired of me," she replied offhandedly.

"Mel?" Brodie asked.

"Gibson," she said, as though it should be obvious. "You didn't know he's been flying in on weekends to see me?"

Brodie made a face. "Ebbie, do you really think a pretty face can make you happy?"

"No, but he's a pretty face with millions."

Brodie looked chagrined. "But…women love my smile."

Ebbie gave a derisive snort. "You can't buy diddly with that, sweetie," she countered. She closed the box, which still contained a third of the cake.

Brodie leaned toward Kelly. "Would you prefer a man with millions, or me and my smile?"

Kelly leaned toward him. "I'm looking for a smile like yours *on* a man with millions. I need someone to support my art habit, but I need him to do it cheerfully so he doesn't inhibit my creativity."

"I thought artists needed to be in pain to work," he said.

She shook her head. "Not me. Pain just makes me miserable. And I can't throw pots when I'm miserable."

"Well—" he seemed to be thinking seriously "—is there anything that'd keep you happy, besides millions?"

"Ah…" She pretended to consider the question seriously, then said firmly, "Nope," and pushed away from the table. She bent down to hug Beth, then went around the table and hugged Ethan, too.

Beth exchanged a surprised look with Ethan, then realized Kelly was pretending she'd known Ethan for some time—something the Richardses would expect of Beth's best friend.

"Great party, guys," she said. "Thanks for inviting me." She pushed Brodie's shoulder as he tried to stand. "Don't get up. Nice to meet you, Brodie. Mr. and Mrs. Richards. See you at the wedding?"

Joanne's manner was cool. "Of course. We'll be there."

"Wonderful. Ebbie, I'll call you about the hors d'oeuvres."

Ebbie looked up from pouring a pitcher of leftover soda into a large carryout cup and covered her momentary surprise with a quick smile. "Thanks. I planned the menu, but left it at the office."

As Kelly waded through the crowd of little boys to find Jason and give him a hug, Joanne said with feigned amiability. "This is a little last minute to be planning a menu, isn't it, four days before the wedding? Or is the entire wedding spur-of-the-moment?"

"The wedding," Ethan said easily, reaching across the table for Beth's hand, "is a tribute to my success in finally convincing Beth I can't live without her." The look in his eyes was intimate and ardent. Beth was ensnared by it and couldn't free herself until he turned to Joanne. "I understand your concern for your grandson and your daughter-in-law, but I promise you I'll take good care of them."

Joanne's mouth worked uncertainly as she obviously struggled with disbelief and the convincing quality of his declaration. Zachary studied Ethan uncertainly, too. Then he exchanged a glance with his wife.

Kelly blew kisses as she passed the table on her way out to the parking lot. Brodie watched her walk away with an interest Beth was thrilled to see. Kelly had sworn off men after her divorce three years before. She'd loved her husband, a football coach at the high school where she taught art. But he'd resented the time she spent on her pottery outside of school and her dedication to the Seattle co-op where Beth had met her.

He'd finally given her an ultimatum—him or her

pottery. It had amazed Beth that he hadn't known better.

Kelly and Beth had commiserated over seafood salads at Pike Place Market the day before Kelly was to leave for Cobbler's Crossing. Most men, they'd concluded, despite their claims of appreciating a woman's skills and talents, still wanted a woman who was traditional, who conformed to their conservative notions of what a wife should be.

Yet those conclusions notwithstanding, here was Kelly now, walking out of the restaurant with her charming derriere being considered with more than casual interest by Brodie Drum, and she, Beth, was about to marry his brother.

What, she wondered, was the world coming to?

The world seemed even a little farther off its axis when the restaurant's front door swung open and five teenagers poured into the shadowy barnlike interior of Dinosaur Pizza.

Nikkie, in a black wool jacket that ended in a band at her tiny waist, an impossibly tight pair of black jeans and boots that looked as though they belonged on a logger, led the way to their table.

Ethan stood up to welcome them, and Nikkie walked into his arms.

"Hi," she said with a shy glance around the table. "Did we miss the party? Hi, Unc. Hi, Beth."

"No," he said, giving her shoulders a squeeze. "We've got cake left, and we'll get you guys some pizza. I thought you had a meeting."

He looked over Nikkie's head to the two girls and two boys who stood behind her. One of the girls was small like Nikkie and had short purple hair with a side part and black lipstick. The other was a tall and glamorous blonde in a long leather coat. Both boys were tall, one gangly with thin-rimmed round glasses and the other thickly built with a blond buzz cut and an earring.

A collective groan rose from the group and Nikkie said morosely, "Mr. Fogarty decided on *Henry V* for our Winter Festival play. We're really bummed out."

Ethan looked surprised. "Why? You love Shakespeare."

"We all love Shakespeare," the buzz cut said, "and it's a play we can get everybody in, but we're looking at Medieval clothes, armor, shields and weapons for twenty."

"On a fifty-dollar budget," the girl with the purple hair said.

"Yeah," the spindly boy concurred. "And he says it's our problem. That learning to mount a production with no money is as important for a drama student to learn as acting."

The blonde sighed. "I wanted to do *Streetcar*. I can do Blanche's lines in my sleep."

The spindly boy turned to her. "Well, you'll have to wake up to do Katharine."

Purple Hair frowned. "*I* want to do Katharine."

The blonde looked down her nose at her. "I have the tiara." Then she spread both arms in a ta-da sort of pose. "And the height to be royalty. You'll have to be happy as my lady-in-waiting."

Nikkie rolled her eyes at her friends, then turned to her father. "And the worst part—besides my cast mates—is that I'm in charge of props *and* I'm playing Isabel, Queen of France."

Ethan smiled sympathetically. "Then you're going to need a really big pizza. First let me introduce you to Jason's grandparents, Mr. and Mrs. Richards. Joanne, Zachary, I'd like you to meet my daughter, Tanika.''

The girl smiled and waved. "Nikkie," she said, then introduced her friends. Bradley was the spindly boy, the blonde was Vanessa, Rosalie the one with the purple hair, and the buzz cut was Cameron.

"Guys, you know Brodie," she went on. They all nodded and murmured greetings.

"And you know Beth," she finished casually.

Beth expected instant denial or at least looks of confusion, but Nikkie must have apprised them of the plan—that she and Ethan would appear to be engaged during the birthday party.

It was easy to see why these kids were in the drama club. Their acting skills were excellent. Beth was treated to friendly smiles, a "How's it going?" and a "Love your sweater!"

Nikkie pulled a small gift-wrapped box out of her pocket and looked around. "Where's Jason?"

As though his personal radar had sensed more loot, Jason appeared at Nikkie's side. He looked up at her in astonishment. "You came!"

Beth read annoyance in her eyes, then Nikkie tossed her hair and thrust the gift at him. "I felt like pizza. Here.''

He had the wrap off in a matter of seconds and held up a watch with Buzz Lightyear on it. Buzz's arms served as the hands.

"Wow!" Jason's eyes were huge. He turned to Beth. "Mom, look!"

"How did you know?" Beth asked Nikkie. Too late she realized that maybe this was not a question she should ask when trying to convince her in-laws that she, Jason, Ethan and Nikkie spent a lot of time together.

"Because Buzz Lightyear is all he ever talks about," Nikkie said with a laugh. She reached down to push a button on the side of the watch, and a tinny voice said, "Buzz Lightyear to the rescue!"

Jason gasped, beside himself with delight. He raced back to his friends to show off his newest gift.

Ethan patted Nikkie's shoulder. "Come on. We'll get you guys some pizza."

Ethan led Nikkie and her friends to the counter. Jason returned to the table with the announcement that he was out of quarters. Brodie, delving into the pocket of his coveralls for change, went with Jason back to the game.

And Beth found herself alone with her in-laws.

Joanne sighed, gathered up her purse, her coat, the foil-wrapped leftover cake and mumbled crossly, "I feel as though we've been set down in the middle of Paramount Studios!" Then she turned to Beth with a coldly polite, "Thank you. We've enjoyed the party. And thank you for the cake."

"Would you and Zachary like to come back to the house for a while?" Courtesy had forced her to ask. She prayed they'd refuse.

Her prayer was answered. "It's been a long day and Zach's arthritis is acting up." Beth saw Joanne shoot her husband a glance that warned him not to contradict her. Apparently she wanted to get away as much as Beth wanted her to. "We might spend the next few days sightseeing if there's nothing seriously wrong with the car, but we'll be in touch before the...wedding." As usual she applied cool disbelief to the word.

"Good." Beth walked the couple to the door of the restaurant. "I have to get you Ebbie's address."

Ethan appeared suddenly behind Beth. He placed both hands on her shoulders as Joanne climbed into the passenger seat of the Cadillac and Zachary went around to the driver's side.

"You'll have to come over," he said, "and help Jason with the Legos you bought. We have a work-table in the basement where we can really spread out."

Zachary looked interested, but Joanne said only, "We'll be in touch."

Beth and Ethan waved till the white Cadillac was out of sight.

Beth stood on the windy street corner with Ethan behind her and knew her life would never be the same. The first time she'd married she'd been hopeful and in love, yet her life had fallen apart, anyway. This time, she was getting married to a man she hardly knew to avoid a legal battle for custody of her son.

Perhaps, she thought, it was the influence of Nikkie and her drama-club friends, but this moment was like being center stage and having the houselights go out as the curtain came down. Stagehands were about to change the set and move all the pieces of her life around.

It would be interesting to know if she was starring in a comedy or a tragedy.

CHAPTER EIGHT

FOR THE NEXT THREE DAYS, Beth went to her cannery studio in the morning and left for Ethan's house in the evening with a grocery bag or a box in which she'd packed some of her and Jason's clothes and personal items. She did this on the chance that her in-laws' detective was watching her.

She had, in fact, noticed a man sitting in a car not far from the cannery the past two mornings, then noticed the same car parked about a block from Ethan's last evening. Was he taking photos of her comings and goings? It would be difficult to convince her in-laws she'd been living with Ethan for a while if she was photographed with a U-Haul and a group of friends to help her move.

Beth had left the room with the bunk beds to Jason and now occupied the fourth bedroom upstairs. She'd brought her bedspread and curtains from the cannery in a laundry bag. The closet had a small built-in dresser, and Ethan brought up an old wooden desk from the basement to put in an empty corner.

"Diana bought it at a church rummage sale, thinking she'd clean it up and paint it one day, but she was always too busy."

Beth thought she heard a wistful note in his voice and went to sit on the edge of her bed. Ethan knelt on one knee by the desk and dusted off the legs. It was a simple maple desk with a spindly-legged chair.

"Are you *sure* you're willing to do this?" Beth asked. "I mean, if you had a great marriage once, this might be harder for you than you anticipate."

He turned from the desk, his forearm resting on his bent knee, the soft chamois in his fingers. His eyes were quiet, relaxed. "Life is full of surprises. It's entirely possible that *our* marriage could be great."

She nodded, then looked away, occupying herself with finding pairs in a pile of loose socks in the middle of the bed.

"Are you sure *you* want to do this?" he asked, pushing to his feet and sitting beside her, leaving only a small space between them. "Considering how you feel about marriage? I know how important Jason is to you, but I really don't think your in-laws could win a case against you in court."

"I don't think so, either," she admitted, concentrating on folding a pair of woolly blue kneesocks, "but it would be expensive and nerve-racking to have to defend myself against them. I also wouldn't want to put Jason through that. Their threats have frightened him enough already."

Ethan nodded, taking the socks from her and putting them aside. He turned to face her and looked into her eyes.

"I know. I'm just trying to make it clear that a halfhearted effort in this marriage won't be good for any of us. If you're having second thoughts, I'd rather help you find a good lawyer and lend you the money to fight Joanne and Zachary. And I'll do my best to be a friend to Jason, instead of a father."

She sat up stiffly, concern budding in her chest,

then doubling and tripling quickly into a big ugly worry. Did he want out of this? Did *she?*

She tried to examine what she felt, a difficult task under his watchful dark gaze. What she found was an understandable fear of something new, the possibly irrational but very real fear of disappointing Ethan in bed and, under all that, an urgent willingness to try, anyway.

"The wedding's tomorrow afternoon," she reminded him.

"Yes, but you haven't signed a contract. If you want to cancel, just say the word."

"Jason," she said softly, "wants a father more than he wants a friend."

He shook his head at her. "That's familiar ground. I'm asking what *you* want."

She shrugged, reluctant to tell him that she found him attractive and appealing and that just being within sight of him calmed her and made her feel secure. And that the thought of being married to him, of sharing his life and his bed, lit a spark in her she'd been sure had died long ago. She'd bared her soul to Steve so many times and been ignored that she'd put a tight cap on what she felt.

And though she knew Ethan Drum could never be confused with Steve Richards, her defense mechanism remained in place.

"I want what's best for my son," she replied.

Ethan would have taken great satisfaction in shaking her. He saw many emotions cross her face and wished she'd explain them in words. But she was like a mystery without a clue, a case without a lead.

"Fine," he said. "I'm in, as long as you under-

stand that I intend to be a husband, as well as a father.''

She bobbed her head. "I'm in, too, as long as you
remember...what I told you."

"Right. Your claim to be sexually inadequate." He
got to his feet and offered her a hand to help her to
hers. "I don't believe it for a minute."

She held on to his hand when he tried to withdraw
it and give the chair one more swipe with the chamois.

She swallowed, put a hand to her hair, then
dropped it, high color filling her cheeks. Her control
seemed to wobble and she looked up at him, her eyes
filled with a curious combination of determination
and reluctance.

He tossed the chamois at the desk and gave her his
full attention.

"You've been honest with me," she said, nervously tucking her hair behind her ear. "I appreciate
that, so I want to be as honest with you. You're a
confident virile man and it sounds as though Diana
was a devoted and wonderful woman. So you had
what it takes for...love to be wonderful."

By love, he knew she meant lovemaking. He listened quietly, wondering what her point was.

She heaved a sigh, as though continuing required
great courage. "My experience has been significantly
different, and I'm not entirely sure that...you'll be
able to change the way I am."

He had every confidence that the problem was not
with her but with the man who'd made his business
more important than his wife. He opened his mouth
to tell her that, but she had more to say.

"So I was thinking—" she looked into his eyes,

then down at her hands, then up into his eyes again "—it would be one thing if we were getting married with the intention of getting an annulment the moment we thought it was safe. But if you want a *real* marriage out of this, you...you might want to make sure, first, that you're not going to regret it later...."

Ethan was blown away by her offer. And guessing by the widening of her eyes, the strong emotion he felt went from him to her through the hand he still held.

He was both touched and angry, and couldn't determine which feeling dominated. He was furious that her self-esteem had been pounded so low she felt obliged to make that suggestion. But it also turned his spine to spaghetti to know that she'd made it because she was trying to be fair to him.

As tempting as her offer was to his longtime celibate body, he knew that accepting it would only strike another blow to the pride her husband had driven into the ground.

He took her face in his hands and kissed her gently and slowly. Her lips were soft, pliable. A bit surprised.

"Thank you," he said when he raised his head, "but that won't be necessary. I'm sure I won't regret anything." He smiled. "Excuse me. I'm going to shower before dinner."

"SHE'S MAKING *frozen* lasagna for dinner," Nikkie said, her voice laced with disdain. She stood in the doorway of Ethan's bathroom, arms folded, shoulder leaning against the doorjamb.

Showered and dressed in jeans and a chambray

shirt, he stood before the mirror over the sink and combed his hair.

"You do that all the time," he said, leaning forward to frown over a spray of three or four gray hairs in his sideburns. Damn. He'd have sworn they weren't there yesterday.

"But she's a mother."

Ethan gave the back of his hair one more swipe with the comb, then tossed it onto the blue-tiled counter and turned to face his daughter.

"Your mother brought home take-out from the deli a couple of nights a week, and we ate fish sticks and tater tots a lot." He leaned a hip against the counter and smiled. "But we didn't love her because she was a great cook. We loved her because she was warm and funny and she loved us."

Nikkie's expression firmed. "You're not expecting me to love *her,* are you?"

"No, I'm not. I'm expecting you to be polite and helpful and understand that she's doing her best in a strange and difficult situation."

"Do you?"

"Do I what?"

"Love her."

"I like her a lot," he answered, the words coming easily. "Liking often turns to love."

Nikkie absorbed that, then straightened away from the doorjamb with an expression of disapproval. "Well, I think it's barbaric." Then she marched off through his room and across the hall to hers.

He followed, stopping in her doorway and watching her yank a silky white blouse off her bed and move to the closet to hang it up.

"Would you find it less barbaric," he asked, "if

she was fixing roast chicken and twice-baked potatoes for dinner?"

She glanced at him over her shoulder with a look he could only describe as parental. "Please, Daddy. You don't like it when *I'm* snide," she said, hooking the hanger on the rod in an angry motion, then closing the closet door.

"Why did you come to Jason's party?" he asked as she smoothed a bedspread that didn't need smoothing.

"Because our meeting broke up early and I wanted pizza."

"I think," he said carefully, preparing for an explosion, "that you secretly like the idea of having Beth and Jason around."

When his daughter gasped and gave him a look that said he was crazy, he raised a silencing hand. "I know. You're concerned about what it'll do to the life you and I have grown used to. In a way so am I. But deep down, I think you sometimes get a little lonely. I think you're afraid you might like having a stepmother and a brother."

She glared at him, fists clenched, and he congratulated himself. He knew that look; he saw it regularly. He didn't know if it was the teenager in her or the woman, but she hated it when he read her mind.

"I think you should know," she said, her chin angling stubbornly, "that if she tries to push me around, I'm not going to stand for it."

"I don't think she's the pushy type."

"You've only known her five days."

"It only took me two days with you," he said, wandering a few steps into her room, "to know that *you* were pushy. Had us up all night. Allergic to this, allergic to that. But we kept you, anyway.''

Her shoulders sagged and she appeared on the verge of a smile. "Daddy, I'm half you. You're, like, the motherlode of pushy! Hey!"

Suddenly her expression changed to anger and she rushed past Ethan into the hallway. He followed, wondering what had upset her, and caught up with her halfway to the stairs. She stood glowering at Jason.

The boy had Simba in his arms, the cat's furry legs and tail hanging heavily.

"That's *my* cat," she said, taking the gray bundle from Jason's arms.

"He was on my bed," Jason said, sounding more hurt than defensive. "I was gonna give him some milk."

Nikkie cuddled Simba like a baby. "Milk's bad for cats!" she snapped.

"But everybody gives cats milk."

"It makes old cats sick. Just leave my cats alone and go play with all your new toys."

Jason's voice rose. "Well, excuse me all to hell!"

Nikkie turned to Ethan, the picture of mortification. "Daddy. He said *hell*." She stalked back to her room and closed the door.

Jason looked up at Ethan beseechingly. "He was on my bed. And I thought cats liked milk!"

Ethan put a hand on Jason's head and led him toward the stairs. "They do, but that cat's pretty old and it does make him sick."

"Nikkie hates me."

"No, she doesn't. She's just grumpy because things are changing a little around here."

"She's jealous 'cause I had a birthday and got lots of stuff."

While that observation did have some truth, Ethan said, "I don't think so. But she hasn't had to share my attention with anyone else for a long time. Just like you haven't had to share your mom. But Nikkie'll be okay, don't worry."

They'd reached the stairs and Ethan caught Jason by the shoulder before he could start down. "No hells and damns around here, okay? No four-letter words."

Jason appeared confused about that. "H-e-l?" he spelled. "D-a-m?"

"Hell has two *l*s. And damn has an *n*."

Jason's eyebrows went up. "It does? Where?"

"On the end. I know it's weird and you don't hear it, but it's there."

"Oh. Taylor Bridges says that all the time. And I don't usually say hell, but Nikkie was yelling and she's bigger. I wanted her to hear me."

"Yeah, well, you can say regular words just as loudly as swear words. So don't pollute the conversation with bad language."

"Okay." Jason looked abashed. "Sorry."

Halfway down the stairs Ethan caught the acrid smell of something burning. With Jason right behind him, he raced to the kitchen and found it filled with smoke.

Beth had opened the window over the sink, as well as the back door and was waving at the smoke with a dish towel. On the counter was the foil pan of lasagna. It was incinerated.

"God, I can't believe it!" she said when she saw Ethan. "I usually prepare frozen meals just fine, but I'd gone down to the basement to put a load of laundry in and got distracted by all the paintable things you have down there—clay flowerpots and wooden boxes and that galvanized tub. I didn't hear the timer.''

She tossed the towel at the counter, opened the refrigerator and pulled out a large white bowl. "How do you feel about salad *without* lasagna?''

Ethan was not one to be dismayed by small domestic crises when his work showed him repeatedly that the world was filled with such big ones. He could see that Beth was very upset, however, so he dismissed the ruined lasagna with a shake of his head. "Don't worry about it. Salad's great. Jase and I'll pick up some ribs and chicken to go with it.''

He took his jacket from a hook near the back door and tossed Jason's at him. The boy pulled it on, eager to accompany him.

"Oh, boy!" Jason's blue eyes shone as he zipped up his jacket. "I like chicken and ribs better, anyway! I'm *glad* you're a rotten cook, Mom!''

Beth met the amused look in Ethan's eyes and had to smile. "Thank you, Jason,'' she said, leaning down to kiss her son's cheek. "It's nice to be appreciated.''

Jason raced through the open door toward the Blazer. Ethan adjusted the collar of his tweed jacket and challenged her with a raised eyebrow. "Want to practice kissing me goodbye?''

She went toward him, her pace lazy, her heartbeat picking up. Steve had hated it when dinner wasn't ready or not as painstakingly prepared as he preferred. And though he seldom shouted, he'd always shown his disapproval with icy politeness or stiff silences.

And here Ethan was going out with a smile to bring dinner home. Unbelievable.

She stopped within inches of him and asked in surprise. "You're not annoyed?"

"Over food?" he asked. "No. I save annoyance for bad calls by referees or deputies who call in sick on Mondays—stuff like that. Anyway, I seem to remember we'd agreed you don't have to fix meals."

She laughed mirthlessly. "I was trying to make a good impression."

"You could still save it with a kiss."

An unfamiliar sense of well-being made her close the small space between them and tip her face up toward his.

He lowered his head without touching her until their lips met, and the kiss he gave her was sweet but lingering.

Beth unconsciously rose on tiptoe to maintain contact. He responded by parting his lips. She dipped the tip of her tongue into his mouth—and the contact changed suddenly from casual to intense. He wrapped an arm around her waist, pulling her against him. She put both arms around his neck, and the kiss deepened.

She experienced the sensation again of having ingested lava. It shocked her to realize that what she felt was sexual excitement. She pulled her lips from Ethan's and looked into his face, wondering if he could be right about her. Was it possible she *did* possess a strong sexuality?

His eyes were stormy with a decidedly desirous gleam. He drew an uneven breath and grinned. "That kind of a kiss will never send a man on his way," he said, running a hand gently up and down her spine. "It only makes him want to stay."

That sense of sexual well-being seemed to double. "The kids'll be hungry," she said. "You should go."

"I can't."

"Why not?"

"You're standing on my feet." He pointed to his Nikes on which her black flats stood. She must have used them for leverage during the kiss.

She stepped off him, shooed him backward and closed the door behind him, her heart beating like the wings of a hummingbird. She turned toward the counter to find Nikkie, Simba hanging from one hand and Cindy Crawford riding her other shoulder, standing in the middle of the kitchen and glaring at her.

"That was quite a kiss for two people who've just met," the girl said.

Beth knew she wasn't going to get anywhere with Nikkie if she wasn't just as forthright.

"Yes, it was," she admitted. She went to the counter to toss the burned lasagna into the trash. Then she took the plastic container of cat food from the corner and placed it near the empty bowls on the floor. "But sometimes, when two people find themselves in a situation that forces them to make big decisions together...something happens."

"Love?" Nikkie asked sarcastically.

"Closeness," Beth corrected, pulling the lid off the cat-food container as Nikkie put her furry friends down in front of their bowls. "A kind of mutual dependence that means they have to trust each other. And discovering that your trust is well placed inspires a certain...affection that—" Beth stopped abruptly, remembering her promise to herself to be honest.

"It's pretty complex, Nikkie," she said. "I don't entirely understand it myself. I just know that I like your dad a lot—probably for many of the same reasons you do. He's kind, understanding and supportive.

My first husband wasn't like that, so I probably appreciate those qualities more than another woman would.''

Nikkie scooped cat food into the bowls. Simba, nudging Nikkie's hand in his eagerness to eat, got sprinkled with the multicolored pellets. Cindy Crawford, far more dignified, sat a small distance from her bowl and when it was full approached with a graceful twitch of her all-black tail. Simba sniffed at Cindy's bowl as though to be certain they shared the same menu. The calico growled, and the gray Persian, satisfied, went back to his meal.

Nikkie leaned against the corner of the counter, watching her cats eat, then swung her gaze to Beth. It was clear she had more on her mind.

"I'm not going to give you a lot of trouble," Nikkie said, "Because Dad seems to want you here. But don't expect me to drool all over you like Jason does with my father. I loved my mother, and Dad and I were doing fine by ourselves."

Beth nodded over the merciless statement of fact. Maybe there was something steadying about knowing exactly where you stood. "I've always thought drool was pretty unattractive," she said quietly. "Perhaps you can just treat me as you would any other friend of your father's."

"His friends don't *live* here."

"Life's full of exceptions. But I'll do my best not to get in your way."

"I'd appreciate that." Nikkie gestured to the back door. "Where was Dad going?"

Beth smiled in self-deprecation, suspecting she was in for more flack. "To get chicken and ribs to go with our salad. I burned the lasagna."

Nikkie made a face. "It was frozen."

"I know," Beth said. "I was doing laundry in the basement and noticed all the neat old pots and things down there. The sort I paint for craft shows. I didn't hear the timer."

Nikkie rolled her eyes. "I can see you're not going to be much help around here."

Beth shook her head. "Probably not. But you and your dad were doing fine. It doesn't sound like you need me for that kind of thing." She turned to open a utensil drawer. "I can set the table, though. So if you'll excuse me, I'll do that."

Nikkie walked away.

Beth put napkins and silverware around the table and replayed their exchange in her mind. It wasn't precisely negative and it certainly wasn't positive. It had simply been a sort of honest declaration of territory—like Simba sniffing Cindy's bowl.

BETH'S FIRST WEDDING had taken place before a justice of the peace in a small town in eastern Washington. She'd worn a simple blue dress and carried a bouquet of carnations and baby's breath bought at a nearby supermarket.

But she'd been excited and in love.

Her second wedding took place in Ebbie Browning's backyard in an elegant canvas tent against which a torrential rain beat unmercifully. She wore a long-sleeved ivory wool dress with a roll-necked collar and a tea-length flared skirt. Kelly and Nikkie stood beside her. Nikkie had not been pleased about being a bridesmaid, but she hadn't refused.

Ethan wore a gray suit, the jacket of which he'd draped over her shoulders in the middle of the brief ceremony when she'd shivered against the rawness of the day. All the guests were prepared for the cold rainy weather, but Beth had had nothing to go over her dress but her bright red parka.

Brodie served as Ethan's best man, and Jason as usher.

The two deputies Beth had met at Jason's party and several other people Ethan had introduced to her from his office stood behind them as they recited their vows.

Joanne and Zachary were there fully expecting, Beth imagined, she would turn to them at any moment and admit it was all a farce. But the ceremony continued and finally concluded with the traditional directive to the groom.

"You may kiss the bride."

Ethan complied gently and briefly with a promise in his eyes for later.

Beth huddled a little deeper into his jacket as they turned to face her in-laws and Ethan's friends.

There were cheers and applause followed by a buffet of hors d'ouevres Kelly had put together.

"Coconut prawns?" Beth said in amazement. "Bacon-wrapped scallops? Crab-stuffed mushrooms and heart-shaped watercress sandwiches?" Beth said to Kelly as she stood between her and Ethan in the small buffet line. "I didn't know you could do this kind of thing. All you ever eat is chicken strips and egg rolls."

Kelly grinned at her astonishment. "My mom was a caterer. I learned to prepare a lot of fancy things. I just don't like to bother—unless, of course, my best friend is getting married."

Behind her Brodie bit a huge coconut-dipped

prawn in half and closed his eyes in ecstasy. "That does it!" he said, piling several more onto his plate. "I have to win the lottery."

"Why?" Kelly asked.

"You're looking for a man with millions, remember?" He reached around her while she remained still and helped himself to two stuffed mushrooms. "And I'm looking for a woman who can cook."

"You missed something, Brodie," she told him, slapping his hand when he reached for another mushroom. "Other people might like them, too. I said I *can* cook, but I don't like to."

"You might want to if you adored the man you were married to."

"I'm not married."

"Only because you don't know me well enough yet."

Kelly sighed dramatically and turned to Ethan, who'd reached the end of the buffet and was pouring coffee for himself and Beth. "What is it with him? He seems bright enough, but he doesn't listen."

"It's a problem he's always had," Ethan explained with a straight face. "Our mother always excused him by saying he was a forceps delivery. I think he's just nuts."

"Go ahead," Brodie said. "Have your fun. But when I win the lottery or become an auto-mechanic mogul—" he pinned Kelly with a glance "—and *you're* begging me to marry you—" his glance went to Ethan "—and you need help IDing tire tracks or repairing the county's dilapidated fleet, I'll tell *you* to take a flying leap. And I'll tell you…" He looked back into Kelly's eyes and something there seemed to stop him and snare his attention. "I'll tell you…"

he said absently as Kelly gazed into his eyes. "I'll tell you that I'll take you under any terms. Any."

Ethan turned to Beth with a whispered, "What's going on there?"

She smiled and whispered back, "Can't you guess?"

He looked at his brother and Kelly again and found they were still gazing at each other. People in the buffet line were beginning to move around them.

"You're kidding!" Ethan said as he held both their coffees carefully in one hand and followed her to the head table, one of four set up to accommodate the guests.

"No, I'm not," she said, putting down her plate. She took the cups of coffee from Ethan's hand and put them down, too. "Don't be shocked. Kelly's wonderful. But she has the same problem I have."

Ethan pushed in Beth's folding chair and sat down beside her. "I think she's great. What problem?"

"She has to do her art. Her first husband wanted her attention exclusively and finally left. At least she wouldn't burn the frozen lasagna."

"In the space of a marriage, how important is that?"

"I suppose it depends on how much you like lasagna."

"Oh, just be quiet and eat," he said, grinning. Then he waved at the Richardses as they left the buffet line. "Joanne! Zach! Come join us."

When everyone had gone back for seconds, Brodie rose to make a toast. "To Bethany and Ethan, who have what it takes to make the perfect life—a man dedicated to protect and a woman who beautifies the world with her art. May your lives be joyful and secure, and may there be just enough smudges and just enough risk to make you appreciate what you've found in each other. Happiness and long life.''

Beth noticed that as her in-laws raised their glasses, they both appeared to be struggling with emotion. She wondered if they were remembering how they'd been forced to miss their son's marriage because of the elopement.

Afterward Ethan and Beth cut the cake and Kelly and Ebbie distributed it. By the time guests began to leave, dusk had fallen.

Ethan and Beth were talking to Curtis and Billings and their wives when there was a scream and a commotion from the driveway of Ebbie's house. The six hurried to investigate and found a group gathered around Zachary, who was on his back near the hydrangea that bordered the side of the house.

''Zach!'' Joanne was on her knees beside him.

He was conscious but groaning. ''My leg,'' he told Ethan as he squatted down next to him. ''Broken, I think. I slipped on the wet grass.''

Curtis pulled out a cell phone and dialed 911. Ebbie brought out a pillow and blankets and an umbrella which Beth held over him. Everyone stood around Zach as protection from the weather until the ambulance arrived.

Joanne rode in the ambulance with Zachary, and Ethan and Beth followed in the Blazer. Brodie took Nikkie and Jason home.

The leg was broken, a simple fracture of the tibia. ''We'll keep him overnight,'' the doctor told Joanne, Beth and Ethan in the waiting room. ''It was a clean break, and I don't foresee any problems, but the pain can be a little hard to deal with and we can take care of that here. If he's doing as well tomorrow, I can send him home with a prescription for a pain-killer, but he'll need crutches for at least three weeks.''

Joanne's brow furrowed in concern. "We were heading home tomorrow. If I lay him down in the back seat of the car, do you think…"

The doctor shook his head before she'd finished. "I wouldn't recommend that. He should stay put a couple of days. He'll be too uncomfortable to move."

Joanne nodded. "Whatever you say. May I see him now?"

"Of course. Come with me."

Joanne turned to Beth. "You two can go home." For the first time since Beth had known her, the woman looked vulnerable. "I can get a cab back to the motel."

Beth turned to Ethan, but didn't have to say a word.

"We'll wait for you and take you home with us," he said. "You and Zach can stay at our place until he's feeling well enough to go home."

Joanne looked stunned—also a first in Beth's experience of her. "Thank you," she said after a moment. "I'm sure that would be more comfortable for Zach than the motel. I'll try not to be too long, but I won't sleep tonight if I don't see for myself that he's all right."

"Take your time," Beth said. "And give Zach our best."

Joanne hurried off after the doctor, and Beth and Ethan settled back into the upholstered chairs in the waiting room.

"How did you know," Beth asked Ethan, "that was exactly what was on my mind?"

He leaned back in his chair in an attitude of false modesty. "I'm your husband," he said, smoothing his tie. "It's my job to know what you're thinking."

"You've only been my husband—" she glanced at her watch "— three hours and forty minutes."

"I'm a fast learner."

She sat sideways in her chair, resting her elbow on the back and studying him. His long legs were stretched out and crossed at the ankles. He looked pretty wonderful in a suit, she thought.

"Joanne's worried about Zach and so she's subdued right now," Beth warned, reaching over to brush a speck of something off his shoulder. "But it might be difficult to have her around the next few days. She always puts herself in charge of the situation, whatever it is. It was generous of you to offer to let them stay with you...us."

He shrugged, then sent her a questioning glance. "Have you thought about what it'll mean to *you* to have them in the house?"

"Yes," she said dryly. "Constant tension."

"I mean physically."

"Why physically?"

"Because," he explained, "we'll have to give them your room. We can tell them your things are in there because my closet's too small, but you'll have to sleep with me. It won't do for them to see you and me sleeping in separate bedrooms."

Her heart gave a surprised thud. Why hadn't she considered that? There wasn't an extra room for the Richardses.

She did her best to appear at ease as she said, "Well, I thought that was what you'd intended all along."

"I did," he admitted, "but I was willing to give you time to adjust. To come across the hall when you were ready."

"I'll just have to be flexible."

Amusement shone in Ethan's eyes. "Not *that* flexible," he said. "I'm not into anything gymnastic."

She punched his shoulder. "Ethan, I meant—"

"I know what you meant." He laughed, reaching over the arms of the chairs that separated them and cupping her head in his hand to pull her toward him. He kissed her cheek, then settled her against his shoulder. "I was just trying to lighten the mood. You get so serious when we discuss lovemaking."

"I was trying to be casual."

"I know. But your eyes become the color of a bruise and...I get the feeling there are some things I'll have to help you unlearn."

"I'll do my best," she promised.

He squeezed her shoulder. "One of them," he said, "is the notion that the outcome is entirely dependent upon you. It isn't. And anyway, the fact that we're sharing the same bed doesn't mean we have to share anything else until it seems like a good idea to you. But eventually I'm going to show you how mistaken you are about yourself."

Beth's hand rested on his pectoral muscle and she rubbed it gently in silent gratitude for his consideration.

But again she had that feeling of hot lava pouring through her, and she knew they would one day very soon make love. Though her mind and her emotions were confused about her abilities in the bedroom, her body seemed anxious to be proved wrong.

CHAPTER NINE

ETHAN STARED at the glowing numbers on his digital clock: 2:21 a.m. God. He felt as though he was in a sort of time warp where the last three hours had been a week long.

He and Beth had driven Joanne to the Coast Motel, picked up her and Zachary's things and brought her home. Beth had helped her settle into the room, while Ethan had explained to Nikkie and Jason that the Richardses would be staying for a while.

"How long?" Nikkie had asked sullenly.

"I'm not sure," he'd explained. "Maybe a week, maybe two. Depends on how quickly Zachary heals." He'd given Nikkie a significant look. "And that will probably be affected by how comfortable he is in his surroundings."

Nikkie sat in a corner of the sofa, her legs curled under her, a pillow wrapped in her arms, the picture of defensive resistance. "And I suppose we'll be inviting *them* into the family, too?"

"They *are* in the family," Jason said, his tone as aggressive as hers. "They're Grandma and Grandpa." He sat in the middle of the sofa, arms folded, feet not touching the floor. He frowned at Ethan, who was perched on the edge of a hatch-cover on legs that served as a coffee table. "But I don't want them to stay, either. They're gonna start picking on Mom and trying to get me to go home with them."

"I won't let them pick on your mom," Ethan said firmly, "and your home is right here. Nobody's taking you away."

Jason's frown turned to a fragile smile. "You promise?"

"I promise."

Nikkie got to her feet and threw the pillow onto the sofa. "Well, maybe somebody could take *me* away! If one more person moves in with us, there won't be room for me, anyway!" And she'd stormed off to her room.

Brodie had wandered out of the kitchen, a dish towel over the shoulder of the white shirt he'd worn to the wedding. He'd removed the tie. "I guess I'll have breakfast at the Crossing Café for a while," he said, handing Ethan a mug of coffee. "Looks like you're going to have a full house."

Ethan had hooked an arm around his neck and walked him back into the kitchen. "Bro, if you don't come, there will be no one to cook breakfast. We'll find room for you around the table."

"You mean in front of the stove."

"Yeah."

"Nikkie tells me Beth burned a frozen lasagna."

Ethan smiled. "She was doing laundry and got distracted by all the artistic potential of the junk in my basement. Come on. Weekends are still yours, but save us from toast and peanut butter during the week."

"Okay, okay. I'm such a pushover."

Ethan had put his cup down on the counter and hugged his brother. "Thanks for bringing the kids home and staying with them. And thanks for standing up for me. It wasn't a bad wedding, was it?''

Brodie grabbed his suit coat off the back of a kitchen chair. "We got rained on, I was pursued by a wacky redhead, and one of your guests broke his leg and is moving in with you. No, not bad.''

Ethan was thinking that, when all was said and done, he had Bethany. And that made the wedding pretty remarkable.

Ethan opened the door for Brodie. "Ah, about the redhead... Just who was pursuing whom? It looked to me as though *you* were the one hot on Kelly's trail.''

Brodie stepped onto the back porch. The night was dark, and rain continued to hammer the sloping porch roof. He pulled on his coat.

"Okay, I was," he said. "Then...in the buffet line, she gave me that look.''

"What look?''

Staring out at the rain, Brodie shrugged in frustration. "It's hard to put into words. But I think it means...you're it.''

"It?''

"Him.''

"Who?''

Brodie turned to him, mouth curled in exasperation. "Think, man. You're not usually this obtuse. I think she might think I could be...you know...''

Ethan shifted his weight and leaned a shoulder against the four-by-four that held up the right side of the porch. He thought he knew what Brodie meant, but he wanted to hear him say it.

"Could you spell it out for me?''

"A lasting love!" Brodie shouted. "Husband material!"

"And that's bad?"

"Very. I'm not interested."

"That's fascinating, because I recall you asking her if she could be interested in you if you had millions."

Brodie continued to stare moodily at the rain. "Yeah, 'cause I don't have millions and have no prospect of getting millions, so I thought I was safe."

"Uh-huh. That's why you were coming on to her all day?"

Brodie sighed and shrugged again. "You know me. That's what I do. Most women understand the game."

"You play this game because of Paulette."

Brodie stiffened. "I don't talk about Paulette."

Ethan shook his head. "Bro, you're getting too old for that game," he said, figuring his love for Brodie gave him permission to dispense with tact. "It's a seventeen-year-old, busting-beer-cans-on-your-head kind of game. And you don't talk about Paulette because if you did, you'd have to admit that you fell in love with her and then got dumped."

Brodie went rigid with anger. "Don't preach to me!"

"Somebody should!" Ethan retorted. "You chase down every woman for miles as some kind of proof of your virility, and then when she stops to let you catch her, you pull back. What is it, exactly? Are you hurting them as some kind of revenge on Paulette, or did Paulette destroy your self-esteem so much that when a woman finally does show some interest, you're afraid she won't find anything in you and she'll leave?"

Brodie swiveled his body toward Ethan and drew

back his fist. As though reliving an old scene from their teenage years, Ethan squared his stance and prepared to block the blow.

But Brodie didn't throw it. After one tense moment he dropped his fist and drew a breath, his eyes still dark with fury. "My life is none of your business," he said flatly. "You'd better go inside and take care of your own. I have a feeling this marriage isn't going to be the walk in the park you had with Diana." Then Brodie's eyes shifted somewhere to the left of Ethan, and his tight angry features seemed to collapse in distress.

Ethan turned to find Beth standing beside him. She'd heard Brodie's remark, he was sure, about his seemingly perfect first marriage.

Ethan put an arm around her and drew her close. The night air was cold. "Hi," he said. "What're you doing out here?"

"I heard the two of you shouting at each other," she said, her eyes going worriedly from him to his brother. "Is something wrong?"

Brodie smiled and shook his head. "You haven't been around long enough to know that we usually end up shouting at each other. It's nothing serious."

Beth studied him skeptically, then changed the subject. "Brodie, thank you for staying with Jason and Nikkie."

"My pleasure." He turned to Ethan, his expression neutral. "You'll have to move the Blazer so I can back out."

Ethan followed him at a run through the rain, but stopped at his truck. "What are you doing?" Brodie demanded as he yanked open his door. "You'll get drenched."

Ethan felt rain soak the shoulders of his shirt, but ignored it. "I want to make sure you understand that Paulette was an idiot, not you. When you're not being psychotic, you're really all right. And I hate to think of you spending a lifetime alone because you can't see that."

Brodie looked back at him, his jaw rigidly set. "Will you get the Blazer out of my way before I back over it?" he asked.

Deciding that any further conversation would be profane and irretrievable, Ethan ran to the Blazer and backed onto the street.

In a move that Ethan thought looked like something out of a slapstick comedy, Brodie backed out with a squeal of tires, raced the twenty feet to his own driveway and turned into it with another squeal of tires and a spray of rainwater, then rocked to a stop. He went into his house without a glance in Ethan's direction.

Ethan pulled into the driveway and ran back into the house. The place was silent as a tomb.

The kitchen clock said it was just after eleven. He shot the bolt on the front door and turned off all the downstairs lights. Upstairs he looked into Nikkie's room and found her asleep, a cat curled up on each side of her. Simba looked up and gave him a faint meow. Ethan pulled the door silently closed.

The door of the room Joanne was using was also closed, and there was silence behind it. He could only conclude that meant everything was fine.

Jason's door was open and Ethan looked in to find that he, too, was fast asleep, one arm hanging over the side of the upper bunk. Ethan tucked it back up and resettled the blankets. The boy expelled a comfortable little sigh and settled more deeply into his pillow.

Ethan walked into his own room to find Beth turning down the bed. She wore a simple blue cotton nightie that skimmed her knees. She looked up at him with a smile he imagined was supposed to assure him that she was quite comfortable with the situation, and if he wanted to make love to her tonight, she was willing.

In her eyes, though, was concern, trepidation. When eventually they did make love, he wanted her to be more than willing. He wanted her eager, confident that she was doing what she wanted to do.

"How was Joanne when she went to bed?" he asked, unbuttoning his shirt.

Beth fluffed a pillow. "Exhausted but fine. Now that she knows Zachary's going to be all right, she'll probably be her old self in the morning. So be prepared to listen to suggested changes for your uniform and possibly even the county code." She smiled as she walked around the bed to the other side and fluffed the other pillow. "Do you sleep by the door or by the window?" she asked, still sounding quite composed.

He knew it was perverse, but he took a certain satisfaction in making her control slip. "I usually sleep in the middle," he said, pulling his shirt off and giving it a hook shot into the hamper by the bathroom. "You can have the two sides."

She tossed the pillow on the bed and looked at him, obviously trying to decide if he was being difficult or funny. Then she smiled. "It's nice to know that even so close to midnight you retain a sense of humor."

It was on the tip of his tongue to tell her there were

moments in a man's life when that was all he had
left, but he thought it sounded self-pitying, so he kept
the thought to himself.

He pointed to the side of the bed nearest the door.
"That side," he said. "You go on to bed. I have to
take a shower." He opened the closet door to find
that a few of her things had been hung beside his.
Seeing her colorful fabrics lined up beside his darker
things gave him a weird sense of déjà vu. He remembered when Diana was still alive and his uniforms and
sports coats had shared space with silky blouses and
pastel linen suits. But the sight also projected him into
the future, because he couldn't help but wonder how
well this would work, how long those things would
be there.

Beth gestured at the closet. "I brought some of my
stuff here so I wouldn't have to disturb Joanne in the
morning. I hope that's all right."

"Of course." He pulled off his shoes and tossed
them into the bottom of the closet.

"She believed me when I said my clothes were in
there because your closet was too crowded."

"The best lies are those that have a grain of truth,"
he said, pushing the closet door closed and heading
for the bathroom. But Beth stood squarely in his path,
a line of concern between her eyebrows.

"What's wrong?" she asked.

Again he got an unexpected glimpse of Diana, this
time in the direct way Beth approached a problem.
But at the moment he was tired and would have preferred to forget the whole thing. After all, in just a
few short days he'd fallen for and married a woman
who was afraid to go to bed with him. And he'd been
looking forward to ending what had seemed like an

Play "Lucky Hearts" and you get...

YOURS FREE!

This charming refrigerator magnet looks like a little cherub, and it's a perfect size for holding notes and recipes. Best of all it's yours ABSOLUTELY FREE when you accept our NO-RISK offer!

...then continue your lucky streak with a sweetheart of a deal!

1. Play Lucky Hearts as instructed on the opposite page.

2. Send back this card and you'll receive brand-new Harlequin Superromance® novels. These books have a cover price of $3.99 each, but they are yours to keep absolutely free!

3. There's no catch. You're under no obligation to buy anything. We charge nothing—ZERO—for your first shipment. And you don't have to make any minimum number of purchases—not even one!

4. The fact is thousands of readers enjoy receiving books by mail from the Harlequin Reader Service®. They like the convenience of home delivery...they like getting the best new novels BEFORE they're available in stores...and they love our discount prices!

5. We hope that after receiving your free books you'll want to remain a subscriber. But the choice is yours—to continue or cancel, any time at all! So why not take us up on our invitation, with no risk of any kind. You'll be glad you did!

◆ Exciting Harlequin romance novels—FREE!
◆ Plus a Beautiful Cherub Magnet—FREE!

The Harlequin Reader Service® — Here's how it works:

Accepting free books places you under no obligation to buy anything. You may keep the books and gift and return the shipping statement marked "cancel." If you do not cancel, about a month later we'll send you 4 additional novels and bill you just $3.34 each plus 25¢ delivery per book and applicable sales tax, if any.* That's the complete price—and compared to cover prices of $3.99 each—quite a bargain! You may cancel any time, but if you choose to continue, every month we'll send you 4 more books, which you may either purchase at the discount price...or return to us and cancel your subscription.
*Terms and prices subject to change without notice. Sales tax applicable in N.Y.

BUSINESS REPLY MAIL
FIRST-CLASS MAIL   PERMIT NO. 717   BUFFALO, NY

POSTAGE WILL BE PAID BY ADDRESSEE

HARLEQUIN READER SERVICE
3010 WALDEN AVE
PO BOX 1867
BUFFALO NY 14240-9952

NO POSTAGE
NECESSARY
IF MAILED
IN THE
UNITED STATES

interminable period of celibacy. But he couldn't take what she offered when he knew she'd rather be having an IRS audit or something equally unpleasant. So what could possibly be wrong?

"Nothing," he said, then he leaned down to kiss her cheek and got a disorienting whiff of a spicy rose fragrance. "Go to sleep. Good night." He walked around her and went into the bathroom.

But she followed him and stood in the doorway, preventing him from closing himself in. He saw the rosy tips of small firm breasts under her thin gown and had to tear his eyes away and concentrate on her face. It was pale and anxious.

"You're annoyed with me," she said, "because I'm nervous about...tonight. Is that it?"

"No. I—"

"Well, I'm nervous, but...I want you to make love to me." She looked directly into his eyes, though he could see that took courage.

"Beth," he said patiently, leaning a forearm on the doorway molding, "you say you want to make love with me, but your eyes tell a different story. You don't really want it. And I won't make love with you until you do."

"But I explained." She spoke quietly but urgently. "My feelings are very complex. Part Steve's fault, probably part my fault. But I don't want...the experience diminished for you because of that. I don't want to hurt you—yet there seems no way to avoid it. If you make love to me and I have trouble responding, you'll be hurt. But if we don't make love..." She spread her arms helplessly. "I mean, who *doesn't* make love on their wedding night? I understand that you're annoyed, I just want to make it clear that I—"

He put a hand gently over her mouth to silence her, although he was fascinated by her stream of chatter. The control she always tried so hard to maintain was puddled at her feet. He liked that. And he thought it boded well for their *eventual* liaison.

"Rule number one in this house," he said, lowering his hand when it appeared she'd remain silent, "is that we don't hold ourselves to other people's standards. Each of us does what he or she decides. And if I'm annoyed with anyone, I'm annoyed with myself."

He paused to draw a breath, because being completely honest with a woman, he was just beginning to remember, was harder than it seemed. "I'm used to being in charge of myself and the situation. I thought it would be easy to wait for you to be ready to make love. But I'm discovering that I'm not as strong as I thought. That I'm more vulnerable than I thought. And that's difficult for a man to admit to himself."

A subtle change took place in her eyes. The suggestion that he found her desirable seemed to surprise her. God. He wished he could have had five minutes alone in an interview room with Steve Richards.

She put a hand to his face with a reverence he found humbling. "I hope I can be what you want," she whispered.

He put his hand over hers, turned his lips into her palm and kissed it. "You *are* what I want. That's the problem."

"I meant in bed," she said.

"When two people care about each other," he said, kissing her knuckles now, "they usually have no problem making the other happy—in bed or out.

When that time comes for you, we'll be ready. In the meantime, I really need a shower and you need some sleep."

"Okay." She wrapped her arms around his waist and held him fiercely for so long he was ready to chuck his noble attitude and carry her to the bed. Then she took a step back from him and said with a mystifying disappointment in her eyes that completely confused him, "I usually drop off to sleep the minute my head hits the pillow, so I'll see you at breakfast."

"Right," he replied, and watched her stiff-backed form in the thin cotton walk away before closing the bathroom door.

AND THAT WAS WHY he lay staring at the clock in the wee hours of the morning. He'd taken his time in the shower, grateful to find Beth asleep when he joined her in the bed. She was lying on her back, the fingers of one hand folded against her cheek.

He flipped onto his other side and closed his eyes, thinking how different it was to realize he was married again. Diana's absence had made such a change in his life, and the love they'd had for each other would be with him always. But the image that formed behind his closed eyelids now was Beth's.

As if she'd detected his thoughts, she turned toward him and curled up against his back, her knees tucked up right under his buttocks. His confused libido was confused no longer, and he cursed himself for taking a sympathetic stand with her. They could be making love right now, and he'd have bet everything he owned that he'd have already cured her of her feelings of inadequacy.

But he could tell by the gentle pulse of breath

against his spine that she was still asleep. She hadn't chosen to snuggle against him; she'd done it in an instinctive but unconscious search for warmth and security after a long taxing day.

He tried to clear his mind of thought so that he could get some sleep. That was surprisingly easy. What he couldn't turn off was the reaction of every nerve ending in his body. The part of him in contact with her silky flesh was screaming for him to do something about it. But he'd promised, and she trusted him.

So he lay still even as she snuggled closer. It was character building, he told himself. And he realized he was going to have to be quite some paragon to hold his own in this relationship.

ETHAN AWOKE to the pleasant smell of coffee and…pancakes? French toast? He wasn't sure which, but the aromas wafting upstairs were enough to set his stomach rumbling.

The other side of the bed was empty, but *could* Beth cook anything without burning it? Nikkie was good with eggs, but couldn't seem to get the hang of flipping pancakes, so she never made them. Brodie slept in on Sundays.

Jason appeared in the doorway of Ethan's room, still wearing *Toy Story* pajamas. "Do you smell that?" he asked.

"Yeah." Ethan tossed the blanket back and swung his legs over the side of the bed. "Who's cooking?"

Jason shook his head. "It can't be Mom, and Nikkie's door is closed. It's either Grandma or Uncle Brodie. Come on!" Jason called, then disappeared from view. Ethan could hear his footsteps heading for the stairs.

"Right behind you," he said, going to the closet and pulling on jeans and a sweater. He hadn't fallen asleep until sometime after four, but still he was more ravenous than tired.

And, masochist that he seemed to be, he couldn't wait to see Beth. She should be bright and fresh this morning, all the sleep she'd gotten in direct proportion to all the sleep he'd missed!

Joanne was holding forth at the stove, a pristine counter suggesting that whatever she was preparing had required little effort—or at least none that showed.

It was pancakes. Jason was hard at work on a tall stack drenched in syrup, and Beth sat across from him with two pancakes half-eaten. She wore a red turtleneck and had bundled her hair up in a loose knot. Bangs skimmed her eyebrows when she looked up at him, and silky tendrils of hair had escaped to caress her neck.

The look she gave him was cautious and watchful. He wondered if she'd awakened curled up tightly against him and was embarrassed by it.

Joanne turned away from the stove to see who'd walked into the kitchen. She wished him a pleasant if somewhat haughty good-morning.

He returned the greeting, then went to lean over Beth's chair and give her a kiss. He did it partly for Joanne's benefit, but partly for his own.

"I thought I'd make myself useful," Joanne said, her gaze lingering on him as a new dollop of batter sizzled on the griddle. "I know that cooking isn't one of Beth's strengths."

It annoyed him that she would feel called upon to say so, particularly when she was a guest in what was supposed to be Beth's home.

He gave Beth a calculatedly lascivious look and kissed her again. "She has other qualities that far outweigh cooking in importance."

Beth eyes widened, first in surprise, then in amused appreciation. "Thank you, darling," she said, falling in with his loverlike performance.

"But it's wonderful to have someone around who *can* cook," Ethan said, going to the stove to peer over Joanne's shoulder. He wanted her to know he appreciated her efforts, but he didn't want her picking on Beth. "Anything I can do?"

She stepped aside and pointed to the oven with her spatula. "Your plate's in there."

"Why don't *you* take it?" he suggested. "Since the batter's made, I can probably prepare my own."

"Nonsense." She pulled open the oven door and handed him an oven mitt. "Careful with it. Is your daughter coming down?"

"I don't think so. Sunday's her chance to sleep in."

Joanne nodded. "Well, I'll put a plate in the oven just in case."

Ethan carried his plate to the table. "How's Zachary this morning?" he asked. "Have you called the hospital?"

"Yes, and he had a fairly good night," Joanne replied, expertly flipping a pancake. "The doctor says he can go home this morning if we can pick him up."

"Sure." Ethan reached for the syrup. "We can go as soon as we're finished breakfast."

Joanne turned away from the stove to face him. "We could compensate you for the room and the—"

"No," Ethan said simply. "We're happy to have you here."

"I appreciate that," she said with an upward tilt of her chin that seemed more aggressive than grateful, "but it'll cost you in a dozen little ways. More groceries, more hot water, more laundry, more—"

"No," Ethan said again. And when she opened her mouth to offer further argument, he added quietly, "and that's final."

Her chin went up an extra notch, and she appeared confused, as though receiving generosity and being overruled were foreign experiences for her.

"Zachary might have something to say about that," she persisted.

Ethan cut into his pancakes without looking up. "No, he won't," he returned. "It's my house."

She might have continued to argue, but the smell of something burning turned her back to the stove with a cry of distress. She jabbed the spatula under a smoking pancake and lifted it out, obviously looking for the trash.

"Around the corner of the fridge," Beth told her. "Near the cat food."

The spatula held out in front of her, Joanne followed Beth's directions, then walked back to the stove frowning fiercely.

So Beth wasn't the only one capable of burning food, he thought. He looked up from his plate and caught Beth's eye, then winked and went back to his breakfast.

CHAPTER TEN

ETHAN DROPPED Beth at the cannery on his way to work Monday morning. Their efforts to convince Joanne and Zachary that they were a real family were aided considerably by the built-in stress of getting two adults and two children showered, dressed and fed in order to leave the house at the same time.

Nikkie was carrying a mock-up of a medieval shield she'd made out of cardboard and foil, and therefore she couldn't take the school bus. But she apparently considered arriving at school in a car filled with her new stepmother and stepbrother a severe breach of cool and ignored Beth and Jason completely.

Jason was out of sorts because Ethan had thwarted his plan to ride his bike after school to the old deserted Appleby house in the next block. Ethan had explained that transients often took shelter there, and that though children and teenagers found it fun to dare one another to go in and explore the place, it wasn't safe. Jason had tried wheedling but to no avail.

Beth thought Ethan seemed a little edgy when she suggested he looked as though he hadn't slept well. And by the time the foursome headed for the car, they were all snapping at each other. Beth had a parting glimpse of Joanne and Zachary sitting across from each other in the kitchen. Zachary's leg in its cast was propped on an extra chair, and Beth wondered what they thought of her "happy family."

Nikkie left the Blazer without speaking, and Jason climbed out with only a terse goodbye.

Ethan pulled up to the pier on which the cannery stood and caught Beth's arm when she would have pushed her door open.

"I apologize for my mood this morning," he said with a sincerity that surprised her—apologies had not even been in Steve's makeup. "I haven't been getting much sleep lately."

She turned back, giving him her full attention, wanting to know what was troubling him and to help if she could. "Why not? What's wrong?"

"It's not 'wrong,' precisely," he said with a half smile. "It just keeps me awake."

"What?"

"You," he replied. "You're a cuddler."

Color rose to her cheeks, but she smiled. "That's strange," she said, "because Steve always said that my body up against his made him claustrophobic. So I always stayed on my side of the bed. But—" her color deepened "—when I woke up Sunday morning, I was all wrapped around you. I'm sorry."

"Don't apologize," he said. "It doesn't make me claustrophobic at all. It makes me…" He considered a moment, then apparently changed his mind about telling her. "Never mind. It was no reason to grouse at you. *I'm* sorry. I'll pick you up about six. You said Jason will just walk here from school?"

"Yes. It's not far, so he doesn't have to be picked up. And Nikkie'll get the bus home?"

"She has a drama-club meeting after school, so

she'll get the city bus. That usually gets her home by five.''

''Okay. Do you want me to call and check on her, make sure everything's all right?''

''She'll tell you she's too old to be checked on,'' he warned, ''but I always do, anyway.''

''All right. I'll handle it. Besides, I'll have to check on Joanne and Zachary.''

She pushed open her door again.

''Hey!'' he called.

''Yes?''

''No kiss goodbye? You're forgetting the private detective.''

She leaned toward him. ''Do you really think he's watching?'' she asked, glancing surreptitiously beyond Ethan, then to his left and right.

''I do,'' he replied gravely. ''I imagine he's using binoculars, so you'd better make it good.''

Her smile held amused suspicion. ''You aren't by any chance taking advantage of this situation, are you?''

He tipped his head and closed the few inches that separated his mouth from hers. ''Of course I am,'' he admitted shamelessly, and kissed her until she couldn't breathe or think.

At last he raised his head, and she tried to reestablish a sense of emotional balance, thinking that if he made love with the same artful skill with which he kissed, he might very well be right about teaching her to enjoy it.

She stepped out of the car and blew him one final kiss. He drove away with a tap of the Blazer's horn.

Kelly was perched on a piling by the door to Beth's studio. She was dressed in her studio garb—a ratty denim jacket, old beige cords and a blue sweatshirt stained with clay and glaze. Her short red hair was tumbled, and her eyes were bright with mischief.

"Well, that was quite a kiss," she said, leaping down from the piling as Beth unlocked the studio door.

"We thought the detective might be watching," Beth replied, making her way into the studio, careful not to meet Kelly's eyes.

"Come on," Kelly cajoled. "That was no performance. That was the real thing."

"Well..." Beth flipped light switches, and fluorescent tubes fluttered, then came to life, filling the middle of the cavernous room with a bright glare. Tables around the room were covered with signs and all kinds of hanging wood art that was drying for the Winter Festival Art Fair.

In the middle of the room under another bank of lower hanging lights a large worktable stood, and Beth crossed to it. She dropped her purse under it and pulled off her jacket, hanging it on a nearby coat tree.

"Well, what?" Kelly encouraged, doing the same with her jacket and pulling up a stool without waiting for an invitation.

Beth wondered how to explain to Kelly what she felt for Ethan and decided that she couldn't. It would sound absurd, even to her best friend. "Well, I don't know," she said finally. "He's like a composite of the perfect man. Tough, gentle, firm, kind, funny, warm..." She stopped to grin. "Shall I go on?"

Kelly shook her head and made a gesture Beth interpreted as "Please don't." Then she pulled a circle of pine toward her, one that Beth had yet to decide what to do with, and traced the rings in the grain with the blunt tip of one finger.

"Actually I understand," she said, glancing up at Beth under her lashes. The look in her eyes, Beth noted in surprise, suggested embarrassment. "I've spent quite some time talking to his brother."

Beth wasn't sure what that meant. "You mean he praises Ethan, or you know about Ethan's qualities because you saw them in Brodie?"

Kelly sighed and concentrated on the rings. "If you'd asked me before your wedding, I'd have said it was because Brodie was all those things, too. But on the day of your wedding..." A pleat appeared between her eyebrows. "I don't know. Something changed."

Beth climbed onto her stool and leaned an elbow on the table. She studied Kelly's uncharacteristic frown and put a hand to her friend's knee. "What changed?" she asked. "It looked like the two of you were getting on so well. In fact, in the buffet line, I'd have sworn you made some kind of emotional contact."

Kelly's eyes became unfocused and Beth guessed she was remembering that moment. "Yes. We did. I looked into his laughing face and realized how nice it must be to be fussed over. How much I missed someone laughing about things, rather than finding problems with everything. It came over me as though he'd dropped a net. I was interested. *Very* interested." She sighed and made a face Beth couldn't quite decipher. "But you know what?"

Beth was almost afraid to ask. "What?"

"I think he's one of those men for whom the chase is everything."

"Why?"

"Because the minute I stopped evading him and let him know I could be interested in a relationship, it was as though someone blew up the power station and the lights went out."

"Sometimes," Beth suggested tactfully, "when your emotions are engaged and because you care so much, something that's insignificant can seem bigger than it really is."

Kelly sighed and pushed the pine disk away from her. "I don't think that's the case here," she said, knotting her fingers together and drawing a knee up until her foot was hooked in a rung of the stool. "His ardor cooled considerably the last hour of the reception. When your father-in-law was hurt, I asked Brodie if it would help if I went back to Ethan's with him and the kids, and he told me rather firmly that he'd be fine and that I probably had a lot of cleaning up of food and stuff to do."

That didn't sound good to Beth at all. And suddenly she remembered Ethan and Brodie shouting at each other on the back porch Saturday night.

"Maybe he was just being considerate," she said thinly.

Kelly gave her a look that told her she knew that excuse to be as false as it sounded. "Penny Curtis and Jan Billings were going to help Ebbie clean up so that I could help Brodie. I told him that. But he brushed me off."

Beth tried again. "He might just be a little frightened. You know, the old commitment bugaboo and all that." She smiled. "And you're pretty heady stuff, you know. If he's attracted to you and he thinks you're beginning to notice him, he might just be over-whelmed.''

Kelly considered that grimly for a moment, then tipped her head from side to side as though it could be a possibility about which she remained undecided. ''Well, I'm not going to give him another thought. I was well rid of my ex because he could never under-stand me. I'm not going to get involved with someone else who's going to make me feel unsure of myself. So let's talk about you.'' She caught both feet on the rung of the stool and leaned toward Beth, her eyes gleaming with curiosity. ''How was...the weekend?''

Beth pulled a stack of boards nearer, setting them out in neat rows to prepare them for painting. ''Nik-kie's nose is a little out of joint because not only is she dealing with a stepmother and brother, now there's Joanne and Zachary. Of course, Zachary's stuck in bed for a few days, but Joanne takes a little getting used to. She did make breakfast yester—''

Beth abruptly stopped when she looked up and found Kelly staring at her and shaking her head.

''What?'' Beth asked.

''You know what I want to know,'' Kelly said. ''Did a couple of nights with him spark your interest in sex again?''

Beth sighed and met Kelly's gaze. ''We haven't had sex.''

Kelly blinked. ''You're kidding!''

''I know. I know. I would have, but the day of Jason's party when I asked him to marry me and he agreed, we talked about what each of us wanted out of it, and we agreed that it wouldn't simply be a con-venience thing—''

''So far,'' Kelly said, ''I don't understand.''

"Well, let me finish," Beth returned with mild impatience. Not that even the complete story would clarify anything for Kelly. Beth herself still felt confused. "I told him how it was with Steve and me and how I've...been ever since. He seems to think I'm wrong and that making love with him will be entirely different."

"Well, why didn't you?"

Beth leaned both elbows on the table and rested her chin in her hands. The weekend seemed like something that had happened to someone else—a wedding, a trip to the hospital, a beautiful but suspicious stepdaughter, a man who kissed her with dark-eyed ardor, then gently pushed her away when she said she was willing to make love with him.

"I told him I was willing," she said, running her fingertips over one of her boards. "But he said my eyes told a different story. That he wanted to wait until I was sure it was what I wanted."

"Willing," Kelly said with a wince, "is a pretty insipid word."

Beth straightened and jumped off the stool. "I know it is," she said loudly. The words echoed in the nearly empty room. "But what if I'd behaved otherwise, then he put a hand on me and I froze, sure he'd start telling me at any moment I was cold and unresponsive and completely unappealing? That would have been harder on him than waiting...wouldn't it?"

Kelly slid off her own stool to put an arm around Beth's shoulders. "Steve was a jerk, Beth. And before you get all defensive, I know you had a good thing going in the beginning, but he didn't uphold his end of the relationship. He ignored you when he was busy. He was too ambitious to spend any time with you, to remind you that he cared. Then when he made some big deal, he came home and treated you like...like the spoils of victory. What woman wouldn't conclude that this was no fun and she wanted no more of it?''

Kelly turned Beth to face her and grasped both her shoulders. Her gaze was fierce. ''The thing you have to remember here, Beth, is that you're no longer dealing with Steve. This is Sheriff Ethan Drum—the man who scoured the countryside at night in the rain to find Jason. The man who supported Jason's story so he wouldn't humiliate him in front of your in-laws, who agreed to marry you to help you through this. It's not going to be like it was with Steve. *You're* not going to be like you were with Steve.''

Beth knew that. She just wasn't sure her brain could translate that information to a body that had turned itself off long ago.

''All right, enough about men,'' Kelly declared, hooking an arm in Beth's and leading her toward the door that led into the rest of the cannery. ''Let's talk about something we understand—art. Show me where my studio will be.''

Beth spent the next hour and a half walking Kelly through a series of large separated spaces that would ultimately become the long-dreamed-of art mall. She showed her how each room could be partitioned to make a small showroom in the front and still leave a big working area in the back. There'd be north light from the long series of small-paned windows facing the river and the state of Washington on the other shore.

Kelly chose the space closest to Beth's and insisted on writing her a check. Beth tried to refuse, protesting

that it would be another week at least before she had
the place painted.

"For a slight reduction in price," Kelly bargained,
"I can paint it myself. You've had the building inspector in, so we know the pier and the structure are
safe. All I have to do is paint the walls something
soft and light, spruce up the showroom area, and
pretty soon I can be here working beside you every
day and checking on the progress of your love life."

Beth snorted. "Oh, good."

They laughed, then Beth walked Kelly out to her
car.

JASON CAME to the cannery from school looking no
more cheerful than he had when she and Ethan had
dropped him off.

"Taylor Bridges," he said, munching on an apple
Beth had brought for him, "doesn't believe Ethan's
my dad. He says I'm making it up."

"Maybe you should invite him over sometime,"
Beth suggested. She knew it wasn't fair to hold a
grudge against a child, but the Bridges boy had been
a thorn in Jason's side since her son's first day at
Cobbler's Crossing Elementary. "Maybe for dinner.
Then he can see Ethan for himself."

Jason chewed, swallowed and perked up. "Yeah!"
he said. "That'd be cool! Can I do it tomorrow?"

"Let me check to make sure Ethan doesn't have
anything scheduled." With a fine-tipped brush dipped
in silver paint, she put whiskers on a cat on one of
her door plaques. "He has meetings at night sometimes."

"Okay." Jason came up beside her and leaned into

her free left arm as she worked. "You know, coming here's turning out to be a good thing, isn't it?"

Beth wrapped her arm around him and pulled him closer. She dabbed silver dots in the cat's wide green eyes. "You mean because of Ethan?"

"Mostly." As she turned to look at him, he added, "You like him, too, dontcha?"

"Yes, I do," she replied, kissing his forehead.

Jason grinned, his eyes alight with secret information. "You kiss him a lot. I seen you."

There was no denying that. "Uh-huh."

"You're not gonna be having babies, are you?"

"No. No babies."

"Nikkie said you were." He threw the apple core into the wastebasket under her table. It landed with a thunk. "She says if you and Ethan had babies, you wouldn't need us anymore."

Beth stopped in the act of tipping the cat's ears with silver and set down her brush on her palette. She wiped her hands on a rag and gave her son her full attention. "Jason, you know that isn't true. You have always been and will always be the most important thing in my life."

He leaned against the edge of the table. "Yeah, but if you had a baby that was part you and part Ethan, then it really belongs to you. I'm part somebody else and so's Nikkie."

Horrified that he might have been worried about that all day long, she waved him onto the other stool.

"First of all," she said, choosing her words carefully, "all children belong one hundred percent to both their parents."

He frowned, unable to grasp that. "But my dad's dead and so's Nikkie's mom."

"Yes," she said, "but though people die, love doesn't. Your dad and Nikkie's mom still love you from heaven, just like you both love them from down here. Only now you have even more love because you have Ethan."

He considered that and added cautiously. "And Nikkie has you?"

"Yes." She wasn't certain Nikkie would hold the same enthusiasm for the concept that Jason did. "And it doesn't matter to Ethan that he wasn't there when you were born, and it doesn't matter to me that Nikkie was born to another woman. I love her because now we're all a family. And it wouldn't matter if Ethan and I did have a baby, because we wouldn't love it more than we love you and Nikkie."

"So she was wrong." Jason seemed pleased by that possibility.

"She was mistaken," Beth corrected diplomatically. "It's a new situation for all of us, so it's easy to be confused about the way things will work. But I promise you that Ethan and I will always love you and Nikkie, even if we did have a baby."

He smiled, that problem solved. "Can I have a board to work on till Ethan picks us up?"

"Sure." Beth found him a board with a slight irregularity on one edge, and the box of odds and ends paint tubes she'd given him to use when she'd first set up her studio.

On a sudden impulse she drew two cats on a board with a pale yellow background, a fluffy gray Persian and a sleek calico with a black spot above the muzzle. She had the cats painted in an hour or so, then added pink collars on which she carefully printed their names with her fine-tipped brush—Simba and Cindy.

Then she added Nikkie's name in mossy green block letters at the bottom of the board.

She made a few fine-lined flourishes for a border, then pushed the board aside to dry.

"That's cool, Mom!" Jason was her biggest fan. He jumped off his stool. "I'm gonna get my sign. We can put it up at Ethan's, can't we?" He ran across the studio to the small apartment they'd lived in before to retrieve his name plaque from his bedroom door. She saw the yellow kitchen wall through the door Jason had left open; it seemed like an eternity, she thought, since they'd lived there. Their lives had changed so completely.

Remembering her promise to Ethan, Beth called home. Nikkie answered.

"Hi," Beth said cheerfully. "It's Beth. I'm just checking to make sure everything's okay."

"Why wouldn't it be?" Nikkie said rudely.

"Because there's a man there with a broken leg," Beth replied patiently, "a woman who isn't really familiar with the house and a young woman who's helping to plan a play that's in a crisis over props. So my checking to make sure no one needs anything doesn't really seem out of line, does it?"

There was a moment's silence, and Beth could imagine Nikkie sticking her tongue out at the receiver but keeping any further rude remarks to herself because her father had insisted she be polite to her wicked stepmother.

"Zachary is fine," she said with rigid courtesy. "I know because he shouted at me to turn my music down. Joanne is fine. I know that because she told me that chocolate has empty calories and will give me zits."

Beth couldn't help but feel sympathy for the girl at home alone with the Richardses. "And how are you?" she asked, her concern genuine. "Is there anything you need?"

"If you want to help me," Nikkie said with a despondent sigh, "you can find me medieval shields and weapons for twenty. Mr. Fogarty thought my foil-and-cardboard stuff wouldn't be convincing. I'm supposed to try to come up with something else."

"I'll look around the studio," Beth volunteered, "and see if I can find anything that'd help."

There was another silence, then Nikkie said politely but despairingly, "Thanks."

"No problem. See you in an hour or so. We'll bring home something for dinner."

"Don't bother," Nikkie said. "Joanne took a cab to the market and came back with all sorts of stuff. She's making pot roast for dinner."

"See? Everything has an upside."

"If you say so. Bye."

Beth rummaged through a stack of wooden shapes she'd cut out and hadn't had a chance to use. At last she found what she was looking for. It was shield-shaped and full-size. Pleased with herself, she took it to her table and began to trace a shape with pencil.

It was an hour later and she and Jason were admiring each other's work when a cheerful voice shouted from the doorway of her studio. "Bethie! How the hell are you?"

She turned to the studio's entrance to see a tall lanky figure standing there dressed in a white jumpsuit stained with paint. He had graying dark hair pulled back into a long curly ponytail. His eyes were pale blue, his cheekbones angular and his square chin had a cleft in it.

Rush Weston was too attractive for his own good, and he bore the burden with a self-awareness Beth had never seen before in an adult. He was funny, charming, sometimes thoughtful, and always a brilliant sculptor, but he had the ego of a spoiled two-year-old.

"Hello, Rush," she said, meeting in the middle of the room to shake his hand.

He wrapped her into a crushing bear hug, instead. "Bethie, how are ya? Feels like it's been an age! I met Kelly at the coffee bar and she said she'd just rented a studio from you. So I thought I'd better get my deposit in before all the studios are taken."

Beth patted his shoulder, then pushed him firmly away. "No danger of that," she said. "Kelly insisted on giving me money because she thinks I need it. And she's painting her own space so she can get in earlier. Oh, and I've had the building inspector in since you looked around, and everythng's secure."

He nodded. "Good. Good. So if I paint my own space, I can get in early, too?"

"Sure. If you want to. We'll have to see how efficient the furnace is. I might have to get something bigger, which could take a little time. Can you put up with that?"

Rush snaked an arm around her shoulders and squeezed. "I'm unveiling my piece for the county's art association at the festival, and I'd like my studio set up here by then so everyone can come in and look around. And, baby, I can put up with an ice floe in my studio if it means I get to be near you."

Beth looked up at him and said with a certain relish, "Rush, I'm married."

He stared at her a moment, clearly stunned, then dropped his arm.

"I'm married," she repeated. "To Ethan Drum, sheriff of—"

"I know who he is," Rush said with a sharp downturn of his features. "Are you crazy? I thought you didn't want any part of marriage again."

"I didn't. He...changed my mind." That was true. She needed a husband and he was available and willing.

"He's going to let you keep this place?"

"Why wouldn't he?"

Rush wandered around the room, pausing to look at the boards spread out on her table. "I told you I've met the sheriff. Struck me as a hard nose. Doesn't believe in gray areas. Things are black or white. Not the kind of man an artist should tie up with."

"He isn't at all like that," Beth insisted.

"Maybe not now." Rush glanced up, warning in his eyes. "Now that he's landed you, I'll wager he becomes more demanding and possessive."

Beth made a sound of exasperation. "I'm not a fish, Rush. He didn't land me. He decided to spend his life with me—the way I am. He knows how I am about my work and he's willing to live with that."

"So he says."

"So he *is*."

"We'll see." He waved an index finger above the cat plaque she'd painted for Nikkie, then shook his head over the shield. "When are you going to stop doing this cutesy stuff and concentrate on *real* art?"

Beth bristled. She'd be the first to admit that the

plaques weren't art, but she didn't have the luxury of being an art snob at this point. "They pay the bills, Weston," she said. "And if I'm going to be your landlord, don't pick on my stuff. I might raise your rent."

He turned back to her, his eyes brimming with the passion that always lay just under the surface. It was what made him a brilliant sculptor—and something of a Casanova. "Maybe we could make a deal where you take it out in trade." The lewd suggestion was made quietly and he tried to put his arms around her again.

Beth raised both her arms to block the attempt, so he simply caught her wrists, instead. "There's something between us, Bethie. You know it and I know it."

"You're right, Weston," Ethan's voice said lazily from the doorway. "The something between you is me."

CHAPTER ELEVEN

"I'M SURE that little scene played really well for your in-laws' detective," Ethan said as he pulled the Blazer up to a stoplight. His profile had all the animation of a figure on Mount Rushmore.

Beth was growing tired of explaining. She'd done it once when Ethan walked into her studio to find Rush with his hands on her. She'd done it a second time after Rush had left. And she'd done it a third time while Ethan had helped Jason on with his jacket and walked him out to the Blazer.

"If I explain it all a fourth time," she asked, a weary, slightly antagonistic note in her voice, "do you think you might actually listen?"

He turned to look at her, anger bright in his eyes. Before he swung his gaze back to the road, she saw something else there she found a little thrilling. Jealousy.

The light changed and he accelerated with more speed than necessary. "I heard you all three times," he said as the tires screeched. "It still doesn't make sense."

Swallowing an angry retort, Beth glanced over her shoulder at her son, who was sitting quietly, his eyes uncertain. She gave him a reassuring smile, then turned back to Ethan.

"Can we save this for a more private moment?" she asked stiffly.

"Yes," he said without looking away from the road. "But we *will* get to it."

"Oh, yes," she said, perversely unwilling to let him have the last word. "We will."

He gave her a dark glance, which was soundless but served as the last word, anyway.

As they marched from the driveway to the house, Beth caught Ethan's arm and pulled him to a stop. He turned to her, his eyes glowering with temper and impatience.

"I was just going to suggest," she said calmly, dropping her hand, "that you try not to look quite so much as though you intend to eat us all for dinner. Joanne and Zachary saw the four of us leave the house this morning snarling at each other. If we come home the same way, it might not matter what their detective reports. They'll be sure our marriage is doomed, anyway."

She was right. Which only served to irritate Ethan further.

He'd lain stoically awake beside her for two nights while she'd wrapped herself around him in her sleep and drove him to the brink of insanity. But except for a few moments of general irritability, he hadn't complained.

Then he'd walked into her studio and found her in the arms of a former client of the Butler County Jail. She hadn't appeared to be offering much resistance.

Well. Maybe it was time to stop being patient.

But not in front of her in-laws. Jason was standing between him and Beth now, looking anxiously from one to the other, wondering, Ethan was sure, if his life was going to fall apart. If his mother's three-day marriage was about to end and launch him into the custody of his grandparents, after all.

"You're absolutely right," Ethan said with a forced amiability. Then he pulled the back door open and gestured Jason inside. "Come on, buddy." He continued to hold the door for Beth.

Her expression remained icy for a moment, then with a toss of her head, she swept past him with a smile and a "Thank you, darling."

"There you are," Joanne said, meeting them at the door. She wore a flowered apron over her slacks and shirt and wielded a meat fork. "Potatoes are almost done. You just have time to wash your hands."

The aroma filling the kitchen would have soothed Ethan's mood if he hadn't had to follow Beth's shapely derriere up the stairs and into his bedroom.

While she tossed her jacket onto the bed and went into the bathroom to wash her hands, he hung up his uniform jacket and threw his shirt at the hamper. He pulled on a dark blue sweatshirt and was changing his uniform pants for a pair of jeans when Beth walked out of the bathroom.

"All yours," she said, her tone brittle. She carried her jacket to the closet, and he noted her quick glance at him as he drew up the jeans and zipped them. Her cheeks pinkened, and she looked away.

"You're embarrassed at seeing me dress," he challenged, heading for the bathroom, "yet you can let another man hold you in front of your son and be comfortable with that?"

He concentrated on washing his hands, hearing her firm footsteps come around the bed to the bathroom door. "First of all," she said, her voice breathy with anger, "for explanation number *four*—" this last word was spoken very loudly "—I did not let him hold me. He'd tried to, so I raised both arms to prevent him and he caught my wrists. That was when you walked in."

He glanced at her as he reached for a towel, his eyes rejecting the explanation—for the fourth time.

"And Jason knows Rush. He knows we're... friends, that Rush tends to be physically demonstrative and that it means nothing. I'm sure he didn't give it a thought."

Ethan tossed the towel over the rod without comment and stalked past her into the bedroom and out to the hallway, Beth following. He noticed Zachary's partially open door and went to it, intending to say hello. But Zachary was sound asleep, his leg in the colorful blue cast propped on a pair of pillows, the pajama leg trimmed to midthigh. A sock had been fitted over his partially bare foot.

Ethan pulled the door closed without latching it so that if Zach called out, he would still be heard.

But Ethan didn't want to risk Beth's father-in-law overhearing their argument.

Cooperating, Beth lowered her voice as she trailed Ethan to the stairs. "And I looked away when you were pulling on your jeans," she said as though they hadn't been interrupted, "because it occurred to me that you have nice muscular legs, and I was too angry with you to entertain a complimentary thought."

He stopped in his tracks at that admission and she almost collided with him. He turned to look at her, hands on his hips, torn between anger and pleasure that she found *something* about him appealing.

She stood quietly in front of him, apparently as

ensnared by the moment as he was. Then she angled
her chin and added haughtily, "Unfortunately your
brain seems to be all muscle, too. Let's move it.
Joanne doesn't like to have to wait dinner for anyone."

Ethan could have eaten a mastodon raw—and not
because he was hungry. He couldn't remember ever
feeling so elementally angry. Even when a perp was
resisting arrest and started swinging, he was able to
keep his cool and react only in department-approved
ways.

But seeing Beth being handled by Rush Weston,
then listening to her defensive responses to his questions about the incident, had done something to his
equanimity. He didn't have the control over his emotions he usually had—and he didn't like that at all.

During dinner he asked Joanne about Zachary,
complimented her on the excellent dinner, asked Nikkie about her day and learned that the drama teacher
had been less than enthusiastic about her shield and
weapon cardboard prototypes for the Winter Festival
play.

"But Beth was going to look for something in her
studio," she said with a grudgingly hopeful glance
across the table.

"Oh," Beth said, pushing back from the table. "I
did bring something home for you to look at. I was
so ang—" She stopped, obviously not intending to
let her ex-mother-in-law know about her anger at
Ethan. She continued with a smile, "I was so anxious
for dinner that I forgot it in the car. We could smell
the pot roast even in the driveway," she said to
Joanne. Then to Nikkie, "I'll go get it. Excuse me a
minute."

Jason, seated beside Ethan, paused in his hearty attack on his plate and asked eagerly, "Can we have Taylor Bridges for dinner tomorrow?"

Ethan grinned at him, grateful for the boy's cheerful presence. "You think he'd be good to eat?"

Jason frowned while Nikkie groaned at Ethan's joke. Suddenly the boy caught on and laughed.

"No. I mean can he come over here for dinner. Mom said it was okay, but I should check with you 'cause you might have a meeting."

Tomorrow was Tuesday. That meant a county commissioners' meeting. "I do have to go to the courthouse for a couple of hours, but you can have him over even if I'm not here." He turned to Joanne. "That is, if your grandmother doesn't mind cooking for one more."

Joanne actually smiled. "Of course not."

"No." Jason was adamant. "You *have* to be here. That's why he's coming."

"What do you mean?"

"'Cause he doesn't believe you're my dad now. He thinks I'm lying. So Mom says the best thing to do is show him."

Beth returned with something large wrapped in white paper. Ethan had been so furious when they'd left her studio he hadn't noticed she'd been carrying it.

She'd caught the end of Jason's report and now met Ethan's gaze with an apologetic look. It wasn't quite convincing, because her eyes still snapped with annoyance.

"Taylor's been giving him a hard time for months," she said. "So let's have him come for dinner and see that Jason isn't lying."

"Okay, then let's make it Wednesday," Ethan said. "Is that all right with you, Joanne?"

"Perfectly," she replied, passing platters around the table for seconds.

Ethan half expected Nikkie to react negatively to an attempt to prove he was now Jason's father, too, but she was concentrating on the package Beth was unwrapping.

Shaped like a medieval shield, it had been fashioned out of half-inch-thick board and divided into quarters, the upper left and lower right painted blue with three gold fleurs-de-lis, and the upper right and lower left painted red with three gold lions guardant.

Nikkie's mouth fell open in awe. Ethan's annoyance with Beth was overridden with pleasure and satisfaction at what she'd done. It was a hard-won first step in building a relationship with his daughter.

"Wow," Nikkie breathed, getting up to inspect it.

"I'll have to look up the coat of arms of Henry V to be accurate," Beth said, "but I think it's something like this. And we can check out the coats of arms for Henry's nobles. These are easy enough to make if you think they'll work. I can cut them out, draw the patterns, and you and the drama club can paint them."

Nikkie took the mock-up of a shield in her hands and inspected it in detail, then looked at Beth in astonishment.

"Mr. Fogarty will think this is brilliant!" she said, her usually careful pose of disinterest dissolving in the face of such an impressive solution to her problem of props.

"How would we hold them?"

"Two leather straps on the back, I think," Beth said. "One off to the side to slip an arm through, and another toward the other side for your hand to grip.'' She looked at Ethan. ''That's right, isn't it?''

He nodded, guessing she'd consulted him not because she needed to, but because she was feeling generous in her success. ''Yes, Madam Armorer. I believe that's right. Of course you could use something less expensive than leather. Vinyl or some kind of plastic. No one'll notice from the audience.''

''And I have a heavy-duty stapler for putting them on.'' Beth touched Nikkie's arm in a manner not intended to be maternal but simply friendly. ''You take it to school and see what the consensus is. If your drama teacher and the club like it, we'll go into production.''

Nikkie was still staring at the shield, touching a fingertip to the beautifully executed lion guardant. ''I will,'' she said. ''Thanks.''

''Sure.'' Beth pulled out the sign she'd made with Nikkie's cats on it. ''I was making these for the fair and thought you might like one.''

Nikkie studied it wordlessly and Beth asked with a wince, ''Too childish?''

Nikkie shook her head. ''No. Not at all. Thanks. I really like it.''

Beth went back to her chair. ''I'm sorry,'' she said to everyone else around the table. ''I didn't mean to interrupt dinner.''

''Can you make me a shield?'' Jason asked eagerly. ''With Buzz Lightyear on it?''

''A wooden shield,'' Ethan said, holding the platter of meat and vegetables for the boy while he forked more food onto his plate, ''is a little primitive for Buzz. Shouldn't he have a cloaking device or something?''

Before Jason could reply, a deep voice bellowed from upstairs. "Jo! I'm starving!"

Joanne smiled wryly at Beth as she pushed herself away from the table to make a plate for Zachary. "Maybe you could make me one with a wooden spoon on it," she said. "Or a knife and fork. There's a brown Betty in the refrigerator if someone wants to dish it up."

Ethan cleared the table and Beth loaded the dishwasher while Joanne took a plate upstairs to Zachary and remained there. Nikkie and Jason had gone to their own rooms to do homework.

Ethan put the small amount of leftovers into a plastic container and handed Beth the platter. The kitchen had taken on a kind of peaceful ambiance he wouldn't have thought possible, considering his and Beth's anger at each other, his daughter's usual moody defensiveness and Joanne's aggressive personality.

But something had happened at dinner. There'd been an unexpected and surprisingly successful give-and-take that came close to creating a familylike atmosphere.

Joanne had been happy to have people to cook for while she was stranded in Cobbler's Crossing with a temporarily invalid husband, and everyone else had been most appreciative of her meals. Nikkie had been astounded and grateful for the shield Beth had produced to help her with props for the play, not to mention her delight at the sign for her door. Jason had been happy when Ethan agreed to let him invite Taylor Bridges to dinner, and Ethan had been gratified by the boy's obvious pride in having him for a stepfather.

Peace reigned everywhere, but he wasn't going to

be happy until he was sure Beth had no feelings for Rush Weston. And he was going to see that she wasn't happy, either.

"So you're telling me that Weston's in the habit of putting his hands on you," he asked, resuming the argument with a vengeance, "with your consent?"

As he gathered up place mats and tossed them into a hamper in the hallway, he heard the slam of the dishwater door, then the rush of water as Beth started the wash cycle.

When he came back into the kitchen, she was standing in the middle of the floor with an expression that could have ignited fuel. She pointed to the back door. "I'd like to speak to you outside," she said, her voice barely steady.

Even though the subject had really been settled hours ago, he still wasn't ready to give in. He hated Weston and felt outrageously possessive about Beth, and he was spoiling for a fight.

"Certainly." He pulled the back door open for her and followed her onto the back porch.

"I would have thought," she said, turning to face him the moment the door closed behind them, "that a man who'd had such a happy marriage for all those years would understand a little something about trust."

That punched a hole right in the middle of his anger, but it was easy to fill it up again.

"I never found Diana being groped by another man," he said. He knew he was being unfair, but he wanted convincing, damn it.

She put a hand to her forehead and he saw her lips move unsteadily. Regret brimmed in him, fighting the anger for space.

"I know Diana was a paragon," Beth said, lowering her hand to her throat and tugging at the high collar of her red sweater, "and I'm just a woman you think is using you just to hold on to her son. You probably imagine that this isn't really a marriage, and therefore I don't feel called upon to be faithful."

That was precisely the fear he'd experienced when he'd walked into her studio and found Weston there, touching her.

"And I'm sexually repressed," she admitted, looking him in the eye, "which means that after two nights of sleeping alone...well, not alone but apart, you're thinking you can be patient until doomsday and you'll get nothing out of this marriage."

That rankled. He sat on the railing near the porch support and leaned back against it. "I might think that," he said, "if all I wanted out of this marriage was sex. But it isn't. That's why I hated seeing you with Weston."

"I wasn't *with* Weston," she said, a desperate note in her voice. "I mean, I was physically beside him, but there was no 'groping' and no emotional tie that makes me *with* him, except a sort of casual friendship. He came to ask about renting his space early because he'd run into Kelly, and she'd given me a deposit this morning. They both want to be in and set up for visitors by the Winter Festival, so they're doing their own painting."

"Beth," he said, knowing he was the one who had to be conciliatory here, though not about his opinions on Weston. "I told you I picked him up at a brawl on the waterfront. He was drunk and abusive. I don't like the idea of your life entangled with his."

She moved closer and leaned a shoulder against the

post. "I met him when I first arrived here, and you'll notice that I bear no evidence of bodily harm." She looked tired and strained. He thought he could have refuted her claim, but didn't. "I'm sorry you don't like him, but he's an eccentric. I know he drinks sometimes, but that doesn't matter to me because—" the next four words were delivered with slow emphasis "—*we are not involved*. When I first moved here, he gave me a job assisting in his sculpture class and introduced me to other artists, who are now my friends. I promise you that's all he is to me."

"Did you tell him you were married?"

"Yes." She smiled thinly. "You'll be pleased to know he's no fonder of you than you are of him."

"I don't give a rip about him," Ethan said, hooking an arm around her waist and pulling her to him. "You're the one I care about."

She rested a forearm on his shoulder and asked quietly, "If that is true, why won't you trust me?"

"It *is* true," he said, pulling her closer. "And I trust you, but I don't trust him."

"If you trust *me*," she said quietly, clasping her fingers behind his neck, "you don't have to worry about him. He's going to rent a space from me and that's it. So you can stop yelling at me."

He nuzzled under her hair and kissed the sensitive skin behind her ear. "I'm sorry," he said, planting another kiss, his brain a little muddled by her rose scent. "I'm not usually a man who yells. I'm just…grumpy."

"Hm." She rubbed her cheek against his, then kissed his eyelids, first one, then the other. "Is there a cure for that?"

He groaned with the effort to stop from telling her. ''Just…thinking positive, I guess,'' he said.

Beth knew the answer he withheld and decided it was time she took action. She squeezed him to her and kissed his forehead. ''I have a positive thought.''

He looked into her eyes with suspicion. ''You do?''

''Yes.'' She leaned her cheek against his forehead and prayed she wouldn't disappoint him. ''I want to make love to you tonight.''

He didn't move a muscle and she couldn't see his face, but she felt the reaction in him, the punch of one erratic heartbeat, the sudden tension of every muscle.

He drew his head back so he could look into her eyes. ''Why?'' he asked. She smiled in response, knowing he wasn't interested in lovemaking as a way of making up after a quarrel.

She gave him a quick kiss, thinking what a turn-on kindness was. A curious loosening was taking place within her—strange, she thought, after they'd just had a fairly serious disagreement.

Then she realized it was because he hadn't stalked away from her and left her to absorb the blame. He'd stated his position, fought it out, and when she'd convinced him he was mistaken, he'd apologized.

This was entirely new in her man-woman experience. She felt as though all doors and windows had been thrown open, and she couldn't help the soft laugh that escaped.

''You told me when I was eager to make love with you that I should let you know,'' she said. ''That when it seemed like a really good idea to me that it was time. Well—'' she kissed him again ''—it's time. Except that we have to wait until everyone's asleep.''

He winced and let his head fall back against the post with a thunk. ''What time is it?'' he asked.

She glanced at her watch. ''Seven-thirty-seven.''

''Oh, God,'' he groaned. ''Three hours. Maybe more.''

''Anticipation should heighten the experience,'' she said philosophically, giddy with the rush of freedom she felt.

''I vote we sedate everyone, cats included.''

This time she kissed him slowly, seductively, letting him know with the deep sensuous exploration of her tongue that she'd never been more serious about anything. ''We'll just wait. And think about how it'll be.''

The door from the kitchen opened suddenly, and Joanne stood in the doorway. ''There you are,'' she said, then noting their tangled pose, said apologetically, ''Never mind. It isn't anything that can't wait.''

''What do you need?'' Beth asked, thinking talk was cheap. She might try to convince Ethan of her confidence in her ability to be an enthusiastic love partner, and that the three hours or so that would have to pass until then would only heighten the experience, but she knew she would have to have something practical to do in the interim to keep herself from panicking. She did feel a new freedom and knew he'd given it to her. She was just a little concerned about her ability to give back.

Both she and Ethan straightened and headed for the door.

''Zachary's feeling a little better,'' Joanne said as they walked into the kitchen. ''He isn't needing as much pain medication, so he's getting bored. I was wondering if you had books or magazines he could read."

"How about if I bring the TV and VCR from my room into yours?" Ethan asked.

"But what'll you do?" Joanne asked.

Beth caught the quick amusement in Ethan's eyes and bit her lip. "We're going to bed early," he said. "It's been a rough day."

"But what about tomorrow?" she persisted. "I hate to deprive you of—"

Ethan shook his head. "We hardly ever watch it, anyway. And if there's anything we really want to see, we'll go downstairs."

"Well, if you're sure..."

"I'm sure."

While Ethan moved the TV and VCR and reconnected them in Zachary's room, Beth made a cup of tea to calm her nerves.

Jason appeared with the sign for his bedroom door. "Mom, can you help me hang this?" he asked.

At any other time she might have begged off until she'd finished her tea, but tonight she looked forward to gainful employment. "We need a hammer and a nail," she said, wondering if Ethan kept them in the basement.

"Ethan's got his tools upstairs," Jason informed her. "He brought 'em up to move the television. They're watching a cowboy movie."

Beth walked with him upstairs. "You haven't been bothering Grandpa, have you?"

"They told me to go in," he said, looking offended, "'cause it's a guy movie."

"I see. I'm sorry." She ruffled his hair, enjoying his pleasure in being considered one of the guys.

Beth was pleased and flattered to see that Nikkie had hung up her sign.

The sounds of guns and galloping horses came loudly from the television in Zachary's room. A large metal toolbox stood against the wall just outside the door.

Beth peered around the door and saw Zachary propped up against the pillows, and Ethan sitting in the chair by the bed, his legs stretched out before him.

"There's nobody like the Duke," Zachary said, his eyes riveted to the screen. "Jo always insisted he was going to be her second husband." He grinned, still staring at the screen. "Smart man checked out before it could happen."

Beth waved her hand to claim Ethan's attention.

He walked around the bed and came into the hall, his eyes alight with humor and passion. "Tell me we've moved up the time," he said, catching her hands. Then he noticed Jason standing beside her.

A rueful acceptance replaced the desire in his eyes. The frustration was something they shared, though hers was mixed with more than a little trepidation.

He put a hand to Jason's shoulder. "What's up, Jase?"

"We need a hammer and a nail," the boy said. "I want to put this on my door." He held up his Buzz Lightyear sign. "Mom made it for me before we moved here."

"Ethan," Beth said, "if you can just point me to a hammer and a nail, I can put it up."

Ethan squatted by the toolbox, lifted the top tray,

reached into the bottom and handed up a hammer. "You won't hit your thumb or anything?" he teased.

She pretended to swing the hammer at his head. "I probably use woodworking tools more than you do. At the studio I have saws, sanders, dremels, lathes, you name it, and I have yet to lose a thumbnail or a pinkie finger."

He straightened and waggled an eyebrow. "Ooh. I love it when you talk tough."

"Ethan, come and see this!" Zachary shouted.

Beth pushed him toward the room. "Go. We'll rendezvous later."

He sighed and kissed her again, his eyes lazy with desire. "Words I've longed to hear," he whispered.

Beth hung the plaque with several experienced strokes of the hammer. Jason's pleasure in it made her feel as though it should have required much more effort.

She went into his room to encourage him to get ready for bed and was a little horrified to discover that in less than a week he'd managed to make it look like a warehouse for boy's clothing—one without hangers.

"Jason," she scolded gently, picking up jeans, shirts and underwear off the floor, "you know better than this. Underwear and shirts and dirty jeans go in the hamper. Stuff that's still clean should be hung in the closet."

He followed her as she gathered his things. "But I can't reach the hanger thing."

"The rod," she said, folding clean jeans at the zipper and draping them over a hanger. She was about to suggest he stand on a chair, but a maternal second sense told her that wasn't a good idea. "Then you can put things on your chair and I'll hang them up for you until we can put in a lower rod.''

She collected underwear and carried it to the bathroom hamper. He waited for her in the doorway of his room, a pair of battered tennis shoes in his arms. ''Are you happy here, too?'' he asked, appearing anxious for the right response. ''I mean, you weren't really at first, but you are now, aren't you?''

''I'm happy wherever you are,'' she said, taking a jacket off the bedpost and hanging it up in the closet.

''I mean you're happy you got married to Ethan,'' Jason said in exasperation.

A man in the making, she thought wryly, direct and insistent.

But at least she could give him the answer he wanted. ''Yes, I'm happy I married Ethan.''

''And Nikkie's starting to like you, too.''

Beth plucked a pair of pajamas off another bedpost and handed them to him. ''We might have to wait a little while for that to really happen. She liked the shield I made, but I'm not sure she likes me yet.''

Jason took the pajamas, then wrapped his arms around her waist. ''She will 'cause you're a great mom,'' he said, his eyes alight with a contentment she hadn't seen there in some time. ''Aren't we lucky I ran away and all those campers were lost so that the only one who could come and look for me was Ethan?''

He lowered his voice and glanced toward his open bedroom door. ''And aren't we lucky I lied to Grandma and Grandpa, and then Ethan helped me?''

Beth almost hated to be reminded of how their situation had come about. It made it seem so fragile, and the possibility that it could all dissolve one day was something she didn't like to contemplate. Particularly tonight.

"We're lucky nobody's caught us," she whispered back conspiratorially.

Jason seemed to like that and ran off giggling to take a shower and get ready for bed.

CHAPTER TWELVE

By TEN O'CLOCK Jason and Nikkie were asleep, and Zachary had turned down the sounds of battle in deference to the late hour.

Beth piled her hair in a loose knot on top of her head and took a shower, wondering where Ethan was. He'd left Zachary's room a short while ago and she'd heard him go down the stairs, but he had yet to return to their bedroom.

Heart thudding nervously, she spritzed cologne and slipped on a berry-colored silk nightie Kelly had given her years ago but she'd never worn. The color made her flushed cheeks appear to be on fire, and she put her hands over them to cool them.

"You look like you're about to ignite," she told herself with a moan.

"You are," a quiet male voice said from the doorway.

She spun around. Ethan stood there in jeans, bare-chested and barefoot, a tulip glass of something bubbly in each hand. His hair was damp, suggesting he'd showered in the other bathroom. A mild frown creased his brow. "Second thoughts?" he asked.

"No," she denied, moving toward him. "A little nervous, though."

He smiled and handed her a glass. "Me, too," he

said with a sincerity that turned her spine to oatmeal and made her heart swell with love.

He beckoned her out of the bathroom and toward the bed, where he'd turned back the blankets and banked the pillows against the headboard. He held her glass while she climbed into the bed and sat against the comfortable backrest he'd made.

He followed, drawing her into his arm and tipping the rim of his wineglass against hers in a toast. "To learning to communicate."

She drank to that, then leaned against him. His warm shoulder was muscled and smooth under her cheek. She tipped her head back to kiss the underside of his jaw. "That means 'I love you' in…in Romanesque," she said fancifully. His arm around her and his easy manner were beginning to banish her nervousness. She watched his eyes darken at her admission and it was a moment before he whispered, "God, I love you, too." Then he cleared his throat and smiled.

"Romanesque? Really?" He kissed the top of her head. "I thought Romanesque was a style of architecture."

She made an airy gesture with her glass. "It's a mistake everyone makes. It's actually a language."

"Ah. A romance language?"

"No." She turned her face into his chest and kissed his pectoral muscle. She felt his heartbeat accelerate and her own race to match it. "The language of romance. There's a difference."

"I see." He sipped his wine. "And you're fluent in this?"

"Not really," she admitted, leaning her cheek

against him again. "It wasn't spoken where I lived before, so I've had little chance to practice."

"Well." He ran a hand tenderly up and down her bare arm. "I don't want to one-up you, but I happen to be a Romanesque scholar."

She smiled. "I guessed that."

"Yes." She heard the light clink of his glass against the top of the bedside table. "I have a Ph.D. in it. Unfortunately I've also had little chance to practice. But I'd be happy to share what I know." He took her glass from her and placed it beside his. When he turned to her, his eyes were dark with intent. "Together I'll bet we could write the definitive text on it."

She slid down into the bed, her heart thudding, and he leaned sideways over her to rearrange the pillows under her head. Then his eyes met hers and she saw everything he was in them—tough, strong, gentle, funny. And at the moment she held his complete attention, and the realization gave her both profound comfort and unbearable excitement.

She put her hands to his face and rubbed a thumb gently over his upper lip. "I know how to say, 'I'm glad I found you.' Want to hear?"

"Please," he replied softly.

She pulled his head down to her and kissed him with all the tender passion he inspired in her. She parted her lips, he opened his mouth, their tongues met and stroked...and she finally had to draw back to catch her breath.

"Excellent pronunciation," he said, his voice low and a little rough. "What else can you say?"

She traced the line of her jaw with her fingertips,

then trailed her index finger down the middle of his throat to his collarbone.

"I can say, 'You've changed my life,'" she suggested.

"Mm." He ran a hand down her side, over her hip to the top of her thigh. "I'd like to know how to say that, too."

She felt the warmth of his hand through the thin layer of fabric, and a frisson of anticipation arced through her.

She leaned up to kiss the base of his throat, then dropped a series of soft kisses down the middle of his chest. She pushed away from the mattress, forcing him backward until he lay on his back on the bedspread and she kneeled over him.

Ethan felt her lips and her breath at the waistband of his jeans and prayed that his cardiovascular system was up to this. Letting her remain in control so that he didn't frighten her was almost more than he could do.

With the denim blocking her path, she strung kisses across his waist from his left side to his right. He couldn't withhold a groan.

"Do you want," she asked on a whispered breath, "to try to...repeat that after me?"

Everything inside him roared, but his reply was a throaty, "Yes, I would."

He reached under the hem of her gown and moved his hands slowly up the backs of her smooth legs, then down and up again, inching his way to the warm flesh of her bottom.

She eased her weight on top of him, buried her face against the side of his and lay still as he explored her.

Her long sigh fractured as she finally sat up on him

to pull off her gown. The action took the loose clip in her hair with it, and the dark mass tumbled to her shoulders, curly and fragrant.

He reached up to touch it, but she caught his hand and brought it to her breast. The small mound filled his palm, and he felt its tip pearl.

"This means," she said, her voice a little unsteady, "'You've changed *me*.'"

He slipped his hands around her and, sitting up, eased her onto her back among the pillows.

He kissed the slight convexity of her stomach, her hipbones, the juncture of torso and thigh.

Her hands at the waistband of his jeans unzipped them. He sat up to push his jeans down and off, and the instant he was free of them, she reached for his arm to draw him back to her.

He lay beside her and pulled the blankets over them. She pushed herself against him and bent her knee, rubbing it along his thigh as her hands moved down his back and over his hip.

"This means 'I need you,'" she said, her whisper a little feverish. She nipped at his shoulder.

He caught her in the crook of his arm and held her to the mattress when she tried to wriggle against him. She stroked a hand over his belly and downward, but he caught her fingers and stopped her, enfolding her hand in his and carrying it back to her waist.

"Now I have a few things to say," he murmured softly. She settled back with a languorous smile. He stroked a hand down her abdomen and placed it possessively right where she longed for his touch.

Beth was certain she would explode. Her heart couldn't beat this fast, her breath couldn't come in such shallow gasps, her nerves couldn't be stretched this tight without snapping.

He dipped a finger inside her, then found the spot Steve had never believed was there, and said, his lips just above hers, his other arm holding her to him, "This means 'I love you and you're everything to me. Everything.'"

His clever hand began to move, and as she absorbed the wonder of those words, pleasure rushed at her headlong so that the declaration still echoed when fulfillment overtook her.. The sensory impact of the miracle created by love and understanding given and taken pinned her to the mattress with its force. It filled her, bathed her, and just when she thought it might drown her, she rose with a gasp of astonishment, and let it wash over her in breathtaking waves.

She opened her eyes to see Ethan's pleased and slightly self-satisfied expression. Then she closed both hands over him and felt her own satisfaction when his expression turned from smug to seduced, and he grew ready under her touch.

"This means," she said as he moved quickly over her, "'Let me be as generous as you are.'"

Even as he lifted her hips and entered her, she saw his eyes react to her eagerness to please him. She closed her eyes and ran her hands up his arms, hoping that it would be as good for him as it had been for her.

He drove into her and she lost all ability to concentrate. Pleasure rose again all around her, and just as she'd begun to suspect that she'd somehow gotten this wrong, that her intention had been to give Ethan the same delicious pleasure he'd given her, he burst inside her with a cry that he silenced in her hair.

She'd done it. She'd given him pleasure. The past wasn't her fault.

As his body pulsed over her, she came alive again like the molten middle of the earth. In astonishment, she clung to him as they shuddered together for long, long moments.

As the ripples of pleasure cleared, Beth burst into tears.

Ethan cradled her to him, his voice filled with concern. "What?" he demanded. "What?"

How did a woman tell a man, she wondered, that he'd just restored her faith in herself as a sexual being? How did she explain that though she was logical and clear-thinking in every other way, she'd allowed a selfish lover to convince her that the unsatisfying results of his lovemaking had been her fault?

Ethan tried to ease her away to look at her, but she put a hand over her eyes. "Nothing," she said, sniffing. "Nothing. I'm fine."

There was a sharp pain on her left buttock. She yelped and dropped her hand, staring at him in stunned surprise. He'd pinched her!

"In Romanesque," he said gravely, "that's 'Don't lie to me.' What is it? Did I hurt you? Upset you?"

And suddenly the momentous revelation she'd just had about herself seemed to lose all importance in this very sane and comfortable world Ethan had provided. Her tears turned to laughter and she wrapped her arms around his neck.

"Oh, good," he said, turning them so that she lay in the hollow of his shoulder, "I've married a split personality."

She hitched a leg up over his and kissed his throat. "But I'm multilingual. You liked my Romanesque."

"I did indeed. I, however, am single-minded, and I want to know what you were crying about."

"They were good tears," she said, snuggling closer. "Not bad ones."

He drew her arm across his waist. "Great. Then it should be easy to explain to me."

She did. It didn't take very long, and it was like being purged of the past. He listened, understood, commiserated.

"But as of tonight," he said, "it no longer matters. That's over, and I think we proved—" she heard the smile in his voice "—rather forcefully, I might add, that he was wrong and I was right."

"I love you," she said, suddenly exhausted.

"Brilliantly." He stroked her hair, then kissed it. "I love you, too."

"Also brilliantly. Jason said we were lucky."

LIFE WAS IDEAL. For the next week Beth worked like a fiend in her studio and made love with Ethan like a wild woman every night.

The night Taylor Bridges came to dinner, Ethan took the boys to the gym with him afterward, then dropped Taylor at home.

Jason was the picture of self-satisfaction when he and Ethan returned. As Beth tucked Jason in that night, he said that Ethan called him "son" when they were shooting baskets, and that later, when Ethan took them for ice cream and Jason and Taylor went to the bathroom, Taylor told him he was the luckiest kid in the whole world.

Beth thought he probably was.

She wished she was doing as well with Nikkie as Ethan was doing with Jason. Yes, Nikkie was visibly pleased with the shields, but her friends from the drama club, who came nightly to work on them, were warmer to Beth than she was.

Nikkie was polite and no longer overtly hostile, but except when her friends were over, she kept to herself and showed Beth no sign of friendship.

Zachary was comfortable with his crutches by the end of the week, and Joanne declared it was time to return to Seattle.

"You're welcome to stay a few more days," Beth said, "if you think it would—"

"No," Joanne insisted. She looked from Beth to Ethan with a new ease in her manner. "We appreciate your hospitality and your generosity, but you have to get back to your routines and we have to get home. We've enjoyed watching your progress with the props for Nikkie's play, though, Beth. And of course, we'd like to be here for the opening of the cannery over the Winter Festival weekend."

"Please come back for it," Ethan said. "We'll try to get along without your cooking until then."

Joanne tried not to look too pleased, but Beth could see it was an effort.

They left on Sunday morning, and Beth and Ethan made love all afternoon by the fire in the family room. Nikkie and her friends were rehearsing the play at school, and Jason was spending the afternoon at Taylor Bridges's.

On Monday evening the blissful peace was shattered.

Beth had put in a good day at the studio. Ethan had helped her pack up the clay pots in the basement and transport them to the cannery. She'd spent the day washing them and giving them all coats of brightly colored background paint.

She and Ethan and Jason had gone for burgers after work because Nikkie had stayed late at school to re-hearse, and Ethan had a Search and Rescue meeting after dinner. Ethan had dropped Beth and Jason at home and given her a lingering kiss goodbye and a whispered promise to be home early.

Jason turned on the television and Beth puttered about the kitchen, making herself a cup of tea and running the dishwasher. The house was quiet without Ethan and Nikkie, she noticed, thinking how quickly and closely their lives had become entwined. Even though Nikkie seemed to do her best to keep her dis-tance, Beth found herself caring and worrying about the girl and wishing she could discover some magic way to bridge the gap between them.

There was a knock at the back door. Beth opened it to find Brodie standing there in a brown tweed sports jacket over a tab-collared denim shirt and ca-sual brown slacks. In one hand he held a rather tou-sled mixed bouquet of flowers. He looked handsome but angry and stormed past her into the kitchen.

Apparently remembering his manners, he stopped in the middle of the room and said with an apologetic twist of his lips and a thrust of the flowers toward her, "Hi. Are you busy?"

"Not at all," she replied, closing the door. "But Ethan's at a meeting tonight."

He jammed his hands into his pants pockets. "Good. I wanted to talk to you."

"Ah…sure." She looked doubtfully at the flowers. "These are…for me?"

"Why not?" he asked defensively.

Okay. She decided to simply coast until she could figure out what was happening here. She pointed him to the table. "Sit down. Can I make you a cup of tea?"

He looked uncertain for a moment, then nodded. "Okay," he said finally, then held up large-fingered hands permanently stained in the lines and hollows with grease and oil and whatever else mechanics dealt with. "Just don't give it to me in anything delicate."

Beth laughed as she rummaged through the cupboard for something to put the flowers in. She finally decided on a teapot with a chipped spout. She filled it with water and set the flowers in it, wondering what had happened to them. They were beautiful, but crinkled and bruised.

"Not to worry," she said. "We seem to be big on sheriff's-office mugs. Sit down, Brodie. Milk and sugar?"

He pulled out a chair and sat. "I don't know," he admitted. "I've never had tea before."

She stopped in the process of opening a teabag's protective paper envelope. "You're kidding. Well, I can make a pot of coffee if you prefer."

"No." He waved a hand dismissively. "This is my day for doing things I'm not used to."

Beth filled the mug with water and brought it to him.

"That sounds a little ominous," she said, sitting opposite him with her cup. "Do I want to know what you've done today?"

He leaned away from the table, crossed one ankle over the other leg and studied the ceiling tiles overhead. "I called in sick," he said, then quickly added when Beth began to express concern, "I wasn't, I just told my guys I was sick so they wouldn't guess I was being an idiot.''

It was on the tip of her tongue to ask why, but she held off. He seemed to be collecting his thoughts, and judging by the storm in his eyes and the complete absence of his usual good humor, she guessed they weren't pleasant.

"Then I got a haircut," he continued, "went to Buckley's and bought this jacket,"

"Which looks very dapper," she interrupted.

He gave her a glance she found difficult to interpret, then leaned forward over the table and drew the steaming mug toward him. "Thanks. I'm giving it to Ethan. And this shirt with the dumb collar. I feel like I should have a handlebar mustache."

Beth was beginning to suspect where this was going. She propped her elbow on the table and leaned her chin in the palm of her hand. "I think that's the appeal of those shirts for women. Victorian men wore something like it under those old, stiff celluloid collars. But...I'm guessing Kelly didn't like it."

He looked momentarily surprised, then took a sip of his tea and shook his head. "Kelly never saw it," he said. "I went by her place tonight to see if she'd like to go to dinner. She was packing up stuff from her studio to move into your cannery. She hardly even looked at me.".

"Well..." Beth struggled between an inherent preference for diplomacy in such matters and the undeniable effectiveness of the plain and simple truth. She did her best to combine both. "I think the night of the wedding, you left her with the impression that...you're not really interested in a relationship."

He drank more tea, then put the cup down, his expression moody. "I thought I wasn't," he said, leaning back in his chair. He folded his arms over his chest and let his head fall back. "I once had a relationship with this woman I met when she and her father were driving from Portland to their vacation home across the river. He owns Techno-Ware in Portland. Their Rolls-Royce broke down just this side of the bridge. It was only a hose, and I went to them to fix it because, I'm not sure, but I think you'd probably go to mechanics' hell for towing a Rolls."

Beth smiled, but Brodie didn't. He straightened restlessly in his chair, blew out a breath and took another sip of tea.

"Anyway, Paulette—that was her name—looked at me. I looked at her and it was fate. You know, *fate*, in capital letters. Her father was so pleased with me he invited me to their place, she came over a few evenings to see me. I spent a couple of weekends with them. We got along famously, and when it was time for them to go back to Portland, I asked her to marry me."

His eyes seemed to lose focus for a moment, then he rubbed a hand over them, and when he looked at Beth again, his gaze was self-deprecating and sad. He went on as though he could suddenly see it all from a comfortable distance.

"She looked so surprised," he said, shaking his head. "And now I think that's what hurt the most. That I was *so* in love, and all along she hadn't a clue. Then she blinked these velvety brown eyes and said in this husky rich-girl voice, 'But Brodie, you're just a mechanic.'"

Beth reached a hand across the table and covered his, her heart filled with sympathy and anger. "Obviously a zero, Brodie. If she was here, I'd deck her for you."

His thin smile told her he appreciated the offer. "Anyway, it was hard for me to admit I'd been that blind. In fact, I think I've resisted admitting it by deciding that love was never meant to be taken seriously and treating every woman I met that way."

"But you feel something for Kelly?"

"I don't seem to be able to put her out of my mind. Is that the same thing?"

"I'd say so."

"So how do I get her to realize I regret acting like an adolescent and I want to spend time with her?"

"Tell her that."

He blew out another breath. "I did, and I handed her those flowers." He pointed to the ragged bunch in the chipped teapot. "All she did was hit me with them and lock the studio door on me."

Beth went for the teapot to refill her cup. "Want more?" she asked, holding the pot over his.

He shook his head and made a face. "I don't think tea's my thing. But thanks."

Beth laughed and put the kettle back on the burner. "You know," she said, sobering, "I think Kelly feels about marriage the way you feel about tea. She had it once, didn't like the taste, and even though there are other kinds available, she doesn't want another cup."

Brodie frowned at her metaphor. "You mean, she doesn't want *me*."

"No," Beth corrected, leaning toward him. "She doesn't want to risk getting what she had before— which was someone who didn't appreciate her and wouldn't let her be who she is. I think she would want you if she really knew the man under the Don Juan facade.''

He brooded over her words for a moment, then pushed his cup away and stood. He didn't seem any happier than he had when he arrived, but he did seem a little more hopeful. He hugged Beth. ''Thanks for listening. I'm glad I've got you for a sister-in-law.''

''Well, you're all right for a brother-in-law, too.'' She smiled, then walked him to the door and opened it for him. ''And keep the jacket and shirt. You look great in them, and if you handle this right, you might get to wear them again.''

''Let's hope so,'' he said.

Just as Brodie went out the door, Nikkie came in, looking flushed. She called a greeting to her uncle, gave Beth a polite hello, then hurried through the kitchen toward the hallway and the stairs, all the while careful to avoid Beth's eyes.

Beth noted that, then dismissed it; her husband's daughter was simply continuing to keep her, Beth, out of her space.

''Have you eaten?'' Beth called after Nikkie.

''We had pizza delivered!'' Nikkie shouted back.

Ethan phoned at nine o'clock. ''This is going on longer than I'd hoped,'' he said. Then his voice dropped a tone and took on a quality she could almost feel through the electronic connection. ''But if you wait up for me, I promise to make it worth your while.''

''I'll be waiting.''

''More than an hour,'' he said with sudden briskness, ''and I'm out of here. I love you.''

''I love you, too,'' she answered, sharply aware of how sincere she was.

She hung up the phone, then turned and almost collided with Nikkie. The girl's eyes were wide and stricken, and Beth presumed she was upset because she'd heard Beth tell Ethan she loved him.

Beth summoned patience and prepared to defend her position. But before she could say a word, Nikkie asked anxiously, "Have you seen Simba?"

Surprised by the question, Beth had to take a moment to think. When Ethan had dropped her and Jason home after dinner, Cindy had been eating, but she couldn't recall seeing Simba.

"No," she said finally. "Why? Is he missing?"

Nikkie made a nervous gesture with one hand. "I think so. Cindy's on my bed, but I've called Simba and looked in all his favorite places and he isn't there."

"Did you check Jason's bunk?"

"Yes."

"Did you ask Jason? He's watching TV."

"Yes. He hasn't seen him, either."

Relieved to find herself in one of the areas of motherhood she understood and in which she felt qualified, Beth was prepared to help Nikkie find her cat. She reached into a utility drawer for the large flashlight Ethan kept there.

"Come on, we'll look around outside," Beth said, going to the hooks by the door for her jacket. "You check the yard and I'll—"

Nikkie stopped Beth with a hand on her arm before she could open the door. Beth looked at her in puzzlement, and saw more than worry in the girl's eyes. Guilt was there, as well.

Jason walked into the kitchen, his expression concerned. "So, we gonna go look for Simba?" he asked.

Instead of snapping an answer at him, Nikkie averted her eyes from Beth and studied her fingernails. "I...I think I know where he might be."

She glanced back at Beth, clearly expecting reproof of some kind.

Beth called on her reserves of calm and good sense. "Where's that?"

Nikkie pointed vaguely west. "In the Appleby house," she said.

"But he never wanders that far. And the house is boarded up."

"You can get in through the basement window," Jason said, apparently pleased to be able to share that information. "The board's loose at the bottom."

"Ethan told you to stay away from there," Beth scolded, missing the connection.

"I have," he said in the voice of the unjustly accused, "but all the kids know you can get in that way."

The light began to dawn for Beth. She turned to Nikkie. "But how would a cat get in there?"

Nikkie met her suspicious gaze and admitted reluctantly but frankly, "He probably followed me. The drama club did have a rehearsal after school like I told you, but Cameron and Bradley thought it would be fun to have it somewhere else, since it was just us. So the club voted and decided on the Appleby house. I ran home to get some Cokes and cookies, and Simba followed me."

At Beth's surprised look she explained, "I know he's a really lazy cat, but when he's been alone all day, he sometimes just wants to be with me, no matter what.'' Nikkie returned to her story. ''Anyway, when we left, it was dark and later than I thought, and I forgot all about him. He probably went to sleep somewhere and…'' A big tear slid down her cheek. ''All we did was rehearse the play, but Dad'll be really mad.''

Beth glanced at the clock over the stove. Nine-ten. ''All right.'' Beth pointed at Jason. ''You stay here. Nikkie and I will be right back.''

But Jason reached for his coat as Nikkie pulled hers on. ''I wanna come,'' he said.

Beth took the coat from him and returned it to the hook. ''No. I want you to stay here. Watch TV until we come back. And Uncle Brodie's right next door.'' She blew her son a kiss and dashed outside, Nikkie right behind her.

They hurried to the end of the block, looked both ways at the corner, then ran across the street and down another half block until they reached the deserted Appleby house.

Beth headed for the main entrance, but Nikkie caught her arm and pulled her around the house and behind a dormant rhododendron.

The house was a dark rectangle against a moonless sky. The many trees and bushes that surrounded it formed irregular shadows. The wind blew, leaves and branches rustled—and Beth did her best to ignore the gooseflesh on her arms.

''Shine the flashlight down here, Beth!'' Nikkie whispered, taking Beth's wrist and pointing it downward.

The beam revealed a piece of plywood that had been nailed over the window. There was graffiti on it and obvious gouges on the bottom edge where a tool had loosened the nails that held it in place.

Nikkie removed the plywood with very little effort. Then Beth hunkered down beside her and peered through the window into the darkness. Even from outside, the place smelled dank and musty and faintly alcoholic.

"Simba!" Nikkie called in a loud whisper. "Simba! Come on, baby!"

No response.

"Simba!" Nikkie tried again.

Still no response. Beth lay on her stomach on the grass and cast the beam of light over what she could see of the basement. There were stacks of dusty boxes, some of them rotting from the dampness. Rusty old gardening tools were propped against an ancient furnace. The concrete floor was littered with the debris left by the occasional transient—paper cups, empty bottles, fast-food wrappers, a filthy jacket.

Nikkie continued to call, and at last they heard a thump. She called again excitedly, but all they heard was silence.

Beth handed her the flashlight. "Hold this for me," she said, taking all her instinctive fears of dark and unknown places and thrusting them away. "If, God forbid, there's a *person* down there, just run to the nearest house and call 911."

"Beth, I should go in," Nikkie argued, trying to push the flashlight back at her.

"No, I will," Beth said firmly. "Just do as I say and stay here."

Nikkie gave in and directed the flashlight beam to the floor just under the window. Beth sat on the window frame, cleared long ago of broken glass by transients, and swung her legs into the basement. Her feet encountered a rusty laundry sink. She stepped into it and squatted down to hold the sides and lower one leg to the floor, then the other. She reached up for the flashlight.

"Be careful, Beth!" Nikkie cautioned with a sincerity Beth would have found touching under other circumstances. Right now all she could think of was finding the cat in good health, getting out of this place and getting home before Ethan did.

She swept the light before her and picked her way across the cluttered floor calling the cat. Things scurried in corners, and it occurred to her that if the cat was alive and well, being in this basement was probably the feline equivalent of a two-for-one day at the Burger Bistro.

She swept the light under and around boxes, tools and broken parts of things she couldn't identify, then went around to the other side of the furnace. She swept all corners with the light first and was relieved to find nothing human crouched in a corner.

"Simba!" she called. "Come on, kitty! Here, kitty!"

A sudden thump behind her caused her to turn with a little scream. The thumper responded with her own scream. It was Nikkie.

"I told you to wait!" Beth whispered.

"Well, I couldn't see you," Nikkie answered defensively. "And I'd feel awful if something happened to you because you were looking for my cat."

"Then next time," Beth said, "don't leave your cat in a haunted basement!"

Nikkie took a step back. "You're yelling," she accused.

"Do you know what your father would be doing if he was here?" Beth asked, turning around again and inching her way forward in the beam of light.

Nikkie grabbed hold of the back of Beth's shirt. "I'm trying not to think about that. Do you see any— There!"

"Where?" Beth asked, and Nikkie caught her wrist and directed the beam to a set of shelves built against the wall. Simba sat between an auto-parts box and a broken light fixture, looking like just another dusty remnant of the past.

"Simba!" Nikkie cried with delight and reached up for him. Her reach was one shelf short.

The cat yawned and watched her straining fingertips with interest, carefully keeping all parts of his body beyond her reach.

"Simba," she said, impatience mingling with her delight at finding him safe. "Come on. I'll give you a can of tuna! *People* tuna!"

A sudden clatter of metal caused Beth and Nikkie to spin around, the beam of light in front of them.

"Jeez!" Jason complained, putting both hands up protectively. "It's just me."

"Jason Richards!" Beth grabbed his arm and pulled him toward her.

"I know, I know," he protested, "but Ethan says a man's got to take care of his family, and he says when he isn't here, it's my job."

"Your *job*," Beth said, leaning over him, "is to listen to your mother!"

Jason looked beyond her shoulder and smiled.

"There's Simba!" he said, pointing. "I can see his eyes!"

"Yes," Beth said wearily. "Nikkie found him. But we're having trouble getting him down."

"Oh." Jason moved around in front of them and studied the predicament. Simba could be heard purring, but he wasn't moving. Jason thumped his chest like Tarzan, and Simba leaped off the shelf and into his arms.

He turned to a surprised Nikkie with a wide smile and handed her the cat. "That's how I get him off my bunk," he said. "I was just playing around one day, and he jumped on me when I did that."

Nikkie held the cat to her cheek and buried her nose in his fur, dust and all. She looked up and said gravely, "Thank you, Jason."

His eyes widened. He glanced at his mother, then back at Nikkie, and replied with another big smile, "Yeah, sure."

"All right, we're out of here," Beth said, urging Jason and Nikkie, with Simba now clinging to her shoulder, before her.

She boosted Jason up onto the laundry sink and pushed on the seat of his jeans until he could wriggle out the window. Nikkie handed up the cat, then followed Jason through.

Beth stepped into the tub, then reached a hand out into the darkness for help as she clambered up. "If we're all very quiet, we might get home without anyone—"

She knew the moment the helping hand clamped her wrist that it didn't belong to Jason or to Nikkie. It pulled her with startling ease and speed through the window to the grass and onto her feet.

On her way up she noticed a familiar pair of boots, uniform pants and jacket. Over the shoulder of the jacket she saw several cars in the middle of the street, their red-and-blue lights illuminating the sheriff's department's logo.

She groaned defeatedly and looked into an angry pair of brown eyes under the low brim of a Stetson hat.

"Hi, Ethan," she said in a very small voice. "You're home early."

CHAPTER THIRTEEN

"ETHAN!" BETH CLUTCHED the bars of the prison cell and shouted at the top of her lungs. "Ethan Drum, you come here this instant!"

Beth heard footsteps hurrying down the hallway from the outer office and into the small bank of holding cells. She could tell by their urgent pace that they didn't belong to her husband.

Deputy Curtis's harassed face appeared on the other side of the bars. "Yes, ma'am?" he asked.

"Where *is* he?" she demanded.

"Um...he's on the phone with the governor's office, Mrs. Drum." Curtis pointed awkwardly behind him. "I'm supposed to ask you to be quiet. You're disturbing the drunk tank."

Beth could not remember ever being so enraged. If she could have gotten her hands on Ethan at that moment, she was certain the seventy-pound difference in their weights would have made no difference.

"The governor?" Beth repeated. "What—is prowling a capital offense? And don't I get a trial first?"

Curtis smiled nervously. "I don't think your case will go to trial, Mrs. Drum. The governor's visiting Butler County in a couple of months. That's what they're talking about."

"You're damned right it isn't going to trial! I haven't done anything!"

"Pardon me, ma'am, but the sheriff's got quite a list of charges," Curtis disputed courteously. "There's breaking and entering, two counts of endangering the safety of a minor, resisting arrest—"

"I did *not* resist arrest!"

"He carried you in, ma'am," Curtis reminded her. "And you were beating on his back."

"Because I hadn't *done* anything!" she shouted.

"You resisted arrest, ma'am," he repeated.

"You tell the sheriff," she said, forcing herself to speak more quietly, "that if I'm not out of this cell and on my way home in five minutes, he's going to be single again. Do you understand me, Curtis?"

"Yes, ma'am." Curtis hurried off to relay her message.

Beth checked her watch. Midnight.

It was twelve-thirty-five when Beth heard another, lazier set of footsteps and identified the tread. Ethan came around the corner, shrugging into his jacket. He gave her one dark look, pressed a button, and her cell door opened electronically.

She snatched up her jacket and stalked past him into the hallway.

"Am I free?" she asked, "or are you taking me down some dark country road where I mysteriously disappear? This is very interesting, you know. I've never seen small-town justice in action before. I always thought *Cool Hand Luke* was an exaggeration."

He pushed the cell door closed and crossed to her, every muscle in his face tight and hard. "I would be happy," he said with a calm that belied the anger in his eyes, "to exaggerate a little justice for you right now, so don't push me."

She would have, but after the past hour and the raging surge of adrenaline brought about by her arrest, resistance and subsequent trip to the car, then from the car to the jail over his shoulder, she was exhausted. She wasn't sure that even her fury could keep her on her feet much longer.

"Where are the children?" she asked coolly.

"At Brodie's," he replied.

"Good." She punched her way into her jacket, adjusted the hem with a yank that should have made her an inch shorter, then zipped it, seriously endangering her trachea. "Then when we get home, we can talk about the divorce!"

ETHAN WASN'T generally a drinking man. He had a beer occasionally, a mixed drink at a party once in a while, but the alcohol he kept around the house was mostly medicinal. When he got home with Beth, he poured himself a third of a barrel glass of Irish whiskey, certain his blood pressure would burst his heart within the hour if he didn't relax.

He was doing his best to *appear* relaxed because Beth was raging like a woman possessed, and he knew his control was making her crazy. It was small satisfaction in light of what she'd put him through tonight, but he was enjoying it.

Still, it would be a long time before he forgot what it had felt like to get a call from Ebbie, who picked up messages whenever he was in a meeting.

She reported that one of his neighbors had called to say she'd been watching the pilot boat through her binoculars and happened to notice several figures by the Appleby house. When he'd asked why she hadn't called the police, Ebbie replied that the woman said she thought one of the figures looked like his daughter.

What particularly troubled the woman was that she'd seen a couple of young men go into the basement that afternoon.

"Well, hell, why didn't she report it then?" he asked.

"Her son had just pulled up to take her to her doctor's appointment, and afterward she forgot. Curtis and Billings are doing back-to-backs tonight. I'll dispatch them for you."

He'd raced to the site, mindless with worry. If there was a transient in the basement, there could be trouble. He knew better than anyone that the homeless weren't necessarily criminal. A certain element was, however, and even for those who weren't, the sudden intrusion of someone else into their sanctum could surprise them into reacting with fear, instead of common sense.

Then he'd arrived. Curtis and Billings behind him, to find Nikkie and Jason on the grass. He'd been giving serious thought to paddling both of them where they stood when he'd heard a voice coming from the basement. Then he'd stared in disbelief when a hand reached out, groping for help. It was wearing the simple gold band he'd put on it a little more than a week ago.

At that moment he'd had no idea what their adventure had been about, but it had sounded as though she'd been suggesting that they conceal it. In view of the fact that he'd forbidden both children to go into the Appleby house, he'd lost all willingness to listen to explanations before he acted.

He'd asked Billings to take the children to Brodie's, then told Beth he was taking her in for questioning.

She'd argued, which he'd expected, but when he'd tried to lead her to the car, she'd kicked him, which he hadn't expected. That was when he hoisted her over his shoulder, carried her past an openmouthed Curtis and put her in the cage in the back of his patrol unit.

Things had gone from bad to worse. Her fury had set off his, and now here they were, two volcanoes about to erupt.

"Would you like a drink?" he asked with strained civility before replacing the bottle in the open kitchen cupboard.

"No," she said, pacing the kitchen like some out-of-control bumper toy. "I want a divorce."

Just as they had when she'd spoken them earlier, the words struck terror into his heart. But he kept his calm facade in place and headed for the hallway to the living room, barely avoiding a collision with her as he interrupted her pacing pattern.

"Okay," he said, and continued into the living room.

He'd called a lot of bluffs in his time, and some of them had even involved weapons aimed at his heart or his temple, but he'd never awaited a reaction with the trepidation with which he awaited this one.

"Okay?" she repeated, right at his heels as he made for the telephone. "Okay? That's all Jason means to you? *Okay?*"

That was a promising response, but he ignored it

and stabbed out Brodie's speed-dial number on the cordless phone.

Brodie answered instantly.

"Hi," Ethan said. "It's me. Everything all right?"

"With me and the kids or with you and Beth?" Brodie asked.

"Not now." Ethan took a pull of whiskey. "The kids all right?"

"They're fine. They're asleep. But they were pretty worried when they got here. They said you went a little Dirty Harry on Beth."

"With good cause," Ethan replied. "So are they okay there for the night?"

"Of course. They wanted to go home, but I figured you had a reason for having them brought here, instead of asking me to go to your place." He paused. "Ethan?"

"Yeah."

"Calm down, okay? If you guys are about to have it out, count to ten or something first. Have a drink. Remember that she and the kids went to the Appleby house to get the cat. They didn't have criminal intentions. And even though you think you know what's best for everybody, that doesn't require them to do it. Kids, sure, but not a woman. Even if you love her."

"I thought you weren't into taking women seriously."

"I've changed my mind."

Ethan laughed mirthlessly. "Do yourself a favor. Change it back. See you in the morning."

He pushed the Off button on the phone and put it back on its base. He took another sip of whiskey and turned to Beth. He felt fractionally calmer.

"Jason means a lot to me," he said in answer to

the question she'd flung at him before he'd called Brodie. "That's why I got just a little upset knowing he'd been in the Appleby place."

"A *little* upset?" she said, her voice reaching a high register. "You didn't even let us explain! You have the kids thinking you're going to kill them in the morning and you *arrested* me."

He pulled the drapes closed and took another sip of whiskey. "I didn't arrest you," he amended. "I only brought you in."

"Just to punish me!" she said angrily. "You had no right to subject me—"

He turned on her, temper boiling despite the whiskey and his best efforts to remain calm. "I had every right!" She stood in the middle of the room and he strode toward her. "I went to a meeting leaving my kids in your care, and what do you do? You take them with you as accomplices to help you break into a private residence. Do you have any idea what it feels like to be the sheriff and arrive at a call only to find that the perpetrators of the crime are your family?"

"The house was empty!"

"It doesn't matter!" he roared. "It's someone else's property! They just don't live here. But that's not the point, anyway. You heard me tell the kids that transients go in and out of there all the time. If some wacko had been in there, you and the kids could be hurt or dead right now!"

She was quiet a moment, assimilating that information. "I had a flashlight," she said defensively.

"Oh, good," he said flatly. "How many rounds does it hold? Or does it just allow you to see the gun before it fires at you?"

She put a hand to her forehead, and he realized

suddenly that she was very pale and that her hand shook a little. Concern for her diminished his anger slightly.

"All right," she admitted in a quieter tone. "I exercised poor judgment. I knew it at the time. But Nikkie was very upset about the cat and she came to me for help."

He guessed she was being carefully nonspecific. He knew how it had all come about, but she didn't know he knew. Nikkie had told him all about it when he'd put her and Jason in Billings's car. She'd assumed all blame and made it clear that Beth had told Jason to stay home and her to stay outside on the grass.

"And you thought to look in the Applebys' basement?" he asked.

She went to the window, drew the curtain back and looked out. "Cats love dark hiding places."

"But the place is boarded up. How did you think he'd gotten in there?"

She turned away from the window and met his gaze, her own direct and suspicious. "If you wanted to interrogate me," she said, "you should have done it when you had me in a jail cell."

"If you'd just told me what happened without a lot of attitude," he countered, "you wouldn't have ended up in a jail cell."

"Oh, I understand." She let the curtain fall back into place and came around the chair to lean against its well-upholstered side. "Your deputies were there and you had to flex your muscles."

"No," he said after counting to ten as Brodie had recommended. "Our children were there, and it was important for them to see that ignoring the rules has consequences. I didn't have all the details, but I figured out what had happened, though I didn't know if it was Nikkie or Jason at fault. I'd have let them believe I was taking you to jail, let them see us drive away, then I'd have taken you for coffee somewhere and chewed you out quietly for not waiting to check on the cat until I got home.''

She arched an eyebrow. "So, it's all right for *you* to disregard the rules and break in?''

"I'm an officer of the law," he replied. "I can go anywhere. And I'm armed.'' He paused. "Anyway, you wouldn't *let* me handle the situation easily. You turned on all this attitude. What was that about?''

"You were just beginning to convince me that you were different from Steve," she said, "and suddenly you were acting just like him. Full of criticism and accusation, without even bothering to ask for the details.''

Ethan downed the rest of his whiskey and put his glass on the coffee table. "Beth, I'm not Steve. I don't know how many times I have to remind you of that. If I acted at all like him, it's unfortunate, I guess, but I won't apologize. I answered a call in which my entire family was involved, and the knowledge of what could have happened scared the hell out of me. I'm not going to spend a lifetime tiptoeing around you so that nothing reminds you of Steve. I get upset with you, you're going to know it.''

Her jaw remained taut, her chin angled. "I should have stayed with my promise to myself not to get married again. I should have taken Jason and hidden somewhere.''

So. She wasn't tiptoeing around, either. Good. He had a few other things to get off his chest. "You didn't marry me to keep Jason," he said quietly, resting his hands on his hips. "You married me for me. And now that you have me, I don't behave quite the way you expected, so you don't know what to do. Your life was dictated by what Steve wanted for so long that when you were finally free, all you could think about was never having to answer to anybody again. Well, that won't be life with me."

He closed the space between them and took her chin between his thumb and forefinger. "You know me, Beth. You know I'd never hurt you and I'd never stop you from being what you want to be or doing what you want to do, as long as it doesn't endanger you or the kids. But you do something that scares me or worries me, I'll stop you."

She caught his wrist in her hand and pulled it down. "That kind of...paternalism in a husband," she said stiffly, "is so Victorian."

He refused to budge. "So are frivolous women. I don't want to run your life. I just want to keep you safe. If you can't see the difference, maybe you're not mature enough to be married at all. Good night." He left her standing near the chair and went upstairs.

She went to bed in the room she'd used before the wedding. He'd felt sure she would, but he was too angry and too determined to make concessions.

And apparently so was she.

HE SETTLED THINGS with Nikkie and Jason in the morning. Brodie brought them home just after seven and disappeared into the kitchen. They looked terrified, more affected by the events of the previous night than he'd expected.

He took them both in his arms, then sat them on the sofa and listened again to each one's interpretation of what had happened.

Nikkie finished with, "I told you, Daddy. It was all my fault. I went with the kids to rehearse there, and I'm the one who forgot Simba. Beth just went to help me. She told me to wait on the grass."

"Yeah," Jason added. "And she told me to stay home. But you said a man takes care of his family, and you were gone, so I was the man."

In the light of day and after a long and lonely night, Ethan was wondering if he'd made more of the incident than he should have. But then he looked into his daughter's and stepson's trusting faces and remembered how very real his anxiety had been, how important it was that they understood danger and, in that regard at least, obeyed him unconditionally.

He put an arm around Nikkie's shoulders and one around Jason's. "Nikkie," he began, "I appreciate your honesty, and I'm proud of you for not letting Beth take the rap, because she tried to."

Her lip quivered. "She did?"

"Yes, she did. She tried to make me believe you had just decided to look outside for the cat and it was her idea to check the Applebys' basement."

He let that sink in for a moment, then gave her the bad news. "But while I'm proud of you for telling the truth, I'm grounding you for ignoring the rule about the Appleby house in the first place and rehearsing there."

She nodded as though she'd expected as much.

He turned to Jason. "You're grounded, too," he said, "for not listening to your mom."

Jason looked surprised. "I was listening to *you!* You said—"

Ethan cut him off. "—that it's your job to look out for your mom and Nikkie when I'm not here. I know. And I can see where you might have gotten confused, but your mom gave you specific instructions to stay home. Disobeying her isn't the best way to look out for her.''

Jason puzzled over that. Ethan knew that deep down his argument wasn't sound, but he felt obliged to back up Beth's authority. This had all come about because everyone was trying to help everyone else, but he had to hold to the Appleby-house rule.

He looked from one child to the other. ''Two weeks. Nothing but drama-club stuff for you, Nik, because I know they're counting on you, but don't try to stretch it. Nothing after dinner.''

''Okay.''

''And, Jase, the bike stays in the garage and you stay in.''

''Okay.''

''Good.'' Ethan stood, pulling the children to their feet. ''Let's get some breakfast.''

Beth came down the stairs just as Ethan was urging Nikkie and Jason toward the kitchen.

''Good morning.'' Beth smiled at the children and opened her arms as Jason launched himself at her. She didn't bother to raise her glance to Ethan's.

''Mom!'' Jason held her tightly, then looked up at her, his eyes wide with respect and admiration. ''You were in the slammer! What was it like?''

Ethan kept going toward the kitchen, thinking grimly that his point about obeying rules and laws may have fallen short of its mark.

He stopped in the kitchen doorway, turning at the sudden sound of sobs. They were coming from Nikkie, who'd thrown her arms around Beth's neck and was apologizing brokenly for being the reason she'd been taken to jail.

Beth held her and spoke quietly. Ethan couldn't

hear the words but guessed they were something like, *It's all right, Nikkie. It wasn't your fault. Your father's a prehistoric muscle flexer with delusions of power and we're his unfortunate victims.*

In truth, he was happy to see his daughter and his wife finally making an emotional connection. It was just unfortunate that it had to be over what he feared was the death knell of his marriage.

He went to pour a cup of coffee and sat at the table.

"Morning, Cruella," Brodie said. "One egg or two?"

"Two. And lay off me," Ethan advised. "Cruella's a woman, so your sorry little joke doesn't work."

Brodie broke two eggs into a pan and while they cooked placed half a grapefruit in front of Ethan. "I think it does—she's the ultimate villain, man or woman, and only someone who'd collect puppies to make a coat of *their* coats would haul his own wife off to jail for helping his daughter rescue her cat."

Ethan glared at him. "I don't remember asking for your assessment of the situation."

"Too bad," Brodie replied. "It comes with breakfast."

Before Ethan could tell him what to do with breakfast, Beth and the children trooped in and the conversation was terminated.

Beth and the children chatted cheerfully as Ethan drove the Blazer on the now familiar round of elementary school, high school and cannery.

But the cheerful conversation stopped the moment Jason was dropped off and Ethan was left alone with Beth. The vehicle was filled with icy tension for the next two blocks.

Ethan pulled onto the pier and saw two cars parked at the side of the building. One he recognized as

Kelly's MG. The other, a decrepit Volvo station wagon with lumber sticking out of the back, Ethan remembered being there when he'd walked into Beth's studio and found Rush Weston with his hands on her.

He said nothing, simply let the engine idle while Beth shouldered her purse and pushed open her door. She held the door an extra moment and he wondered if communication might be reestablished between them. She seemed to be struggling to put something into words.

"Nikkie asked me if the drama club could come over tonight to work on the shields," she said, her face expressionless. "I told her it was all right."

"It *is* all right." He kept his expression as blank as hers.

"Good." The wind tossed her hair, and a wicked gleam in her eyes marred her attempt to remain completely impassive when she added, "I'd hate to end up in jail for having forgotten to tell you."

She reached back inside for the lunch she'd left on the floor on her side, and he leaned over to catch her wrist. She looked at him in surprise, not frightened but clearly uncertain of what he intended. He liked that.

"Innocent forgetfulness isn't a crime," he said, injecting a warning note into his voice. "But smart sarcasm is a felony, not to mention foolish. You might keep that in mind." He freed her hand. "Have a good day."

She slammed the door.

CHAPTER FOURTEEN

BETH SLIPPED her arms into the two leather handles she'd attached to the back of her prototype shield. She flexed the muscles in her arm and was pleased that the heavy-duty staples she'd used kept the strips in place.

She'd tried vinyl and simple staples earlier, but one flex of Cameron's forearm and a staple popped. Considering Henry V's army would be composed of Cobbler's Crossing's football team, she knew she had to find an alternative. And old leather belts from the thrift shop were an economical alternative to twenty feet of two-inch wide leather from a fabric or craft shop.

Now that she knew the belt worked, she'd run back to the thrift shop in the afternoon for more.

Her studio door opened and she turned around to greet the visitor, the shield still on her arm.

It was Kelly, in black jeans with ripped knees and a man's shirt that had once been white but now looked like a Jackson Pollock canvas. Her red hair was stuffed under a paper painter's cap.

"Whoa," she said, her eyes going to the shield as she walked toward Beth's worktable. "Where's your horned helmet and pointy bra?"

"Lent them to one of the other Valkyries," Beth

said, smiling as she eased her arm out of the straps. "Go away unless you have a caramel-vanilla latte."

Kelly rolled her eyes and leaned over Beth's table to study the coats of arms she'd drawn on the shields. "I brought a bunch of stuff down this morning, but forgot the box with my coffeepot. Brodie came over yesterday while I was packing and I lost track of what I was doing."

Beth showed Kelly the finished product. "I was the recipient of the bouquet you dusted him with," she said.

Kelly admired the shield and said nonchalantly, "I can't imagine why he'd come to see you."

Beth folded her arms. "Why, hoping for a clue to your complicated psyche," she said, then added dryly, "As though I had it."

Kelly gave her a chiding glance and turned the shield over to inspect the back. "You should talk, Ma Barker. I was up late last night and listening to the scanner when I heard about the dustup at the Applebys'. So you're a big bad mama with a record now?"

Beth took the shield away from Kelly and put it aside. "No, I do not have a record. He couldn't arrest me. He just went through the motions to make me pay for having gone down there with Nikkie in the first place. And as my friend, aren't you supposed to be sympathetic to my plight and offer comfort and support?"

Kelly asked seriously, "Is it going to lower my rent?"

"It might forestall eviction."

"Can you evict me if I haven't even moved in yet?"

"We'll ask Ethan," Beth said, taking the shield

from the table and adding it to one of the boxes in which she'd placed the other nineteen wooden discs. "He's good at manipulating the law in his favor."

"I imagine," Kelly ventured, "that he took you to jail to impress upon you and the kids that, as beguiling as a haunted house is, that place can be dangerous at night. And also because you kicked him. He's an officer of the law."

"He's my husband and he was being a jerk."

"At home he's your husband. At the scene of a disturbance he's the sheriff, counted upon by the citizens of Butler County to keep the peace. And you were shouting at him and fighting him, according to what I heard on the scanner."

Beth groaned and went to the open door of the studio to look out at the river beyond the pier. The water was the color of gunmetal and met a sky of the same color. The line of the horizon was almost invisible in the monochromatic world of the wintry Oregon coast.

Seagulls flew around a red-and-black tug pulling a barge mounded with wood chips from the mill on the other side of the bay. Cormorants watched its passing from their perch on old pilings, remnants of other cannery piers.

It occurred to Beth that it was a beautiful setting, but her world felt as sunless as the sky.

Kelly came up beside her. "So what happened to you last night? I saw the two of you shopping after work just a couple of nights ago, and it looked as though you'd found some common ground."

Misery welled up in Beth's chest. "He was shouting at me," she said, her voice dull, "and acccusing me of being foolish..."

"Astute of him, I would say," Kelly offered mercilessly.

Beth leaned a shoulder against her open door, feeling suddenly heavy, burdened. "He was sounding a lot like Steve," she explained, seeing vivid pictures behind her eyes of her and Ethan shouting at each other. "All I could think about was how confining some of those times had been, how demoralizing, and here I'd been beginning to think that with Ethan, those days were gone forever."

Kelly leaned against the other side of the doorway, her hands pressed behind her. "Beth, you're not comparing Steve's selfish claims on you to Ethan's gut reaction when he arrives at a call to find his family in danger, are you?"

Beth put a hand to her head where an ache had been gaining momentum ever since she'd climbed out of the shower that morning.

"I did last night," she admitted.

"He's a man and you scared him," Kelly said simply. "They get really ticked off when they have to admit that to themselves. And it's instinctive to take it out on whoever inspired the fear, whether or not it's entirely justified. It means he cares. I think you should forgive him."

Beth turned to her friend with a disbelieving look. "I have a broken bouquet in my kitchen that says you don't practice what you preach."

"I don't have to." Kelly stared out at the river. "My situation's entirely different."

"How so?"

"Ethan yelled at you because he cares. Brodie backed away from me because I never meant anything to him at all. It was just the sort of hormone-driven game kids play.''

''Not exactly.''

Kelly met her eyes with a frown. ''What do you mean?''

Beth related the story of Paulette.

Kelly listened. There was a momentary softening of her expression, a small gasp of indignation, then she sighed and turned her gaze out to the river again. ''Stupid snot. But it just proves that he's out to pay *her* back by taking it out on every other woman he comes across—get her interested, then drop her.''

''He admits he was doing something like that. Until you.''

Kelly laughed scornfully. ''Right. 'But you're different, Kelly.' I've been around too long to fall for that one, Beth. I'm no different, I just called him on it and he caved, but he can't have any holdouts. He has to make me come around, too—and *then* he'll dump me.''

''I don't think so.''

''Well, I won't be finding out.''

''Fraidy cat.''

''Smarty-pants. I'm playing it safe.''

Beth caught Kelly by the arm and pulled her back into the studio and across it to a poster hanging over her tool chest. It pictured a tiny boat on a seemingly endless ocean under a vast sky. ''What does that say?'' Beth demanded.

Kelly shifted her weight and read in a disgruntled monotone; '''A ship in a harbor is safe, but that is not what ships were built for.'''

Kelly turned to Beth and challenged her with a

look. "Okay. If I'm going to stick my neck out, you're going to make things right with Ethan."

Beth offered her hand, secretly pleased to have an excuse to try to rectify things between her and Ethan. "Deal."

Kelly studied her skeptically for a moment, then shook hands to seal the deal. She winced and asked in a small voice, "Doesn't this feel a lot like Butch and Sundance jumping hand in hand off that cliff?"

Beth smiled and tried to think positively. "They lived, didn't they?"

THE KITCHEN was full of laughter and loud music. Beth had spread newspaper all over the table and all over the floor. Nikkie and Vanessa knelt on the chairs and painted the shields' backgrounds while Rosalie, Cameron and Bradley sat cross-legged on the floor and painted in the details, according to the sketches Beth had made.

Jason prowled the room peering over shoulders and admiring their work. Beth was pleased to see that they were tolerant of him and that Nikkie even let him try his hand at stenciling. When his tense hand moved the stencil and created a lion with a lump protruding from its back, she patted his shoulder and told him not to worry, no one would notice.

Then she looked up at Beth when Jason was distracted by something else and made a comically distressed face.

Beth returned a wink and a nod and the unspoken assurance that she would repair the damage.

Ethan kept bowls of popcorn and corn chips filled, soda glasses topped up and the cats out of the paint.

Beth noted worriedly that he made no effort to talk

to her, though she was sure their silence wasn't obvious to Nikkie and her friends. Considering her behavior the past twenty-four hours, she couldn't blame him for ignoring her. But how she was going to fulfill her part of the bargain she'd made with Kelly remained a mystery.

Brodie came over to investigate the source of the noise.

"Jeez," he grumbled theatrically, "do I have to call the sheriff and have this place raided?"

Nikkie and her friends laughed.

Ethan put a glass of soda in his hand and a corn chip in his mouth. "Eat that and be quiet," he said. "We have enough noise around here already."

Brodie took the chip out of his mouth. "I thought maybe you needed help running the roulette wheel or dealing blackjack."

Ethan shook his head and offered a supermarket tub of salsa for Brodie to dip the chip into. "The only gamble around here is whether or not these shields come out right. The guys are talking football, and the girls are talking Brad Pitt. Who knows what we could end up with?"

Rosalie held up the first finished shield. "This!" she said, her voice conveying surprise and awe.

Everyone turned to look, and silence filled the room for a moment. The shield was Henry's. The lions stood out brilliantly against the red paint, and the fleurs-de-lis were beautifully formed on a blue field.

"Beth!" Nikkie breathed, the glow on her face saying everything. "Look at what you did!"

Beth denied the credit with a shake of her head. "You guys did it. All I did was provide the wood and make the stencils. If you act as well as you paint, you're all headed for Hollywood.''

"Oh, I just came from there," a female voice said from the back door. "Unless you're interested in beautiful people, big cars and lots of money, it has nothing for you. That's why I'm *here*.''

The kids laughed. Beth's heartbeat shifted into second gear. Kelly was *here*, she guessed, to keep her part of the bargain.

The kids went back to work, turning their music up a notch to be heard over the adult conversation.

"Can I get you a soda, Kelly?" Ethan asked. "Coffee?''

"No, thank you," she replied with a smile, then seemed to lose control of it as she turned to Brodie. It narrowed, wavered, then disappeared altogether when Brodie didn't smile back.

Kelly glanced at Beth for support. Wanting desperately for her best friend and her brother-in-law to have at least an opportunity for another go at their relationship, Beth pushed aside her own difficulties and tried to spur Kelly on.

Ethan stood only a foot away from Beth in the corner of the kitchen into which the press of teenagers had forced them, and she reached out to hook her arm in his and lean into him. She gave a smile for Kelly that suggested she, Beth, had already taken her steps in their deal and it was time for Kelly to follow suit or be a welsher.

Ethan didn't move away from Beth, and he didn't remove his arm, but he did nothing positive, either. As she inhaled the fresh rainwater fragrance of him and felt the warm textured wool of his sweater under her cheek, she was very aware that he didn't respond.

She knew precisely how Kelly felt.

Kelly tossed her red hair and refocused her attention on Brodie. "I was hoping," she said in a voice that wasn't at all familiar to Beth, "that I could buy you a cup of coffee."

Beth watched him study her warily a moment, then lift his glass. "Got a root beer."

Kelly put her hands in the pockets of her short leather jacket, her jaw firming perceptibly. "You don't have pie. I could buy you that to go with the coffee."

He considered her another moment, bounced a glance over Beth's head to Ethan, then said to Kelly. "But it's almost ten o'clock. This is Cobbler's Crossing. Nothing's open after ten."

Kelly shrugged. "I'm a caterer, remember?"

The merest trace of a smile pulled at his lips. "I never forget anything."

"Good," she said, drawing the first even breath Beth had seen her take since she'd walked into the room. "I like that in a man. If we take my car, I can have you home in time for Leno."

Brodie put his glass on the counter, slapped Ethan on the back and leaned down to kiss Beth's cheek. "Thanks for the hospitality, guys, but I've got to run." He opened the back door for Kelly. "Can I drive your car?"

She passed through the door before him. "It's very precious to me. Are you a good driver?"

"Nothing special," he replied, "but I'm a good mechanic. I break or dent anything, I can fix it." The door closed behind them and Beth couldn't help her relieved sigh.

"God, that was an ordeal," she said, forgetting for

an instant, in her delight over Kelly's preliminary success, that her own part of the bargain remained undone. She pulled her arm from Ethan's.

Jason brought her an empty plastic bowl, then returned to the table to look over Nikkie's shoulder.

Ethan moved with Beth as she went to the cupboard for the second bag of corn chips. "And what was your stake in that little scene?" he asked.

He didn't look hostile, she noted, just comfortably removed from the situation.

"Kelly's my friend." She poured chips into the bowl and carried it to the table, then went back to the counter and carefully folded the top of the bag. "And Brodie's wonderful. I think they'd be good for each other."

"And you encouraged her to try to straighten out their problems," he speculated, "by letting her think we'd dealt with ours."

She clipped the bag closed and gave him a small friendly smile. "Precisely."

"Artful trickery," he said.

"Everyone should have a skill."

There was a shout from Cameron as he looked at his watch, then a sudden flurry of activity as the young people who'd ridden in with Cameron began to pack up the project.

"Drop the brushes in the water jar," Beth instructed, "and leave all the wet shields side by side on the floor against the wall. I've got something rigged up to protect them. Don't worry about the newspaper. I'll clean that up."

Ethan volunteered to take Rosalie home because everyone else was on Cameron's way. Nikkie went with him.

Beth waved in response to the cries of "Thanks, Mrs. Drum!"

Beth hugged Jason, then shooed him off to bed while she picked up the newspapers and stuffed them into a plastic garbage bag. She covered the painted shields with overturned boxes to keep out the cats, stashed all the paints and supplies in another box and took the brushes down to the laundry sink to wash them.

At last, feeling as though she'd won Henry's Battle of Agincourt single-handedly, Beth left on the back porch light and the kitchen light, then locked up the front of the house and went upstairs to get ready for bed.

ETHAN WALKED into the kitchen with Nikkie and noticed the silence. There was something poignantly familiar about it. It reminded him of all those years when it had been just the two of them, before Jason decided to run away and changed all their lives forever.

Forever. It struck him as a strange word to use in connection with the woman he'd married on an inexplicable impulse, particularly in view of the state of that relationship at this very moment.

Still, he thought fatalistically as he reached behind him to lock the back door and turn off the porch light, the word applied. Even if she left tomorrow, he would still be changed forever. There was a lot of confusion in her, but also so much light, so much spontaneous laughter, so much grace. And so much love.

The shadowy quiet of the house reminded him of the first time he'd made love to her. It surprised him to realize that had been only last week. Every time they'd made love since had expanded and amplified his spirit so that there were moments when it felt too big for his body, as though he would have to live to be four hundred to make use of all he felt.

"Daddy?" Nikkie turned to him from the rack where she'd hung up her jacket. She helped him out of his and put it on a peg. Her eyes were bright from the hectic evening. "Thanks for letting the kids come over and work tonight. We had a great time, and we got a whole lot done."

He nodded, opening his arms in surprise when she leaned into him and stayed there. Over the past few years he'd gotten used to kisses and hugs dealt out sparingly, and usually on the run.

"I'm really sorry about going to the Applebys'," she said, her grip on him tightening "I knew better, but...you know. When you're the sheriff's daughter, everybody thinks you're a Goody Two-shoes."

He held her tightly and kissed the top of her head. "I know that's hard for you sometimes, but let me tell you that Goody Two-shoeses are underrated. They don't usually find themselves in situations where they can get hurt. Try to remember that rules aren't just to make your life uncomfortable. When you're young and enthusiastic about everything, it's hard to recognize potential danger, so I have to do it for you. You have to trust me to know what I'm doing."

"I know." She looked up at him, still holding him, her bright pretty face alight. "I'm just beginning to understand how smart you really are."

His first instinct upon hearing that was to get a tape recorder and have her repeat those words. He was certain there'd be times in the future when he'd desperately need to hear them again.

"And what brought on this revelation?" he asked.

"Beth," she said. Nikkie looked a little mystified, as though an adult truth had invaded her teenage life and confused everything. "I didn't want to like her. I didn't want things to change. But every time I turned around she was being nice to me, trying to do something for me without being pushy like Jason's grandma or sappy like some movie version of the perfect stepmother."

Her voice tightened a little. "When I couldn't find Simba, she was ready to go out in the dark and help me look. Then when I told her where I thought he was, she didn't yell or threaten or anything. I think she probably even might have told you about it when it was all over—or made *me* tell you—but we didn't take time to talk about it. We just went looking for him. And she did tell Jason to stay home, but he thought we were taking too long, so he came to help because you told him—"

"Yeah, I know. A man takes care of his family and I was gone, so he was the man."

She stood up on tiptoe to kiss his cheek. "Anyway, I love you for being so smart," she said. "And I kind of like the way things are turning out around here. Good night, Daddy."

"Good night, Nik."

Ethan turned off the kitchen light and headed for the stairs, resolved to end the standoff with Beth. He couldn't change his position on the Appleby house, but he could certainly concede that, though his entire family had ignored his instructions, they'd done it for reasons that had everything to do with responsibility and generosity, however misguided.

Nikkie's door was already closed, and the only

light in the hallway came from the night-light in the bathroom. Ethan peered into the room Beth had used the night before, expecting to find her curled up under the covers, asleep.

She wasn't. The bed was undisturbed.

She'd gone to his room? He took a few steps into the room, but his bed, too, was undisturbed, the coverlet carelessly thrown across it, just as he'd left it that morning.

Where was she? Feeling that same familiar but unwelcome silence he'd recognized just a little while ago in the empty kitchen, he suppressed any notion that she might have left.

She needed him. Even if she was angry, she was too responsible to leave in a fit of pique.

Just to be certain, he went to check on the one thing she'd never leave behind. Jason was there, fast asleep in the top bunk in the room at the end of the hall, one arm hanging over the side. Simba was curled up in a ball on Jason's pillow, his head against the boy's.

Ethan felt great relief, and then a swelling of the deep affection Jason's straightforward ways inspired. He tucked the arm up onto the bunk, then stroked the cat, who'd awakened with a start.

Simba purred and went back to sleep.

Ethan walked into his bedroom and over to the window, wondering if Beth could have gone to Brodie's. But Brodie's house was dark. Of course. He'd left with Kelly.

"Ethan."

Beth's voice came from a corner of the darkened room. He turned away from the window, his heart giving an erratic lurch. "Beth." He spoke quietly, hoping to calm himself. "What are you doing in the dark?"

"I was sitting in the chair, thinking about things," she said. She was wearing his white terry-cloth robe. It fell almost to her ankles, and her face and throat gleamed above it, her dark hair disappearing in the shadows. He felt weak with the need to touch her.

She lifted her chin. "I still think your tactics last night were uncalled for," she said, her chin coming down as she spoke, the line of her shoulders softening under the big robe. "But in all fairness, so were mine. And you did have good reason, I guess, to get a little out of control. I, on the other hand, was reacting to the past, instead of the present and..."

She expelled a breath, tried to put her hands in the pockets of the robe, but they were too low for her to do more than slip her fingertips in. She folded her arms and said, "I'm sorry."

He crossed the distance between them in two strides and took her in his arms. "*I'm* sorry," he said, absorbing the rightness of holding her against him after a separation that had seemed interminable, though it had been only a day. "I was beside myself with worry when I saw all of you there, but I should have handled things differently. I should have understood. But I was feeling, rather than thinking."

She nuzzled his throat, her hands gently exploring his waist. "Me, too." She tipped her head back and asked, her voice dropping an octave, "Why don't we shower yesterday away—together? Water is a sort of dialect of Romanesque."

He didn't say anything for an instant, and Beth experienced the panicky fear that she'd overstepped.

She'd often done that with Steve, offending or embarrassing him.

Then she saw Ethan's white smile in the dark and he wrapped an arm around her, and walked with her into the bathroom, stopping at the shower stall. He hooked a finger into the belt of the robe and pulled until it was undone. Then he slipped it off her shoulders.

His eyes shone with the same expression she'd seen in them the first time he'd made love to her. A very male appreciation of her body, coupled with a kind of disarming humility.

She reached her fingers under his sweater and T-shirt and pulled them up and off. Unbuckling his belt and unzipping his jeans, she slipped her hands between his briefs and his warm flesh and pushed the briefs down to his ankles. He toed them the rest of the way off.

He opened the shower, pulled her in with him and backed her into the cold tile corner to protect her from the onslaught of water until he had the temperature adjusted.

Then he brought her in front of him under the spray. It was a warm and comfortable drumming on her shoulders, and it seemed to create an answering beat within her. She put her hands to Ethan's chest. "Want me to soap you?" she asked.

He leaned down to kiss her greedily. "Later," he said, and lifted her into his arms, encouraging her to wrap her legs around him.

She complied, holding tightly to his neck, and felt a small jolt of surprise when his fingers parted her and slipped inside.

He tipped his head back to look into her face. "I won't drop you," he promised, humor in his voice.

She shook her head, his fingers distracting her. "That isn't...it."

"What, then?" he asked, kissing her lightly. "Is making love in the shower new to you?"

"Yes. Remember...I told you I wanted to...try something with...with, um..."

"Steve?"

"Yeah, Steve. And he..."

"Right. He was disgusted by it. This? Making love in the shower?"

"And standing up. He...said it...wouldn't work. That the shower was for hygiene, and the only way to have sex was...in bed. Ethan!"

"All right. I'm with you. And I'm about to prove to you that he was wrong about that, too."

Her body caught in the tight spiral that was the prelude to fulfillment, Beth held on to him in an agony of waiting. He propped a foot against the tile and entered her surely, making a seat for her with his hands as he leaned his shoulders back against the wall in the small space.

She cried out at her sudden release. It shot through her like fireworks, hot and colorful and lighting up the night.

She clung to Ethan as he erupted inside her at the same moment.

He clung to her, his hands stroking her hips and her back until the celebration finished and the sky cleared.

They soaped each other's bodies and washed each other's hair. When they got out and dried off, they sat in the middle of the bed while he rubbed her hair with a towel. Then they pulled the blankets up over them and, arms and legs entangled, drifted off to sleep.

Beth's last thought before she drifted off to sleep was that she felt sure she'd never doubt Ethan's opinion on anything again.

CHAPTER FIFTEEN

HENRY V'S ARMY lined up backstage in three tight rows, their shields held out before them, and smiled as though war was the last thing on their minds. Beth imagined that after the roaring success of their opening night and the cast party ahead of them at a waterfront restaurant, it would be the restaurant staff who would need the shields.

Ethan photographed them for posterity, and then the army tried to break ranks. But Ethan pointed them back into place and posed Nikkie and her friends in front of them, then pushed Beth into their mix. She tried to protest, but Bradley and Cameron brought her physically into the middle of the front row.

"Thanks, guys," Ethan said finally. "I'm finished." The cast exploded from their tidy rows into a moving knot of excitement. Parents and teachers milled around them, offering their congratulations and their parting instructions for the night ahead.

Nikkie rushed to where Ethan stood with Beth and Jason, and Brodie and Kelly. "The football team's going to the cast party on the rooter bus, but Mr. Fogarty's taking the drama club to the party in his van, and he says to tell you he'll have us home by eleven. My curfew's ten, so I thought I'd better make sure."

"Eleven's fine." Ethan flicked her chin and

grinned. "Just remember that you're the queen of France and act accordingly."

She struck a haughty pose. "*Mais, oui.* I have several beheadings scheduled for zee morning."

"Good. I'm glad to see you have an enlightened legal system in place."

Beth gave Nikkie a hug. "You're aware, of course, that your father's system is about as enlightened, so watch yourself. His spies are everywhere."

Nikkie looked heavenward. "Be sure to watch *your*selves, too. You're going to that dance-and-dessert thing with Uncle Brodie and Kelly. That sounds like trouble to me."

"We resent that!" Kelly said with feigned offense as she hugged Nikkie. "You were wonderful, sweetie. And all your props looked perfect from the audience."

Brodie took Nikkie from Kelly and hugged her in turn. "You were brilliant, Nik. Genius is unpredictable, isn't it? I mean, I have it, you have it, yet it managed to skip your father altogether!"

Ethan gave his brother a mock punch on the arm. "Careful," he warned. "This room is full of weapons."

"Duh! They're all phony."

Ethan gave him a cold smile. "The way you irritate me, Bro, I could run you through with a paper sword."

Brodie kept an arm around his niece. "This could prove to be a troublesome evening, Nik. We'll call you if we need bail money."

Ethan laughed. "The way she saves, we'd rot in jail. No, I think we have to count on graft and corruption if we get arrested."

"Oh, good. The job's going to be fun again." Curtis appeared beside Ethan. "I'll look the other way for a pickup."

His wife, a plump blonde in a bright pink suit, elbowed him in the gut. "Are we talking trucks or women?"

"Trucks, Penny," Billings assured her. He and his wife, a gorgeous brunette half a head taller than he was, came up on Ethan's other side. "He's been off women ever since that gorgeous little DUI rabbited in the middle of her field sobriety test and he had to chase her down the riverbank and into the water."

"Nikkie, you did a wonderful job!" This praise came from Joanne. She and Zachary had approached the group. They'd arrived that afternoon for the Winter Festival weekend.

Zachary patted Nikkie's shoulder. "Good work, young lady." He appeared quite well, though he leaned on a brass-handled cane. "Your shields, by the way, looked very authentic."

"Beth's responsible for that," she said with a smile in Beth's direction. "We're going to sell them at the Parents' Club auction at the end of the school year to make money for the drama club *next* year."

"Wonderful idea." Joanne leaned toward Beth to be heard in the crush of people. "Would you mind if Zach and I go home rather than on to the dance? We're pretty beat."

Jason's grandparents were staying at Beth's and Ethan's for the weekend. Beth shook her head. "Of course not. I laid in some snacks, so help yourselves."

The conversation ended abruptly when the announcement was made that the rooter bus was leaving in fifteen minutes. With costumes to change and determined to be on time, the "army" cut a wide swath through parents and friends.

The friendly insanity, however, went on well into the evening. Ethan, Beth and Jason, Brodie and Kelly, and Curtis and Billings and their wives shared a table in the fairground hall for the after-theater dance and dessert.

Ethan and the deputies recounted stories of their more humorous cases, with Brodie, as the man who repaired their vehicles, making a few contributions. Jason sat beside Ethan, leaning over his arm, laughing with the men and absorbing every word. The women talked children and jobs and men, remembering wryly what it was like worrying about them when they were late.

"Who'd have guessed," Penny Curtis asked, indicating with a jut of her chin the laughing men, "that they were late because they were having such a good time?"

Jan Billings shook her head. "Bert could have fun at the dentist. What do you do with a man like that?"

"Thank God for him every day," Kelly advised.

Beth had to agree.

"All right, what'll you have for dessert?" Ebbie suddenly materialized at their table wearing an apron with the Ladies of Law Enforcement logo. The group had provided and was serving desserts as a fund-raiser for the county's new women's crisis center. "And make it snappy. Don't think that because I work with most of you that I'll take any guff. Now. We have double chocolate torte, blackberry cobbler with vanilla ice cream, or crème caramel with whipped cream. No substitutions."

She studied each face in turn. "It would help me a lot if you'd all have the same thing and then consider seconds. It's been a long day, and this is a good cause."

Beth saw the mutiny brewing as the men from Ebbie's office exchanged glances.

"Cake," Ethan said with a straight face, "and I'd like that à la mode."

"Only the cobbler comes with—" Ebbie began.

"I'll have the crème caramel with ice cream," Curtis said.

"You can't—"

"I'll have the cobbler with whipped cream." This from Billings, who turned to his wife.

Picking up the game, Jan asked, "Is there a sampler plate with a little bit of everything?"

"Cake with whipped cream," Penny ordered briskly.

"Cake with crème caramel," Brodie said. "And the same for Kelly."

"I'll have the cobbler with ice cream." Beth gave her companions a scolding look, then when Ebbie offered her a smile for her cooperation, she added, "But I'd like my ice cream on the bottom, please. And could I have a raspberry vanilla latte to go with that, with nonfat milk but real whipped cream? Dusted with cinnamon."

Everyone laughed heartily and Ethan pulled Beth into his arms and kissed her temple in congratulations. Then they all awaited Ebbie's reaction.

She drew a breath so deep that the bib of her apron rose and fell, and she looked around the table again, desire for retribution just barely masking the laughter in her eyes. "Eight chocolate cakes," she said, scribbling on her pad, "and eight regular coffees. Jason?"

She leaned over the child whose head rested on Ethan's arm, apparently willing to give *him* a choice. But he was fast asleep.

"If he wakes up," Ethan said, "I'll share with him."

Ebbie nodded, then looked around the table one more time. "The tip," she said, her voice soft with significance, "had better be worth my while."

Curtis looked up innocently. "I didn't know you tipped at charity functions."

Ebbie patted his head. "Then you're going to be our first registration at the new home for battered *men.*"

The men groaned and booed at her threat, and she blew them a kiss as she returned to the kitchen.

Conversation and laughter began again, and Beth leaned comfortably into Ethan, his arm still around her. He eased his other arm out from under Jason's cheek and let the boy's head fall to his chest. Jason stirred restlessly, found a comfortable spot on the wool of Ethan's jacket, tucked his hand under his chin and didn't move for the next hour.

Beth couldn't remember ever being more content in her life.

SATURDAY DAWNED cold but sunny. Beth looked out the kitchen window with gratitude, knowing that even though the art-fair organizers had put up tents to protect the artwork in the event of rain, people would be far more likely to walk around—and to linger and look—if the weather was fair.

Brodie and Joanne prepared breakfast, and Beth

and Kelly tried to skip it in the interest of a little extra time to set out their wares on the pier where all the tenants of the Cannery Art Mall—as Beth had named it—would be showing their work. The rest of the artists would be strung out under tents along the river.

"You have to eat something," Ethan insisted. "It's going to be a long day. You might not get any lunch." He pressed a glass of orange juice into Beth's hand as she tried to dodge him to get to her jacket.

She took several swallows and then handed it to Kelly, who finished it. "Thanks. But there'll be vendors all over the pla—"

"It's ready." Brodie carried two steaming plates of omelettes and toast to the table. "Sit down. You could have this eaten in the time you spend arguing with us."

Ethan took their jackets from them and returned them to the pegs. Brodie pulled out chairs.

Kelly sighed at Beth and, resigned, moved to the table. "I remember now why we made that pact about men and marriage."

"What pact?" Joanne asked from the stove.

Aware of the potential danger in that line of conversation, Beth tried to warn Kelly off with a severe look, but Kelly, her mind no doubt on other things, had apparently forgotten Joanne's connection to Steve on this sunny morning.

"Never to fall for another one," Kelly answered, reaching for the pepper. "My husband wanted everything his way, and Beth's usually forgot she was alive. He—"

Kelly stopped abruptly, awareness dawning on her face.

Joanne frowned and put the spatula down on the

stove. Her expression changed from the almost convivial cheer they'd grown used to to that of the woman Beth remembered all too well from the old days—defensive, judgmental, argumentative.

"What do you mean?" Joanne demanded.

Beth closed her eyes, thinking that the last thing in the world she wanted to discuss this morning was her relationship with Steve. But maybe it was time to set the issue straight. Not the ideal time, certainly, but time all the same.

"I didn't mean anything, Joanne," Kelly said, apology in her eyes when she looked at Beth. "I was talking out of turn."

Joanne moved to the table, pulled out a chair at a right angle to Beth's and sat. The smell of something burning came from the stove. Brodie picked up the spatula and turned the charring omelette. Then Ethan moved to the table, as well, and took the chair opposite Joanne. He leaned back in it as though in the role of observer, but Beth knew better now. He was making himself available if she needed him.

"Kelly was my confidant in Seattle, Joanne," Beth said with courtesy but no apology, "and she listened to my problems when Steve wouldn't. She knows what I went through the last couple of years with Steve."

Joanne went pale. "Steve gave you everything."

Beth nodded. "Everything he could buy, yes."

"He was a wonderful father."

"On the five or six times a year he actually came home before Jason went to bed, yes, he was."

"He was working for *you!*"

Beth sighed. Old pain tried to resurrect itself but failed because there was so much new love. "Joanne, he was working for himself, because some inner demon made him always want to do more, make more, get more. I don't know if he was trying to prove something to you and Zachary or just to himself, but it controlled his whole life.''

"You had that wonderful house on the sound that everyone envied!''

"That's why we had it,'' Beth said. "Not because I wanted it, but so it could be envied. So everyone who visited would want what it contained, and Steve could make more sales, open more stores. I was the answering machine. My job was to make everyone who called Steve at home feel as though he was getting special treatment. I was a business tactic, Joanne, not a wife.''

"Then why did you stay?''

Beth had thought about that often in the year since he'd been gone. Especially lately, knowing what marriage *could* be like.

"Because Jason loved him,'' she said, "and I'd made a vow.''

Joanne's lips pinched closed and she looked away a moment, her eyes welling with tears. "So you're glad he's gone?''

"Joanne.'' Zachary had come into the room. His tone was reproachful.

Joanne looked up at her husband defensively. "Well, she was miserable. She hated him. She *must* be glad.''

"I *was* miserable,'' Beth said candidly. "But it was because I'd loved him so much in the beginning and then it all disintegrated from inattention. Even in my worst moments, I never hated him, never wished him dead. I was just so…disappointed.''

She reached blindly for Ethan's hand. He caught hers and squeezed it.

Joanne excused herself and left the room. With a moody glance around, Zachary shook his head and turned to follow her. Kelly put both hands over her face and burst into tears.

Beth's mouth trembled dangerously. "Kelly, stop it!" she ordered. "It wasn't your fault. That conversation was long overdue."

Ethan used Beth's hand to pull her out of her chair and into his lap as she sniffed back tears of her own.

"It isn't grief for Steve," she said. "It's...I think it's..."

"I know." He rubbed her back and pressed his cheek to her hair. "Grief for how it should have been. But I don't want you to be unhappy." He snatched a napkin from the holder on the table and gave it to her.

She dried her eyes and drew a breath. "I'm not unhappy. I just hate confrontation."

He grinned skeptically. "Really? I've never noticed that."

She laughed and kissed his temple. Then she turned to her friend, who still had tears streaming down her cheeks. "Kelly, it's okay."

Brodie dropped the spatula and crossed to the table. He leaned over Kelly and put his arms around her, then glanced at Ethan, humor glinting in his eyes. "Didn't we make a pact about staying away from women?"

Ethan held fast to Beth. "No," he replied. "As I remember, we made a pact to seek them out."

Brodie looked from the weeping woman in his

arms to Beth, dabbing at her eyes with a napkin. "You mean...we're doing well?"

Ethan grinned. "Damned if I know."

PEOPLE THRONGED the art fair. The colorful tents set up along the water made Cobbler's Crossing look like some medieval encampment. Musicians had been hired to stroll among the exhibits, and the sound of their instruments floated through the air as though sent from another time.

But it was the aroma of waffle cones that was driving Beth crazy. After her set-to with Joanne, she hadn't had time to eat her omelette, and she and Kelly had hurried to the pier on empty stomachs, after all.

Rush Weston had already arrived and, in high spirits at the prospect of the day ahead, had helped them haul out tables and set up their work. All the while he'd boasted of the special project he would unveil at one o'clock, the sculpture that would grace the lawn of the art association's newly acquired permanent home near the maritime museum.

"I beat out fourteen other artists for the commission, you know," he said several times.

Appreciating his help, Beth and Kelly agreed he was wonderful, winking at each other across the long table the three of them had carried out of Kelly's studio.

Rush was set up around the corner of the cannery building, and the tall sculpture stood under what appeared to be several bedsheets sewn together. The sheets protruded with something pointy out the top and out the back, causing Kelly to speculate.

"Knowing him," she said to Beth sotto voce as they dutifully admired his setup of sculpture and bronzes, then returned to their own areas, "it's probably a giant breast! But I'm still anxious to see it. The guy's a genius."

Beth nodded. "I'm with you. And it was nice of him to help us."

"Mm. Only, it makes me wonder what he's up to."

Ethan, with Nikkie, Jason and Taylor Bridges in tow, arrived shortly after the opening with a wonderfully aromatic bag of food from a local takeout place.

"I'll sit for you," Nikkie offered, "so you can have breakfast."

"Brodie brought breakfast for Kelly, too," Ethan said, catching Beth's hand and pulling her aside while Nikkie took her place behind the table. "So why don't the two of you take a little time to relax and look around before the midmorning crush?" He put a hand to her cheek and looked into her eyes, his own gentle but searching. "You all right?"

She nodded. Her disagreement with Joanne had put a bit of a pall over the day. But if things went well, the exposure would help her as an artist and present the Cannery Art Mall to everyone who visited as the place for unique fine art and the more commercial but one-of-a-kind handicrafts.

She turned her lips into his hand. "I'm fine," she said. "I can't believe that deep down Joanne and Zachary weren't aware of all that about Steve, but I thought it was time to say it. I'm sorry it had to be in your kitchen."

"It's *our* kitchen," he corrected with a sweet smile. It turned wicked as he added, "I just don't want you cooking in it very much. Go find Kelly and a quiet place to have your breakfasts. I promised the boys I'd take them to the carnival." He pointed to the Ferris wheel a couple of hundred yards farther down the waterfront. "Nikkie'll watch your table until you're finished."

Beth put the take-out bag down and looped her arms around Ethan's neck. His warmth and his calm seeped into her, and she kissed him lingeringly, trying to tell him how truly happy he'd made her and how much she loved him.

"Yeah," he said, his voice ragged as she finally drew her mouth away. "Me, too."

"Dad, come on!" Jason said impatiently. He caught Ethan's hand and tugged. "You guys can do that later. Me and Taylor want to ride the moon jet!"

"All right, all right." Ethan kissed Beth one more time, then strode after the boys as they ran up the pier to the waterfront path.

Only as Beth replayed the scene in her mind did she realize Jason had called Ethan "Dad." It brought a lump to her throat and seemed to seal her life in place.

"I THINK I'M DEAD," Kelly said, nibbling on a sausage roll as she and Beth wandered slowly through a Peg-Board setup of small scenic paintings done in the impressionist style.

Beth sipped at a paper cup of tea as she stepped back to study a painting of mountains and a meandering stream. "That's funny. You look very much alive to me."

"I mean dead as a single woman," Kelly said.

They were now on opposite sides of the Peg-Board setup, and Beth leaned around it to look into Kelly's face. "I know that being a potter makes your *brain* go to pot, but try to be clearer. Are you trying to tell me we're going to be sisters-in-law?'' Kelly and Brodie had wandered off together the night before in the middle of a dance and hadn't been seen again until they'd appeared in Ethan's kitchen that morning.

Kelly's expression was both terrified and excited. ''Will it mean a reduction in rent?''

''No,'' Beth said. ''If I'm going to have to put up with you day in and day out, it means I'll need *more* money. Will you please speak plainly?''

Kelly came around the Peg-Board, chewing and swallowing her last bite of biscuit. Her cheeks were flushed. ''Brodie asked me to marry him last night.''

Beth squealed and caught her in a hug. She couldn't think of anything more wonderful than having her best friend become a part of her family.

''Brodie's wonderful,'' Beth said. ''You're going to be so happy!''

Kelly took a step back, still holding Beth's arms. Her eyes were filled with amazement. ''Who'd have thought just a year ago,'' she asked softly, ''that we'd both end up in love with and marrying the kind of men most women only dream about?''

As they hugged each other again, Beth realized it would never have occurred to *her*.

BETH SOLD six door plaques to an older woman who was thrilled to find the names of all her grandchildren. After a trip to her car with those, the woman returned to buy four painted flowerpots for gifts, then wandered over to Kelly's table and picked up several bowls.

Beth had just secured the morning's take in a locked box in her studio and intended to take advantage of the lull to tidy up her table when Kelly strode over and took her by the arm.

"Come on," she said. "Let's go see Rush's grand unveiling."

Beth glanced at her watch. It was three minutes to one.

"You go ahead," she said. "I should haul out some more things. These people are in a buying frenzy, and I don't want to miss one patron with an impulse to overspend."

Kelly rolled her eyes. "Jeez, Louise, lighten up. All our customers are collecting at Rush's, anyway. See. Our end of the pier is empty."

Beth looked up from rearranging a pair of children's chairs she'd painted with whimsical mice to find that Kelly was right. A few people were headed for the carnival, but everyone else was formed in a large semicircle, half-a-dozen people deep, around Rush's display tables.

"All right." Beth followed Kelly to Rush's area and discovered her friend had an ulterior motive in insisting they go. Brodie and Ethan were there, too.

Kelly went right into Brodie's arms and into a kiss that made everyone nearby smile and look away. Except Beth. She watched them, feeling as though, in a life filled with miracles, she'd been given yet another.

Then Ethan wrapped his arms around her from behind and found a spot for them in the crowd where she could see. The local radio station was broadcasting remote, and the *Crossings Crusader* had sent a reporter and a photographer.

Beth leaned her head back against Ethan's shoulder. "Did you know," she asked, "that Brodie and Kelly are getting married?"

Ethan smiled. "He just told me. Well, actually he stammered around a lot and I figured it out for myself."

Beth laughed. "Ebbie'll be thrilled to do another wedding." She gasped. "Uh-oh."

"What?"

She widened her eyes in mock alarm. "Kelly catered for us. Does that mean I have to cater for her?"

"No," he replied, kissing her cheek. "I think it means Kelly'll do it and ask you to serve."

Beth pretended hurt feelings. "That's mean."

His arms around her squeezed. "I'll make it up to you later," he whispered in her ear.

Rush cleared his throat, and the broadcaster who'd attached a microphone to the pocket of the artist's chambray shirt stepped out of his way.

Beth leaned back again into Ethan. "Where's Jason?" she asked.

"I sold him to the carnival," Ethan replied.

"Did you get a good price?"

"I threw in Nikkie. She's so good at the midway games she'll bankrupt them in a month, and then they'll be home again. But we can do some high living in the meantime."

"Oh, good."

The strolling musicians had stopped behind Rush and now played a little flourish. Rush began to speak. He talked about what a beautiful spot Cobbler's Crossing was and how the area was a source of inspiration for artists, himself particularly.

"Everything's about 'himself particularly,'" Ethan grumbled softly in Beth's ear.

She jabbed him gently with an elbow, then turned her attention back to Rush, hoping the sculpture would give him the fame his ego seemed to need so desperately.

He went on to talk about himself, giving a rather lengthy history of his career, then said that everything changed for him when he moved to Cobbler's Crossing.

"I found friends here," he said dramatically, his strong profile tipped upward, "and my particular inspiration." He swept a hand toward the shrouded sculpture. "This piece, entitled *Water Woman,* is the culmination of a four-month labor of love. My heart and my soul have gone into it, and I now present it to you, the people of Cobbler's Crossing."

Rush yanked on the sheet and it fell into his arms, revealing a life-size bronze of a nude female figure. A collective cry of approval rose from the crowd.

As Beth admired the statue from the base on which it stood on tiptoe on one foot, the other leg raised and bent at the knee as though the woman had been caught midstride, she thought she noticed a slight change in sound in the common cry of approval.

But the artist in her was too busy appreciating the "movement" in the bronze. The body was poised in an upward stretch, as if toward something just beyond reach. The thighs were long and slender, the hips rounded, the waist slender, the breasts uptilted and generous, the reaching arms graceful.

And then Beth saw the face.

With a little gasp she fell back against Ethan, and that was when she noticed that the arms around her were now like rock and the tension coming from him almost palpable.

She heard someone else gasp and knew the sound had come from Kelly.

The face on the sculpture…was Beth's.

CHAPTER SIXTEEN

THERE WAS A SMATTERING of applause among the other artists assembled, enthusiastic cheers from some men in appreciation of the female form, and startled glances at Beth from acquaintances who thought she must be embarrassed. There were also the disapproving frowns of those who would never understand that nude modeling did not suggest a morally bankrupt character.

The almost painful grip of the arms around her indicated that her husband was among that group. Beth pushed her way out of his embrace and turned, thinking that if she explained calmly and carefully, he might understand.

But she knew the moment she looked into his eyes that that wasn't going to happen. He was wearing the same expression he'd worn the night he'd hauled her out of the Applebys' basement and taken her to jail.

A cold knot formed in her midsection. They weren't going to be able to come together on this. She could hear his argument now. *Do you know what it's like to be present at the unveiling of a nude sculpture and have everyone identify it as your wife?*

Beth saw her in-laws standing in the front row of spectators across the semicircle. Their expressions could only be described as horrified shock.

Embarrassment, frustration, anger and disappointment became a turbulent combination in Beth's chest. She wanted to hide, she wanted to throw things, she wanted to be sick, and then she wanted to die.

But before she did any of those things, she wanted to kill Rush Weston.

But that was self-indulgence, she told herself, and something for which she had no time at the moment. Beth Warner Richards Drum had had it with everybody.

As Rush invited people closer to study the sculpture, Beth realized she was tired of being threatened with the loss of her child, tired of having to be on the watch for her in-laws' detective, tired of having to remind Rush Weston that he didn't love her and she didn't love him, tired of having to remind her husband of the same thing.

Feeling as though she should slip an arm into one of the shields she'd made for Henry V's army, she turned to Ethan and said into his furious dark eyes, "I'll deal with you later. Excuse me."

She knew that genuine shock was the only thing that prevented him from grabbing her and telling her what he thought of her then and there.

She marched through the crowd to where Joanne and Zachary continued to stand gasping at the sculpture. She collected congratulations and pats on the back for being Rush's model and "inspiration," as well as several glares, as she crossed the pier.

She stopped in front of Joanne, arms folded with resolution. "Where is he?" she asked with the air of royal command she'd learned from Joanne.

Joanne met Beth's gaze, her own imperiousness in place. "Who?"

"The detective," Beth replied. "Where is he?"

She saw embarrassment in Joanne's eyes for an instant, then it was gone. "What detective?" she asked innocently.

"The one you hired to check me out," Beth said, shifting her weight, her voice rising a trifle. "The one who's been following me and photographing me. Tell me where he is, or I'll have you arrested for harassment."

"Really?" The imperious look now became scornful. "You're threatening me after you posed naked for that…"

Zachary suddenly pointed his cane at a youngish man in a trench coat who stood several yards away, even now taking photographs. "Right there," Zachary said. "That's Frank Bowker."

Beth pointed to the spot where she and the Richardses stood. "You stay right here or I'll come after you, I swear it."

She turned in the direction of Bowker and was on him even as he took a final photo of her. Then he was preparing to run, backing away and trying to secure his camera over his shoulder. But she had him by the lapels before he could get away.

He was several inches taller than she was, and he appeared to be fairly substantial under the coat. Nevertheless there was no Mike Hammer toughness about him. In fact, she thought she saw fear leap in his eyes when she grabbed him.

"You're coming with me," she said, giving him her best Ethan-in-a-temper look. "And I don't want to hear one complaint or feel the least resistance, do you hear me?"

He seemed to try to pull himself together. "Who do you think you are?" he asked with false bravado.

While he was posturing, she snatched his camera from him. "The woman whose privacy you've been invading," she replied.

"Following you and taking pictures is not a crime," he said, his voice faltering.

She got right into his face. "When your husband is the bad-tempered sheriff of a small town, it is," she said, disregarding the distinct possibility that Ethan wasn't going to be her husband for much longer. "And I'm also holding this...what? Six-, seven-hundred-dollar piece of equipment?"

He sighed. "Nine," he said.

She looped the camera strap over her shoulder. "Then you'd better follow me."

Beth strode back to her in-laws as the rest of the crowd dispersed to the food stands and the other tents. They stood alone, a man and a woman who suddenly looked old and rather frail. But Beth refused to let her resolution slip.

"I'd like you to come with me, please," she said. "And, Zachary, be careful with your cane—those spaces between the planks." Then she marched off toward her studio as though completely confident that her in-laws and their detective were following.

Beth saw that Nikkie was manning her table. "That's quite a bod for a stepmother," Nikkie said under her breath, then giggled. "Are you back? Where's Dad?"

"Would you mind watching the table for a little longer?" Beth asked. Sad, she thought, that it was all falling apart when she and Nikkie were finally becoming friends. "I think your father's...still looking around."

"Sure, no problem. Take your time."

"Thanks, Nikkie." Beth ushered Zachary, Joanne and Bowker into her studio and closed the door. She flipped on all the lights she had, but the cavernous space was still dimly lit everywhere but under the fluorescent bulb above the worktable. So she gathered everyone there.

She pulled a stool up for Joanne. "You might want to sit down, Jo," she said.

"I'll stand," Joanne insisted. "You don't frighten me."

"It isn't my intention to frighten you." Beth made herself speak calmly. "It's my intention to explain a few things to you, then make it clear that there is no way in hell you will ever get Jason from me."

"Beth—" Zachary began.

Beth silenced him with a raised index finger. "I know you're a judge, Zachary, and I know you have influential friends, but even you can't make a case where there is none."

"But there's a statue of your naked body!" Joanne exclaimed.

"Joanne, it's art!" Beth said slowly, carefully. "I posed for Rush's sculpture class when I first moved here to make extra money. I didn't know Rush had sculpted me, but now that he has, I'm flattered to grace the lawn of the art association's new building." That wasn't true, but it wouldn't hurt to let Joanne think it was. "And that is not against the law."

"It's—" Joanne made a face "—disgusting."

And for the very first time Beth had an insight into Steve's sexual reactions to her. Was that what Joanne had taught him? That the body was disgusting?

"It isn't disgusting at all," Zachary said quietly. He used his cane to hike himself up on the stool, then rubbed at his cast as though the leg inside it ached. He gave Beth a thin smile. "I thought it was quite beautiful."

"Zach!" Joanne's eyes widened.

He sighed. "Don't be such a priss, Jo," he said mildly. "You looked like that once, and I enjoyed looking at you. But when I was made a judge, you changed. You became full of self-importance and you assumed a dictatorial code of behavior, which you inflicted on Steve—until he became just as stiff and self-absorbed. You did it to me, too."

Beth stood paralyzed in complete surprise, afraid to breathe for fear she'd be noticed.

"Zachary!" Joanne gasped, leaning against the table for support.

"It's true, Jo," he said heavily. "We used to be fun, you and I, and now you've turned us into caricatures of stuffy old folks. And you turned a boy who was already too serious for his own good into a man consumed with status, with wanting more."

"Are you saying...?" Joanne's mouth quivered, unable to say the words.

"That the adult he became is your fault?" Zachary shook his head. "We all get to a point where we have to look the past in the eye and decide what we want for our own future. Apparently he grew blind to his wife and son, and all he saw was getting and owning. But he did that to himself."

Zachary sighed and ran a hand over his face, then he turned to Beth. "I admit I was a little worried when I first saw your apartment in this place." He looked around, nodding as he noted the fresh coat of paint and the refinements she'd made. "Steve was always telling us that your art took so much time away from him, and I believed him. I was worried for Jason. But now that we've spent time with you and I've seen you with him and with Ethan and the girl, I don't think there was every anything wrong with you. I realize now the problem was with Steve.''

Beth was still afraid to breathe.

Joanne looked even more shocked than she'd been by the statue.

"I didn't want the detective, either," Zachary continued. "But Jo thought it would give us something concrete to go on, and I've found it's often easier to take the line of least resistance when her mind's made up. But no more. Give her the film, Bowker. All of it.''

Bowker backed up a few steps, prepared to resist.

"Now," Zachary said more loudly. He took the wallet out of his jacket pocket. "Hand the cartridges to Beth, you'll get paid in full, and this will be over.''

Beth's heart began to thump erratically. Over? The threat of losing Jason finally over? She'd talked a good line about the solidity of their case, but she didn't believe for a minute that she was invincible where the law was concerned. After all, she'd gone to jail for looking for a cat!

Bowker vacillated a moment, then apparently decided that immediate payment was more appealing than cartridges of film that would have no value to anyone else. He delved into his camera bag, produced six cartridges and placed them on the table.

Beth handed him his camera. "And I want the one that's in there now.''

Bowker took it out and handed it to her. Zachary wrote him a check, which he quickly pocketed, and then he left.

Joanne put a hand to her heart. "Oh, my God," she moaned.

Beth turned to her in concern.

"Don't fall for it, Beth," Zachary said, easing himself off the stool. "She always has palpitations when she doesn't get what she wants. She'll be fine. I want to thank you and Ethan for your hospitality. We're going back to the house now to collect our things, then we'll head for home."

Beth steadied him as he braced against the cane and regained his footing. "I have to tell you something else before you go," she said.

He raised an eyebrow. "What's that?"

She heard herself speak as though it were someone else's voice. "That I did marry Ethan to stop you from taking me to court."

Zachary smiled. "I don't think you did. I think you married him because you saw in him everything you missed with Steve. I like that boy. I loved my son, but I didn't always *like* him."

Joanne now had both hands over her face.

"Neither did you, Jo," he said, slowly closing the few feet that separated them, the thump of his cane echoing in the big room. "How many times did you tell me he should make more time for Jason? You were willing to believe him about Beth because you were jealous of her, but you worried about Jason all the time. I think you wanted the boy just so you could make up to him what Steve didn't give him."

Joanne lowered her hands. Beth could see the lines that bitter disappointment had etched in her face.

"I wanted Steve to be better than he was," she said, her voice thin. "I told him Jason needed him. But he said...he said Beth wanted more."

"Jo, you knew that wasn't true." Zachary cupped his wife's cheek. "You wanted it to be true so you wouldn't have to blame him, but it wasn't. He became selfish and small. Admit it."

Joanne shook her head against the words, and Zachary pulled her into his arms. "He was such a cute little kid," he said to Beth, his own grief visible in his eyes. "It's hard to let go of that when they grow up and turn into someone else."

Tears welling in her eyes, Beth put a hand on Joanne's back. "Zachary, don't leave for Seattle like this. Why don't you spend the night and leave tomorrow? Come on, I'll walk you to your car."

Beth hugged Joanne before helping her into the Cadillac. "Steve and I had a good couple of years in the beginning. I like to remember that. I wish you would, too."

Joanne held her for a moment, then leaned back to look into her eyes. "You weren't ever as happy with him as you are with Ethan."

Beth was glad that had been phrased as a statement rather than a question, considering that Rush's grand unveiling had seriously endangered what she had with Ethan.

"I'll see you at home," she said.

Beth stood in the middle of the parking area that fronted the river and watched them drive away. She felt as though a heavy burden lay suspended in her chest. Much of it had been lifted by Zachary's words, but she'd come to care about her in-laws in the past few weeks more than she ever had when she'd been married to their son. She hated to think of them lonely and in pain.

Her worries had been relocated, not relieved.

She headed back toward the pier at a determined pace, scanning the crowd for Ethan or for Rush. She'd take on whomever she found first.

Then she stopped in her tracks. The pier was empty; the crowd was gone. Tables and booths had been abandoned. Where was everyone?

Then she heard shouts coming from the other side of the cannery. She followed them, picking up her pace until she was running. Had something terrible happened? It must have. What else would have made the artists leave their work unattended?

Then, as she rounded the corner of the building and saw the knot of about a hundred people gathered at the pier's railing, she realized that their shouts were cheers.

She stared in shock as Brodie and several other men hauled Ethan out of the water with a rope. Rush Weston's arms were wrapped around his neck.

Rush was peeled from Ethan's back and laid on the pier, coughing and spitting up water. Jan Billings knelt over him as the crowd gathered around.

Ethan, drenched and perched on the railing, swung his legs onto the pier and leaped nimbly down as Beth approached. Kelly threw a blanket around him. "Ambulance is on its way," she said. "Sorry about the musty smell. I keep it in the trunk of my car. Are you okay?"

"Fine," he replied tersely.

"Daddy!" Nikkie tried to embrace the bulk of him under the blanket.

He allowed her one moment, then kissed her temple and took a step back. "I'm okay, Nik. I don't want you to get wet."

"What happened?" Beth asked. Concern for him,

despite her anger and helpless frustration over the way this day had gone, made her voice and her manner sharp. "Did it make you feel better to throw Rush in the water?"

Ethan dried his face with a corner of the blanket. When he lowered the rough brown wool to look at her, she saw instantly that he wasn't at all hypothermic. A man couldn't be on the brink of freezing and still have eyes that hotly angry.

"Beth, he—" Brodie began, but Ethan silenced him with a look.

"When I can't speak for myself," he said, his tone deadly, "I'll let you know."

"My mistake." Brodie, probably also concerned about Ethan's dunking, snarled back at him. "Second one today. The first one was pulling you out of the water."

Ethan glared at his brother for a moment, then a smile curved his lips. "Did I forget to thank you for that? *My* mistake."

"I suggest everyone calm down," Kelly said diplomatically. "Here, Ethan. A vendor brought you this cup of coffee. Ah. There's the ambulance."

Kelly pulled Beth and Nikkie aside as Ethan moved over to Rush, who was now sitting up. Jan was rubbing circulation into his shoulders and arms.

Rush looked up as the crowd parted to let the EMTs through with their gurney. He focused on Ethan and even from a small distance Beth heard him say clearly, "Thanks. I'm not sure I'd have jumped in after *you*."

Ethan accepted that with a nod. "I just wanted to make sure you lived to serve your thirty days for swinging at me."

Beth heard the exchange with an awful sense of having been impulsive and wrong once again. Oddly it made her feel more defensive than penitent. She put her fingertips to the throbbing that had begun at her right temple.

"Yes," Kelly said wryly, "stupidity does give you a headache, doesn't it? Rush was telling a group of guys that the model had been his lover. Ethan suggested he tell the truth. Rush swung at Ethan, not the other way around. Ethan dodged him and Rush landed in the river. He can't swim."

Rush was in the ambulance in a matter of minutes. The EMTs apparently tried to convince Ethan to go along to be checked over, but he refused.

The ambulance drove off. Jan Billings railed at Ethan about getting out of the cold air and into a hot shower and dry clothes even as she lent him the cell phone in her purse to call the office.

"I'm on my way home," he told Jan when he handed back the phone. "I appreciate your concern, but I'm fine. Beth!"

The note in his voice was authoritative. Considering Beth had intended to make the afternoon about taking charge of her own life, she didn't respond well to the sound of it. Now that she was sure he was all right, she became furious all over again for the way he'd reacted to the unveiling of Rush's bronze.

"Yes?" she asked frostily.

He whipped the blanket off, balled it in his hands and handed it to Kelly. "Thanks, Kelly," he said, then to Beth again, "You're coming with me. Nikkie, will you go back and watch her table?"

Beth tried to protest. "I can't just—"

Ethan ignored her and turned to his brother. "Will

Bridges has Jason and Taylor at the carnival. He's bringing Jason back at two-thirty. Can you bring him home?''

"Sure."

"Nikkie is supposed to meet her friends at three at the taco booth," Beth informed him. "We can't just ignore her plans."

"That's all right," Kelly said traitorously. "At three o'clock, we'll move your table up against mine and I'll watch both of them. We'll get the kids home afterward, don't worry."

War was in the wind, and while Beth had been eager to confront it earlier, she'd felt completely in the right then. Now she was guilty of having accused Ethan of a petty act, when it had really been an heroic one. And she didn't want to walk into a fight at such a disadvantage.

"Joanne and Zachary are at home," she told him. "You go home and shower and I'll be along later."

Kelly pointed to the cannery. "Beth's old apartment is still there. It's tiny, but there is a shower and...you know, room to argue."

Ethan shook his head. "This is going to be a loud argument. We need privacy."

"You need the shower and dry clothes first," Jan insisted, her arms folded resolutely. "And I'm going to hang around until you do it, or I'll call the EMTs back and make them take you to the ER."

Brodie gave Ethan a push in the direction of the cannery. "Go shower. It'll take me five minutes to run home and get you a change of clothes."

Beth showed a stiff-backed Ethan to the shower in her small apartment. She handed him a towel, which he took with a terse thank-you and closed the door on her.

Fuming, she went back outside to help Nikkie as a crowd began to form around her table. It occurred to her that there was something to be said for notoriety.

True to his word, Brodie was back in a very short time with a bag, which he carried into the cannery. Ethan came out shortly afterward in a dark blue sweater and cords. He caught Beth's wrist in the middle of a transaction.

"Ethan, I was—"

But he interrupted her to speak to Nikkie. "Thanks, Nik. Uncle Brodie'll take you home."

"Where are you going?" Nikkie asked, wrapping a clay pot in newspaper. She looked worriedly from her father to Beth.

"We'll be home by dinner," he replied. Then he hauled Beth up the pier toward the parking lot.

Beth dragged her feet and pulled against him. "Ethan, my purse is—"

He threw an arm around her waist, anchored her to his side and kept walking. "You're not going to need your purse."

Beth pulled at the fingers biting into her side. "Every woman in this town is going to vote against you in the next election if you keep acting like a Neanderthal!"

The possibility apparently didn't concern him. He strode across the parking lot with her held close to his side. When he reached the Blazer, he put her in, then locked and closed her door.

He was behind the wheel in an instant and turned the key in the ignition. He switched off the radio, switched on the heater and whipped out of the parking lot and onto the fortunately empty highway with the speed of a competitor at Le Mans.

"You have a bad habit," she said coolly, "of letting your temper affect your driving."

"Don't worry about it," he replied. "I've had pursuit training. But it'd help me if you didn't distract me with conversation."

She leaned her head back against the headrest and closed her eyes. "Another one of those arguments where only *you* get to talk?"

"Yeah. Right. Whose voice are *you* hearing?"

Beth didn't respond, partly because he was right, and partly because she was trying to save her reserves of wit for what was coming. She was going to need them. He was a worthy if completely unreasonable adversary.

She had no idea where he was going. He followed the main road through town to the far end of the waterfront. There he turned off onto another road that led down a slope to a little cove sheltering a long-deserted yacht club. The old frame building had fallen into disrepair, and most of the windows were broken.

There wasn't a soul around.

The parking lot and boat ramp stood empty under a weakening afternoon sun. Clouds massed on the western horizon and began moving toward Cobbler's Crossing. The grass along the riverbank bent with the wind.

Beth looked away from the clouds as Ethan stopped in the middle of the parking lot, turned off the ignition with an angry jerk and rested his wrist on top of the steering wheel.

He stared angrily through the windshield, apparently collecting his thoughts for an attack on Rush's sculpture.

On the theory that the best defense was a good offense, Beth launched her own attack. She yanked off her seat belt and turned toward him.

"I'll save you the trouble, Ethan," she said, sad and disappointed that it had to turn out this way. "I've been through this with you once before, remember? I know exactly what you're about to say."

He turned to her, the anger in his eyes momentarily diluted by confusion.

"At the Appleby house," she said. "This is a slight variation on the theme. 'Do you have any idea,'" she said, her tone deepening as she mimicked his voice, "'what it's like to attend the unveiling of a nude statue in front of most of the town and discover that your wife posed for it?'"

She resumed her natural voice. "You were embarrassed, and like almost everyone else, you think that because someone models in the nude, there has to be lewd and lascivious behavior involved. That modeling was done in a sculpture class Rush was teaching in the presence of eighteen students, many of them other women. I had no idea Rush was planning me for the art association's front lawn, but I'm tired of defending myself to you. It's clear you're not going to have the tolerance for living with an artist that you claimed you would."

"The only thing that's clear," he returned, "is that *you're* the one who's completely misunderstood the situation. Sure, I was surprised to see that the sculpture was you, but I was not embarrassed. My initial anger was not that you'd posed nude for another artist, but that I dislike the man particularly, and I felt a very natural male inclination to kill him because he'd seen the very image I revere.''

Her angry indignation severely dented, Beth tried hard to firm it up. ''Because you thought—''

She'd been prepared to accuse him of presuming Rush had made sexual overtures, but Ethan interrupted her. ''Don't tell me what I thought. You're not inside my head. In fact, I wonder if you've even been anywhere near me for the past month and a half if you can so misread me.''

''Well, if you're not angry about Rush, what's the problem?''

''The problem is you,'' he said brutally. ''I was raving inside that Weston had seen...you. But that was my gut reaction, and I was telling myself that I had to work on that, that what I was feeling wasn't reasonable and I had to get a grip on common sense and see that image of you for what it was— very...beautiful.'' His eyes grew turbulent and grave with that admission, then anger took over again. ''Until you turned around to me and I saw you do it again.''

''Do *what* again?''

''Mistake me for Steve.'' He said the words quietly, but the confines of the car amplified them and seemed to cause them to hang there long after they'd been said.

Beth opened her mouth to defend herself, but he went on, ''Just like you presumed I threw Rush in the river. In the six weeks we've been together, I've proved Steve wrong about you over and over, but that still doesn't seem to separate me from him in your mind.''

Beth watched the clouds move in over the water,

heavy and dark and blotting out the sun. The interior of the car seemed suddenly darker, too.

"Maybe *you're* confusing *me* with Diana," she retorted. "I warned you once that we could never have what you had with Diana."

"I don't *want* what I had with Diana!" he roared. "It was great but that was *her!* I want *you!*"

"Then if you want me, you have to put up with a woman who poses for life-drawing classes! Or who might want to take a class herself! Do you want to go through this emotional struggle every time the subject arises or every time someone teases you because that's me on the front lawn of the art association's building?"

Ethan wondered how it was possible for a man to love a woman and want to murder her at the same time. But that was precisely how he felt.

"You know," he said, "I think you're the one who can't make the adjustment here. This isn't about modeling or not modeling. You're the one who still thinks you can't have your art and a relationship, too, but it isn't because of me. I think you've just decided it's easier to live day and night in your studio doing your thing and not having to worry about working someone else's needs into your life."

Somewhere deep down she recognized a grain of truth in that and closed it off. Assuming an air of feigned surprise was easier than assuming guilt.

"Gee," she said, "when I disagree with you, I end up in a jail cell. Do you think that notion could have anything to do with it?"

"No," he replied evenly. "I think your behaving like a brat has a lot to do with it. Did you really think you could take on another marriage—even one that was just intended for your own purposes—and never have to consult me on anything or explain yourself when necessary?''

She met his gaze, her own unflinching. ''I didn't expect to have to do it at every turn. I guess I thought that at home you'd be my husband and not the sheriff.''

The radio crackled. Then, ''500, come in.''

The voice was Ebbie's, and Ethan yanked the microphone off its hook. ''500. Go ahead.''

''Ethan, we have to transport a juvenile to Portland.'' Her voice sounded apologetic. ''I know it's your day off, but there's no one else available.''

The last thing Ethan wanted to do at that moment was transport a sullen juvenile a hundred miles and drive home in the dark on the winding highway.

Then he glanced at Beth, who looked cold and distant and even less appealing than the long drive in the dark.

''I'm on my way,'' he said, then replaced the mike on its hook and turned the key in the ignition. ''We'll have to finish this later.''

He expected a sharp retort, but she said nothing, folding her arms and leaning as far away from him as she could while he turned around and headed out of the parking lot.

CHAPTER SEVENTEEN

BETH STOOD for a long time under a lukewarm shower, trying hard to revive herself after a brief three hours of sleep. Ethan hadn't come home until just before midnight, and he'd never come upstairs.

She'd heard subtle sounds in the kitchen and lay tensely on her side of the bed, waiting for him to come up. By then her anger had abated somewhat and she'd been willing to have it out with him, to state her case again and listen to his.

But the opportunity never arose.

She'd finally fallen asleep shortly after four in the morning, and when she'd awakened at seven-thirty, he'd already left for the office.

She took that to mean he didn't want to talk. Maybe he no longer considered their relationship worth the argument required to keep it together.

Sadness weighted her limbs and burned in the pit of her stomach. She went downstairs, desperate for a cup of coffee, and found Jason and Nikkie whispering over breakfast cereal. They stopped guiltily when she walked into the room.

"Hi." She smiled from one to the other, trying to force cheer into her voice. The effort failed. "Didn't your uncle Brodie come over this morning?"

Nikkie studied her worriedly. "He isn't home. I made the coffee. How come Daddy left so early?"

Beth poured half a mug of the thick black brew and took a sip before answering. It was strong enough to generate sound when it hit her stomach. She withheld a wince. "I don't know, Nik. You'll have to ask him." She went to Jason, leaned over and kissed his cheek. "Guess you and I have to take a cab to school and to work."

"Cameron's coming to pick me up in his dad's van," Nikkie said. "The drama club's having a field trip today to the Coaster Theater in Cannon Beach. We can drop you and Jason on the way."

"Great." Beth headed for the basement stairs. "Do you think he'd have room for a few boxes, too?"

Nikkie looked surprised. "Boxes?"

"Yes. I have to take a few things back to the cannery."

ETHAN STARED at the coffee and pecan roll Ebbie had placed on his desk. After no sleep and enough caffeine to keep six people awake for forty-eight hours, he imagined that putting that much sugar into his system would be like dropping a match into a can of gasoline.

He felt too incendiary as it was. He pushed the roll away and tried to force himself to focus on the paperwork before him.

But Ebbie appeared in his office doorway looking uncharacteristically apprehensive. He felt himself tense.

"What?" he demanded.

She pointed vaguely in the direction of town. "There's a...a riot. On Ashley and Ninth."

He stared at her. "A riot. In Cobbler's Crossing."

"Yes."

"Well, aren't there two police units on this morning?"

She shifted her weight. "Yes. They're the ones who called for you."

"Curtis and Billings are patrolling."

"They're already there."

"God." Wishing now that he'd eaten the roll, Ethan ran out to his car and made Ashley and Ninth in just under four minutes. The sidewalk was choked with people, but not the type usually associated with a riot.

There were no professional agitators and no angry youths, just men in business suits standing in front of the bakery, older women with shopping bags, younger women with small children by the hand and pushing strollers. A pair of homeless men, one in a trench coat, one in a tattered paisley silk jogging suit, stood on a bench on the sidewalk across the street for a better look.

As Ethan left his car and pushed his way to the core of the crowd, he was grateful to see that there were no apparent injuries and the mood seemed more confused than hostile. Good. The situation was redeemable.

His thoughts on that changed when he finally reached the source of the disturbance and found every single member of his family involved and most of their friends.

He stared, unable to believe his eyes. Nikkie had Curtis by the arm and seemed to be giving him some elaborate explanation that had the vocal support of the entire drama club, whose members were gathered around her.

Zachary and Joanne were bending the ear of one

of two young police officers in the middle of the fray, while Brodie spoke to another.

Beth and Kelly and Portia Pintoretto had Billings cornered. Mrs. Pintoretto owned Gifts Galore, which Ethan noticed had a gaping hole where a display window had been. As he watched, Kelly and Mrs. Pintoretto grabbed each other's arms, apparently prepared to duke it out, but Billings stepped between them, looking desperate.

Just to add interest to the picture, a half-dozen medieval shields—the ones Beth had helped Nikkie and her friends make—were scattered about the sidewalk, two of them in the gift-shop window.

Trying to imagine how all this had come about, Ethan stepped intrepidly into the middle of it.

Jason was the first to notice his presence. "Dad!" he shouted, and raced toward him as though Ethan were God himself.

Ethan opened his arms and Jason flung himself into them. Nikkie was right behind him.

"Daddy, you've got to help us. It's all a big mistake, and…and…" She began to cry. "It's all my fault again, but Mrs. Pintoretto wants them to arrest Beth and Kelly, but they didn't really do it. Well, they did it, but they didn't do it on purpose!"

"Ethan!" Zachary joined them, leaning on his cane. "Thank God you're here. Please try to make them understand that Brodie says he can fix all of them without charge. I'll pay him of course, once he—"

"All what?" Ethan asked reluctantly, holding the children to him.

"The cars."

"What cars?"

"The ones I smashed into when I tried to stop the van."

"What van?"

"King Henry's van. You know. Cameron's."

Ethan remained quiet for a moment, trying to decide if it was him or the situation that simply refused to make sense. He searched his mind for a logical question.

"Why did you have to stop the van?"

"Because Beth was in it," Zachary said. "She was moving back to the cannery."

For an instant the sheriff in Ethan turned off, and the man in him felt a sudden and powerful onslaught of temper. She'd been leaving? While he was gone?

He looked for her face in the crowd, but couldn't find it. Billings had both arms out straight, holding Mrs. Pintoretto off with one hand and preventing a swinging Kelly from getting to her with the other.

"She *wasn't* leaving," Nikkie said, sobbing. "I told her Cameron would take her to work and Jason to school 'cause he was picking me up for our field trip—remember you signed the slip?" When he nodded, she went on, "Well, she asked me if there'd be room in the van for a couple of boxes, and when I asked her why, she said because she had to move some things back to the cannery. Jason and I thought she was moving her stuff back because you guys were gonna get a divorce. I know you had a big fight yesterday."

"So Nikkie called Kelly, and Uncle Brodie was there," Jason said. "And we thought they could come to the cannery and talk Mom out of leaving."

"But Grandma and Grandpa..." Nikkie began,

then corrected herself. "I mean, Zachary and Joanne…"

Zachary smiled. "You were right the first time, Nikkie."

"Well, they overheard me telling Kelly on the phone, and they followed us and made Cameron stop the van so Mom couldn't leave until you got a chance to talk to her."

Ethan managed to assimilate all that, but he still had questions. "How did the window get broken?"

Joanne appeared. "Kelly did that," she said with a wide smile. "When Leadfoot Richards here got the van stopped—" she hooked a thumb at Zachary, who smiled proudly "—Kelly and Brodie were right behind us, and Kelly jumped out and started taking Beth's boxes out of the van, yelling that nobody was leaving anybody."

"Then Mom tried to get the boxes back," Jason said, his eyes shining with the excitement of the drama, "and they were fighting over them, and when Kelly pulled really hard, all the shields flew out and a couple of them went through that mean lady's window. Boy! They fly just like Frisbees!"

"The shields," Ethan asked, just to make sure he was keeping up, "were in the boxes?"

"Yeah," Nikkie said. "She wasn't moving out. She was just taking the shields to the cannery for storage until the Parents' Club auction."

Ethan felt such relief at that news that he gained a new confidence in himself and the situation. He looked around for Beth, but still couldn't spot her.

Billings was listening patiently while Mrs. Pintoretto chewed him out and Brodie was forcibly dragging Kelly away. He brought her toward Ethan and the group gathered around him.

"That woman needs a lobotomy!" Kelly declared, yanking herself out of Brodie's hold. "And you didn't have to take her side!"

"I didn't take her side," Brodie argued. "I just thought you could have been a little more conciliatory about breaking her window."

"I tried. I explained to her that I'd have to repay her for her window in installments and she called me something rude in Italian."

"Do you speak Italian?"

"No."

"Then how do you know it was rude?"

"Because a universal gesture went with the word! And it's going to cost me everything I made at the fair and what's left of my savings, which I was going to use to buy a sign for the front of my studio."

Brodie looked smug. "No, it's not. I paid her."

Kelly's anger fell away and her expression softened. "You did?"

"I did. So you've got yourself a man who is more than a pretty face. Though I'm not a millionaire, I *am* able to take care of your damages."

She giggled and threw her arms around him. "My hero!" she exclaimed.

The drama club cheered. Joanne and Zachary nodded approvingly.

Curtis, Billings and the two police officers approached Ethan.

"Take Jason," Ethan directed Nikkie, "and see if you can find Beth."

"Right."

"Mrs. Pintoretto's willing to drop all charges,"

Billings said, "now that your brother's paid for the window."

"All right. And the owners of the cars?"

Curtis nodded. "Same. Damage isn't serious. A crunched bumper, a couple of lights and a bent mirror. Brodie says he can repair all of it. Believe it or not, everybody's happy."

"It's a miracle," one of the cops said. "When we walked into this, I thought we were going to have to call for hats and bats, just like in 'NYPD Blue.'"

The other cop grinned. "Fortunately for us, Drum, they're all your family. You think maybe you could put an electric fence around your house or something? Possibly post a warning when you guys are coming to town?"

"Hilarious, gentlemen." Ethan looked around at the dispersing crowd. "So we're finished here? No charges, no formal complaints, no tickets, no fines?"

"All clear. Except for you, who has to go home to this crime wave. Just to show you our hearts are in the right place, we'll sweep up the glass for you."

"Appreciate it."

"Daddy!" Ethan turned to find Nikkie and Jason looking concerned. The drama-club members were clustered around them, also worried. "Beth's in your car. In the cage."

He looked up and saw her seated in the back of his unit behind the metal screen that served to isolate the perpetrator. She had a hand to her forehead.

"You're not going to put her in jail again, are you?" Jason asked.

"No." He glanced up at Cameron. "How's your dad's van? Do you need to call him?"

Cameron shook his head. "Nope. It's cool. Not a scratch. We can still take Jason to school."

"I missed him when I went into the spin," Zachary called out. He and Joanne stood out of the way near a parking meter with Brodie and Kelly. "And got the car in front of me with my tail."

Joanne rolled her eyes. "Keep him out of the Grand Prix."

For the first time in about twenty-four hours, Ethan felt like laughing.

"Chinese food at Ming Ha's," he said to his newly adopted in-laws and to his brother and Kelly, who were picking up the shields. "Six-thirty? My treat."

"Sure," Brodie replied. "But why?"

Ethan couldn't think of a good reason, except that now that all their lives were interwoven, they didn't need one. "It's Monday. Family night."

He turned to the drama club, his daughter's eccentric but loyal support. "How about you guys? Chinese food tonight on me? Lots of old folks, though."

Heads nodded and their reply was unanimous. "Cool!"

"All right. See you tonight." He kissed Nikkie and Jason, then headed for his patrol car.

He opened the back door and leaned in to pull Beth out. She looked exhausted and upset and very fragile. "You need a lift somewhere?" he asked gently. "You can ride in the front."

Heavy-lidded blue eyes studied him suspiciously. "You mean we caused this whole—" she waved a hand at the barricades still up on the street, at the damaged cars just now being driven away, at the police sweeping glass off the street "—mess, and you're letting everybody off?"

God, he'd made quite an impression on her over the Appleby-house incident if she thought he could take this mini-riot, which was the result of everyone's love and concern for everyone else, and make them pay for it.

And then, because he felt guilty, he took off his hat and leaned down to kiss her slowly in apology. When he raised his head, he saw confusion in her eyes.

"What was that for?" she breathed.

"Because I'm sorry for ever bearing any resemblance to Steve, for not understanding instantly about the sculpture, for making you believe that anytime we disagreed about anything you were going to end up in jail."

The confusion in her eyes cleared and the love he'd grown used to seeing there shone brightly. She wrapped her arms around his waist and leaned into him with a little groan of contentment. "Oh, Ethan. I didn't think that. But what you said yesterday did make sense. When Steve died, I was so drunk with freedom that I did want to maintain it in a way, even after you married me. I was being selfish. So today I wanted to turn over a new leaf. I figured you'd have to take me in or something, and I was going to go quietly and wait for my chance to explain."

He walked her around the car and put her into the front seat. Then he got in behind the wheel. "You don't have to explain," he said. "Everyone's done it for you. The kids went nuts when they thought you were leaving. Zachary, Joanne, Kelly and Brodie were determined to stop you. And I think the drama club was just happy to be involved. They're all meeting us for dinner tonight, by the way. Chinese food."

She smiled. "How come?"

"Family night," he explained. "I'm taking you home. You're exhausted."

She looked at him across all the gear that sat between the two front seats, her expression disarmingly hopeful. "You don't have a coffee break coming or something, do you?"

"You hungry?"

She sighed. "Last night was horrid and I really really missed you."

Her words fell on him like a caress and made him curse the half mile between them and home.

He snatched the radio mike off its mounting even as he started the motor. "500," he said.

"500," Ebbie answered. "Go ahead."

"I'm code seven, Eb. For a couple of hours."

"It's early for lunch, Ethan."

"I'm not going to lunch, Ebbie. I'm taking Beth home."

"For two...? Oh. Oh! Right. Right. Two hours. Gotcha. Take your time. It's quiet, except for the riot you just cleaned up, and the rioters are all yours, aren't they? See you when I see you."

Ethan replaced the mike. All his. Despite the morning's events, he found great happiness in that knowledge.

"So how did it feel to arrive at the scene of a riot," Beth asked, laughter in her voice, "and discover that the rioters were your family?"

He laughed softly and accelerated. "Routine, my love. Routine."

COMING NEXT MONTH

#766 WHO'S AFRAID OF THE MISTLETOE? • Margot Early

Sarah needs help, and she can get it from only one person—her ex-lover, Tage. But Tage's life and responsibilities have changed since she last saw him. He's recently become guardian to two young children—his orphaned niece and nephew from Sweden. Add Sarah and her impossible dog to this household and you have a Christmas unlike any other! A strikingly original book from an author who's become known for the drama and emotional depth of her writing.

#767 FATHER CHRISTMAS • Judith Arnold

The Daddy School

Hardbitten cop John Russo is hot on the trail of ATM thieves—who turn out to be the precocious children of a powerful lawyer. But neglecting his own motherless son for his job isn't part of the plan. It takes the ebullient Molly Saunders and her Daddy School classes to bring the two back together and teach John the true meaning of Christmas. *Don't miss lesson number three in January!*

#768 UPON A MIDNIGHT CLEAR • Lynn Erickson

The reintroduction of a wolf pack into Colorado is Brigitte Hartman's dream. A dream that has almost become a reality until ranchers like Steve Slater rebel. Is it the wolves—or is one of the ranchers killing local cattle? Brigitte is determined to find out...until it begins to look as if Steve may be more involved than she thought. Suspense and excitement...and Christmas.

#769 A CHILD'S CHRISTMAS • Eva Rutland

Ten-year-old Eric Archer is the child at the center of this inspiring Christmas story. Eric's benignly neglectful father, Lyndon, has left him in the care of his brother, Dave—Eric's uncle. Which is how Dave comes to meet—and fall in love with—one of Eric's teachers, Monica Powell. Then Lyndon meets *her* friend Lisa...and the circle of love continues to expand, drawing other people into its sphere. It all culminates at Christmas....

Take 4 bestselling love stories FREE

Plus get a FREE surprise gift!

Special Limited-time Offer

Mail to Harlequin Reader Service®

3010 Walden Avenue
P.O. Box 1867
Buffalo, N.Y. 14240-1867

YES! Please send me 4 free Harlequin Superromance® novels and my free surprise gift. Then send me 4 brand-new novels every month, which I will receive before they appear in bookstores. Bill me at the low price of $3.34 each plus 25¢ delivery and applicable sales tax, if any.* That's the complete price and a savings of over 10% off the cover prices—quite a bargain! I understand that accepting the books and gift places me under no obligation ever to buy any books. I can always return a shipment and cancel at any time. Even if I never buy another book from Harlequin, the 4 free books and the surprise gift are mine to keep forever.

134 BPA A3UN

Name	(PLEASE PRINT)	
Address	Apt. No.	
City	State	Zip

This offer is limited to one order per household and not valid to present Harlequin Superromance® subscribers. *Terms and prices are subject to change without notice. Sales tax applicable in N.Y.

USUP-696

©1990 Harlequin Enterprises Limited

HARLEQUIN WOMEN KNOW ROMANCE WHEN THEY SEE IT.

And they'll see it on **ROMANCE CLASSICS**, the new 24-hour TV channel devoted to romantic movies and original programs like the special **Romantically Speaking—Harlequin™ Goes Prime Time**.

Romantically Speaking—Harlequin™ Goes Prime Time introduces you to many of your favorite romance authors in a program developed exclusively for Harlequin® readers.

Watch for **Romantically Speaking—Harlequin™ Goes Prime Time** beginning in the summer of 1997.

If you're not receiving ROMANCE CLASSICS, call your local cable operator or satellite provider and ask for it today!

Escape to the network of your dreams.

See Ingrid Bergman and Gregory Peck in *Spellbound* on Romance Classics.

As Seen on TV!

Free Gift Offer

With a Free Gift proof-of-purchase
from any Harlequin® book, you can receive
a beautiful cubic zirconia pendant.

This stunning marquise-shaped stone is a genuine cubic
zirconia—accented by an 18" gold tone necklace.
(Approximate retail value $19.95)

Send for yours today...
compliments of ⊛HARLEQUIN®

To receive your free gift, a cubic zirconia pendant, send us one original proof-of-purchase, photocopies not accepted, from the back of any Harlequin Romance®, Harlequin Presents®, Harlequin Temptation®, Harlequin Superromance®, Harlequin Intrigue®, Harlequin American Romance®, or Harlequin Historicals® title available at your favorite retail outlet, together with the Free Gift Certificate, plus a check or money order for $1.65 U.S./$2.15 CAN. (do not send cash) to cover postage and handling, payable to Harlequin Free Gift Offer. We will send you the specified gift. Allow 6 to 8 weeks for delivery. Offer good until December 31, 1997, or while quantities last. Offer valid in the U.S. and Canada only.

Free Gift Certificate

Name: _____

Address: _____

City: _____ State/Province: _____ Zip/Postal Code: _____

Mail this certificate, one proof-of-purchase and a check or money order for postage and handling to: HARLEQUIN FREE GIFT OFFER 1997. In the U.S.: 3010 Walden Avenue, P.O. Box 9071, Buffalo NY 14269-9057. In Canada: P.O. Box 604, Fort Erie, Ontario L2Z 5X3.

084-KEZR

FREE BOOK OFFER!

With every Harlequin Ultimate Guides™ order, receive a FREE bonus book!

#80507	HOW TO TALK TO A NAKED MAN	$4.99 U.S. ☐	$5.50 CAN. ☐
#80508	I CAN FIX THAT	$5.99 U.S. ☐	$6.99 CAN. ☐
#80510	WHAT YOUR TRAVEL AGENT KNOWS THAT YOU DON'T	$5.99 U.S. ☐	$6.99 CAN. ☐
#80511	RISING TO THE OCCASION More Than Manners: Real Life Etiquette for Today's Woman	$5.99 U.S. ☐	$6.99 CAN. ☐
#80513	WHAT GREAT CHEFS KNOW THAT YOU DON'T	$5.99 U.S. ☐	$6.99 CAN. ☐
#80514	WHAT SAVVY INVESTORS KNOW THAT YOU DON'T	$5.99 U.S. ☐	$6.99 CAN. ☐

(quantities may be limited on some titles)

TOTAL AMOUNT	$
POSTAGE & HANDLING	$
($1.00 for one book, 50¢ for each additional)	
APPLICABLE TAXES*	$ _____
TOTAL PAYABLE	$ _____
(check or money order—please do not send cash)	

*New York residents remit applicable sales taxes.
Canadian residents remit applicable GST and provincial taxes.

To order, complete this form and send it, along with a check or money order for the total above, payable to Harlequin Ultimate Guides, to: **In the U.S.:** 3010 Walden Avenue, P.O. Box 9047, Buffalo, NY 14269-9047; **In Canada:** P.O. Box 613, Fort Erie, Ontario, L2A 5X3.

HARLEQUIN ULTIMATE GUIDES™
What women really want to know!

Official Proof of Purchase

Please send me my FREE bonus book with this order.

Name: _____

Address: _____

City: _____

State/Prov:. _____ Zip/Postal Code: _____

Reader Service Acct.#: _____ **KFZ**

Look us up on-line at: http://www.romance.net   NFPOP